To C

Happy birthday!

Hope you like it!

A.L. Wright

Miss Prince

By

Alicia L. Wright

Tannbourne

Miss Prince

ISBN: 978-0-9567852-2-0

First publication in UK by Tannbourne Limited 2014

Published by
Tannbourne Limited
49 Westleigh Avenue, Coulsdon, Surrey CR5 3AD
www.tannbourne.com

British Library Cataloguing in Publication Data. A catalogue record for this book is available from the British Library.

There are a great many people without whom this book would not have made it into print.

Firstly, my editor, who put up with my constant stream of e-mails and general pesterings for the past two years while I wrote this thing.

My family and friends, who supported me while I could not support myself.

My beta-readers, whose input was invaluable.

And finally, my online friends and readers, who continue to read and support my webcomics.

Thank you all so very much.

Oh and... regarding the story... It's STILL not my fault. Fairytales, folklore, games, films and indeed literature are really like that.

CONTENTS

SOME DRAGON-SLAYING REQUIRED

'I'll get a job', she'd thought. 'Earn my own ticket,' she'd thought. Lucinda's parents had agreed that it was a good idea. 'It'll teach you some responsibility,' they'd said.

Lucinda was currently staring down a dragon, dressed as a man, on only her first day in gainful employment. She suspected her parents would *not* think it such a good idea if they knew.

It had seemed innocent enough. There was an ad in the newsagent's window;

> 'Young person wanted for part time job
> General Assistant
> Must be available on weekends.'

'General assistant', that was a good one. What it hadn't said was 'some dragon-slaying required'. Sara had said that was because it would put people off.

It would probably have put Lucinda off too, but not much. Her goal in life was to do pretty much everything, ever, and something like dragon-slaying was not an everyday occurrence. Lucinda was all about not-everyday occurrences, and caused them to occur quite frequently. She had been causing one quite loudly some weeks before, when her mother burst into the room, to see what the horrible crash had been.

"You're blue," were the first words out of her mouth as she took in the scene of desolation. Lucinda was lying on her back halfway off the bed, covered in books and trinkets that had fallen off the now tilted bookcase, which was wedged between the wall and her bed. She was clutching a camera in one hand. "You're actually blue." Something slid off the bookshelf and made a sad tinkling sound. "WHY are you blue, dare I ask?"

"I'm all right thanks, no need to help me up," Lucinda complained, shedding books and jewellery as she righted herself. "I've only fallen off a bookshelf and got nearly buried alive, I'm *perfectly* fine."

"And why were you climbing the bookcase?" Lucinda's mother asked, ignoring her daughter's complaint. "That camera better not be broken, we need that!"

"It's fine, I kept hold of it when I fell," Lucinda replied. "And I wasn't climbing the bookcase, I was trying to put the camera on top of it at a good angle. But as I was adjusting the tripod, I slipped and grabbed it, so it fell over."

"What on Earth did you want to put the camera up there for? There's plenty of other places to put it, aren't there? Honestly, I don't know where you get these funny ideas from," her mother continued, picking her way around the debris and pushing the bookcase back up against the wall. "You're all right then, are you?" she added, finally.

"Yeah, just a bit sore," Lucinda said, pulling a face at the bookcase. "And *annoyed*! I'm supposed to have my bit filmed for today, I promised!"

"Do I even want to know? Who did you promise?" her mother asked suspiciously as she joined Lucinda in picking up the books and shoving them back on the shelves. "Because I *know* this isn't for homework." Lucinda was dressed in some stylishly tattered jeans, and a similarly abused white blouse. At least, it *had* been white; now it was stained with blue where Lucinda had touched it. Her face, arms and bare feet were covered in face paint. She was also wearing a belt with an oversized gold buckle and small chains hanging from it. The whole thing was topped off by a spiky blue and white wig. She looked like a fashionista zombie.

"Anna, my friend from the U.S.," Lucinda explained. "We're filming our own opening sequence. For a series we made up. We have to start practising *now* or we'll never be good enough."

"Ah. That Japanese stuff again, no doubt," her mother tutted and shook her head. "Do Japanese mums have this much trouble cleaning blue off their bedsheets, too?"

"It's practice for a contest that's coming up next summer!" Lucinda continued, annoyed that her prompt had been ignored. "There's this huge convention and we all want to go and enter the big contest there," she explained. "We're all going to film our own bits of the video in England, and Wales, and New Zealand, and last of all we're gonna film the main bits together at Anna's house in Georgia!"

"Oh, do you send it through the internet?" Lucinda's mother asked, interested despite herself.

"Well, yeah, but we're going to film most of it near Anna's house. 'Cause we all need to dance together and stuff," Lucinda replied.

"'All together?'" her mother repeated, baffled. "How are you going to do that if you're in different countries?"

"We won't be, that's the point," Lucinda explained patiently. "We're going to all meet up and film the main bit at Anna's. All us friends, from different parts of the world in our own little bits filmed at home and then BAM! All of a sudden we're all together in America! It's going to be amazing! There's some cool prizes, but really we just want to say we did it." Lucinda's mother ran the sentence through her head a few times moving her lips as she tried to comprehend what had just been said.

"Let me get this straight. You're going to *actually go* to America to meet these internet friends of yours?" she said finally, her eyes widening in disbelief. "And how are you going to get there? How do you think you're going to be able to *afford* it?"

"Well . . . I was hoping," Lucinda mumbled, "I was hoping that you and Dad would pay . . . " She'd been dreading this moment for two weeks now, since Anna had told her about the contest. "I mean, not all of it!" she added quickly, seeing her mother's expression. "I'm going to get a job!"

"A job, indeed!" her mother retorted. "I should hope so, too! Do you know how expensive plane tickets are? You'll never do it. And you're going to be going abroad all alone!"

"Yes. I looked it up," Lucinda replied sulkily. Why were parents always like this? "And I won't be alone. My friends will meet me at the airport. I'll be staying with them."

"And these friends of yours are genuine, are they?" Her mother was now in full scolding mode. "Have you even met them? What about this Anna? Do her parents know about this plan of yours?"

"Anna's parents know all about it and I've known them online for *ages*. A few years. They're not weirdoes!" Lucinda protested. "We use a webcam half the time, I've

4

seen them and everything! Anyway, one of them is Pens. You know, Andrew," she added for clarification. 'Pens' was Lucinda's best friend from her old town. Her mother couldn't object to him, she'd half-raised the boy; he used to be round for dinner every other day. Until they'd moved last month, that is. Lucinda missed him terribly. She felt like he might as well live in America. Money was tight and her parents complained if she asked for money to go and see him. His family was no better off.

"We'll see what your father thinks about this," Lucinda's mother announced. "You make sure this mess is cleaned up before he gets home! Right?" Lucinda nodded solemnly and began to tidy up. Her mother strode out, muttering to herself about planes and teenagers and cursing cartoons.

After a little while, a voice said, "Is she gone?"

"Yeah. Dad's probably going to yell at me, too," Lucinda addressed this to her laptop, which was sitting on her writing desk in the corner.

"My Mom yelled at me as well," her laptop replied sympathetically. "We're still gonna try and do it, right?" Lucinda nodded. There was a pause. "Did you nod, Cinders? I can't see you."

"I nodded, I nodded!" replied 'Cinders', giving the mess a look of distaste and sitting in front of the laptop. "Ugh, I got paint everywhere, look!"

"Oh man, you did!" replied the brown-haired girl on the screen, peering closely into her own monitor. "Is that gonna come out?"

"It better! Now I'm saving up for plane tickets, I can't be buying new tops all the time!"

Lucinda pulled off the wig she was wearing. It was a

cheap one that she'd bought in a post-Halloween sale last year. Her own hair was long and red; it was currently tied up in a bun and covered with a hair net. She pulled off the net and took out her hair bands, letting it unravel itself down to the middle of her back.

"I wish my hair did that," Anna remarked. "I wouldn't need a wig then."

"No you don't. It's a pain to comb every morning. And it makes it really hard to put wigs on without them looking dumb," Lucinda complained, "and this red hair of mine comes with freckles, you know. You wouldn't like them." Lucinda had quite a few freckles. She felt that up and coming famous people – she wasn't entirely sure what she was going to be famous *for* yet, but she was determined to be famous for *something* – shouldn't have a boat-load of freckles.

"Don't they say that if you have a lot of freckles you're less likely to get cancer?" Anna replied.

"No idea," Lucinda shook her head. "Not sure if I care."

"I'm pretty sure you'd care if you had cancer," Anna replied, forgiving her friend's flippant attitude. One was allowed to say stupid things one didn't mean when one had just had one's dreams crushed by one's parents. "Look, it's okay. Even if they say no . . . we'll figure something out. I'll get my parents to pay for your ticket and you can bring the money with you and pay me back." Lucinda shook her head again.

"My Dad is going to kill me," she pouted. "Cinders doesn't get to go to the ball, Anna. And I don't see any fairy godmothers around, do you?"

"I think it's a good idea," said her father, settling down to read his paper with a cup of tea. "If she can get the money, that is." Both Lucinda and her mother were dumbfounded.

"But George, she's only fifteen!" her mother protested.

"It's about time she got a job and started paying for own things then, isn't it?" her father replied. "It might teach her some responsibility."

"Well. I suppose so," her mother conceded, "but what if she doesn't get enough money for this plane ticket? What if these friends of hers change their minds?"

"If she doesn't get the money then she can't go," her father answered, putting up a hand to stop Lucinda from objecting, "and if these friends change their minds, then she'll have earned some money she can spend on something else. Sound fair?"

"All right then," her mother agreed grudgingly. "But we're sticking to that, you hear me Lulu? You don't get enough money for your ticket and you're not going, end of argument. We don't have a few hundred pounds going spare to bail you out." Lucinda nodded. She was feeling so happy and light headed that she even let 'Lulu' pass.

"Dad, can I have that paper?" Lucinda asked.

"No," he replied, pointedly turning a page and adjusting his glasses. "I'd suggest asking around in shops rather than looking in the newspaper. Or maybe you could try putting the internet to good use for once." Lucinda went off upstairs to her room. She wasn't quite out of earshot when she heard her mother ask crossly;

"What did you go and tell her that for? What if she actually does it?"

"Oh, you know what she's like, Maria," her father

replied, shrugging. "It's one hare-brained scheme after another. She'll get bored and come up with something else."

"What if she doesn't? What if she actually buys a ticket to Australia or wherever?"

"Then we'll have to buy her a lot of sunblock," he answered simply. "You know how easily she burns." Lucinda crept up the final few steps with a grin on her face.

Lucinda's initial happiness at being allowed to save up for the ticket faded quickly. There just weren't any jobs about, and those that were she wasn't old enough for. She was getting worried. She had almost a year to save up, but she knew she needed to order the ticket well in advance. It was nearly the end of the summer holidays already and goodness knows how long it would take to actually save up.

The days and weeks crept on . . .

It had been a month and Lucinda was getting desperate. She'd lost count of how many C.V.s she'd handed out, all to no avail. She wandered around town, trying to find shops she hadn't already asked at. It was hot out, and although she begrudged spending money right now, it was no good. She really, really needed a drink. She headed for the nearest newsagents and bought herself a can of cola. Cracking it open, she took a swig and eyed the adverts pasted on the inside of the window.

'PlayStation 3 for sale, £200ono' she read. She had no idea what 'ono' was supposed to mean. She always read it as 'oh no' as in 'Oh no, I have to sell this cheap'. She considered if she had anything worth selling that would help her raise the money. No chance. What she mostly spent her money on were wigs and materials for costumes and they weren't very saleable.

The next one read 'Lost cat, reward'. There was a picture of a white cat, looking smugly at the camera. Lucinda was sure she'd seen the cat pottering around somewhere, so the ad must be old . . . or the cat was pulling a fast one on its owners.

'Do you need a plumber?' That one was so badly sun-bleached that she could barely read it. Lucinda wondered just how long it had been there. Years, it looked like.

Finally an ad caught her eye. Similar to the plumbing one, it looked old. But it was strange, it was as if it had been made old. The pale, brownish paper seemed hand made and had a 'slightly singed' quality. It was ripped along the edges as if torn off something, and written in barely readable, spidery hand writing. It put Lucinda strongly in mind of a treasure map. Yet, the words seemed perfectly ordinary;

> 'Young person wanted for part time job
> General Assistant
> Must be available on weekends.'

Lucinda blinked. A job she could do? Finally, after a whole month of looking? Something was going to be wrong. The job was going to be gone already, or they wanted someone older, or it was an awful job. But she could always try. She might be just the person they were looking for. And right now she was prepared to do very nearly anything. She went into the shop and asked the man at the counter.

"You want to take a look at what ad now?" he said, giving her a puzzled look.

"The really old-looking one?" she asked.

"About plumbing?" the shopkeeper replied. "I'd be surprised if the guy who wrote that is even still alive, to be honest. It was up there when I started here . . . oh, ages and ages ago now. I dunno why the boss hasn't taken it down."

"No, the really old looking one, with the handwriting?" Lucinda insisted.

"I don't remember one like that." He frowned and squinted at the window. "Knock yourself out. If I didn't see it, someone probably put it up without paying, so you can even take it if you want." Lucinda thanked the man and took the advert from out of the window. It really did look like a treasure map - there was even a little map scribbled on the back, showing where she should go to apply, complete with an X.

Lucinda peered down the alley indicated on the map. She was sure it couldn't be right, but the map was pretty clear. What kind of business could be down an alley like this? Lucinda had never heard anything good about alleys, and she made her way carefully along the dingy little passage, ready to flee at the first sign of nasty men, rabid animals or possibly even monsters. But all she found was a well-kept skip and a rusty, peeling fire escape that had once been a vivid red. Pasted under the 'Fire Exit: Do Not Block' sign was another notice, reading 'Rent-a-Leg'. It had once said something else, but rust had obscured the rest.

There was no bell or other means of announcing her presence, so she tried knocking. When no-one answered, she took a deep breath and pushed open the door.

The room inside was quite large, and dominated by a reception desk. It was a huge, circular, mahogany desk with, in theory, a person seated in the middle, however, for some unfathomable reason, there was no chair. Thus, the unfortunate receptionist had to actually sit on the desk itself and put up with constantly hitting their head on the various shells and horns hanging around it. Some of them seemed to be ringing, and it sounded like they each made a different noise.

The receptionist was perched on the far side of the desk, in the centre. She had a huge, pink conch wedged between her cheek and her shoulder. She was quite tall, with dark skin and black hair, tied in a loose bun at the back of her head. She was wearing a red, Chinese-style dress, at odds with her Arabic appearance. Lucinda wasn't sure if she was imagining it in the gloom, but it looked like she had pointy ears. She glanced up at Lucinda, gave her an annoyed look and continued speaking rapidly into the conch shell.

"Yes, yes I know," she shifted uncomfortably on the mahogany desk, "we've put an ad out." She brushed a strand of black hair out of her eyes, causing the conch to wobble. "Look, I'm sorry, I know you need one, but we just don't have any right now. I could always come and do it myself? No? You'll just have to wait then, I'm afraid."

Lucinda was almost certain she was in the wrong place. If it wasn't bad enough she'd had to take a fire escape up to the entrance, the strangeness of the office wasn't helping at all. Apart from the desk and its collection of paraphernalia, the place was shadowy, as though darkness had gathered in the corners, like dust. The receptionist's attitude wasn't great for her composure either, not that Lucinda could blame her.

It's not that receptionists aren't nice people. It's just that they're receptionists. And it's a receptionist's basic job to organise everything and deal with a lot of other people's problems. This in turn causes them problems, which means they're highly unlikely to want to deal with your problems, especially if you're some kid who seems to have wandered blindly into their office.

The woman, who must have had a sixth sense for timid introductions, said abruptly into the shell;

"Just a minute sir, I'll have to put you on hold." She yanked at it, causing its cord to lengthen considerably, pulled a small radio from under the desk, switched it on and plonked them both next to each other on the far side of the counter. "Yes?" she said pointedly as Lucinda had opened her mouth to speak.

"Er . . . " Lucinda had been cut off before she even began, so she just held up the card from the newsagents in self defence.

"I've got all day, don't worry about me," the woman raised her voice as two more shells started ringing. She gave Lucinda a smile that said clearly 'You don't'.

"Er . . . " Lucinda tried not to wither under the stare. "I've come about this job . . . " She waved the card again. "I saw it in the newsagents." The woman stared at the card like she'd never seen it before. She took it and read it carefully. Then she flipped it over and scrutinised the back.

"This is your advert isn't it?" Lucinda asked, just in case she really hadn't seen it before. The receptionist looked from the card to Lucinda and gave her a critical stare.

"Yes, it is," she replied simply, looking Lucinda up and down. She folded one arm across her chest and rubbed her chin thoughtfully.

"Only-" Lucinda started, desperate to end the silent examination. She was immediately hushed into silence.

"There's been a mistake," the woman said, suddenly brandishing a finger.

"Oh, well in that case I'll just-" Lucinda started.

"Shh-!" The woman waved her finger again. "I'm thinking." She paced around in the middle of the desk, difficult as it was. Suddenly she stopped and fixed Lucinda with a piercing look. "Are you going to run off and get married?" she demanded.

"What?" Lucinda blurted out, surprised.

"You speak English, right? It's a simple question. Are you going to run off and get married?" she repeated sternly.

"No!" Lucinda replied, shocked. "I don't even have a boyfriend!"

"Fabulous!" the woman clapped her hands together and swung herself right over the desk, so she could get out.

"Oi, Freya!" she shouted down a corridor to her left. "Come and take over for a minute, will you?"

"No problem," a muffled voice replied.

"You!" she pointed at Lucinda. "Don't move." She waited for Lucinda to nod. "I'll be back in a minute," she said, and strode off purposefully down the corridor.

As she left, what was presumably a woman, but looked more like an enormous, walking fur coat came in and swung itself over the desk, giving Lucinda a brief view of the most enormous, fluffy, high-heeled boots she had ever seen. The woman was also wearing a huge, furry, white hat, and only her eyes were visible behind a woolly, lavender scarf that was wrapped around her face and neck.

She nodded and waved a white-gloved hand at Lucinda as she picked up the conch and carried on the receptionist's work. She called up an impression of polar bears - really fashion conscious ones.

Just as she realised she was staring, someone tapped Lucinda on the shoulder, making her jump. It was the receptionist. She'd been even less than a minute. It was like she didn't even have time for Time.

"Here, put these on." The woman threw Lucinda some gaudy looking clothes. "Over what you're wearing is fine." Lucinda pulled on a red vest with puffy sleeves, gold edging and matching shorts. It looked even more ridiculous over her shirt and jeans than it would without. "Right, hold this." A sword was shoved into Lucinda's hand, then she was once more subjected to an unnerving inspection.

"So, you say you definitely won't run off and get married?" the woman asked again.

"Yes! I mean, no!" Lucinda corrected herself quickly. "I won't get married."

"Not even if a handsome prince sweeps you off your feet and offers you half his kingdom?"

"Nope. Not even then," Lucinda replied, figuring there was no point in changing her mind now, even if she didn't know what she'd be changing it from. "I don't think that's very likely though."

"You'd be surprised," the woman replied. "And I'm putting that in your contract, you understand. Run off and get married and you're fired. Even think about it and you're fired."

"OK. Wait, so-" Lucinda paused for a second.

"Yes, you're hired," the woman confirmed. "You start tomorrow at nine o' clock sharp. Be on time or don't bother turning up ever again."

"Nine o' clock, right. Oh, and thank you very much!" Lucinda replied, remembering her manners. Talking to this woman was like trying to stand on a ball; it was hard to keep your balance.

"And cut your hair," the woman commanded, "about yea short." She held her hand flat just above her ear.

"What?! Why?" Lucinda blurted out. She liked her hair, despite the freckles and the wig problems that came with it.

"Do you want the job or not?" the woman asked matter-of-factly.

"Yes! Yes I do!" Lucinda wasn't giving up now after looking for all that time. And it appeared to involve dressing up, one of her favourite things. She couldn't ask for better than that. "I'll cut it."

"Good girl!" the woman replied, patting her on the shoulder. "Welcome to the team!" She looked Lucinda up and down one last time and then added, "I suppose you've got to look like a girl sometimes . . . maybe you should cut it to here instead." She held her hand about an inch below her ear this time. "That should do it."

"Thank you," Lucinda replied gratefully. "Oh and, what's your name?" She now had a lot of questions and it seemed as good a place as any to start.

"You don't want to know," the woman replied darkly. "It's terrible."

"It can't be any worse than mine," Lucinda said.

"Can't it?" The receptionist raised an eyebrow. "Why, what's yours?"

"Lucinda."

"That is pretty bad," the woman replied. "Puts me in mind of something that's far too frilly for its own good. We shall have to do something about it." She wrinkled her nose. "Mine's Saharaleia."

"Sahala-?" Lucinda tried.

"Saharaleia," Saharaleia repeated, "Saharaleia Phedoria Cornelia Stollenheim."

"Gosh."

"Call me Sara," she said, holding up a warning finger. "Or else." Lucinda nodded. "Well then . . . " Sara asked, "what do your friends call you?"

"Cinders," Lucinda replied, wondering if Sara would make anything of it.

"Well Cinders, I should push off if I were you. The hairdressers will all be closing soon I should think." Lucinda turned to go, but then stopped.

"Er, isn't there anything I should know about the job?" she asked tentatively.

"You're going to be rescuing princesses, other damsels in distress, overthrowing evil overlords, doing kings a great service, that sort of thing," Sara replied breezily. "Pretty standard stuff."

"Oh," Lucinda frowned, while she thought it over. "Is this an acting job?"

"A bit," Sara explained. "You're going to have to act like a prince. Normally I hire real ones of course, but then they go and get married. I put the 'no marriage' thing in their contracts, but they just don't care. Don't need to, once they've got a wife and a kingdom to call their own." She scowled at this apparent treachery. "And for some reason, once you're a king you sit around and do nothing except get tricked by people and offer half your kingdom and her hand in marriage for the rescue of whatever daughter has been kidnapped this time."

"What, really?" Lucinda asked, unable to believe her luck.

"Yes, really," Sara replied, sounding irritated.

"I . . . I don't think I know how to do any of that

stuff," said Lucinda slowly. She really didn't want to lose the job now. It sounded perfect. She didn't want to come across as dishonest, though. "Am I going to be able to do this?"

"Oh, don't you worry your pretty little head." Sara flashed her a brittle smile. "We've got excellent on-the-job training."

Lucinda arrived home feeling a mixture of excitement and apprehension. Her head seemed to feel especially light now that she'd had her hair cut, too. She still had no idea what she was really going to be doing. But it involved costumes, and that was O.K. by her. It must be some kind of acting job. Or a promotional thing, where she'd have to dress up and hand out leaflets. Well she could do that easily.

"Guess who's got a job?" she told her mother as soon as she saw her, beaming. Her mother looked startled.

"You never have!" she exclaimed. Then she noticed her daughter's hair. "You've cut your hair! What've you cut your hair for?"

"It's for the job," Lucinda explained. "I'm a prince."

"Ri-ight," her mother answered suspiciously. "That's a job these days, is it?"

"Apparently," Lucinda shrugged. "I think it's acting or something like that."

"Oh, acting," her mother sighed with relief. "That should suit you down to the ground, then."

Lucinda was up bright and early. She'd woken up at about 5am and couldn't get back to sleep because she kept having dreams that she was late and Sara had turned out to be a witch and cursed her legs to fall off and other silly things. By the time she was really awake, she was highly dubious of reality in general, and kept pinching herself.

Her first day at work did not help in the slightest.

As soon as she arrived, Sara shoved the red clothes from yesterday at her and told her to get changed in a little office to the side. In addition to the red outfit, she'd also been provided with brown, knee-high boots, some long, leather gloves and a short, maroon cape.

"I thought about what you said yesterday and I think you have a point," Sara announced as Lucinda appeared from the makeshift changing room.

"Oh?" Lucinda was apprehensive. She tried to remember any points she'd made.

"Are you going to be able to do this?" Sara wondered out loud. Lucinda inwardly cursed her own honesty. Was Sara having second thoughts about hiring her? "I'd like to know that, too. So I'm going to give you a few tests. Three is the standard number. They're all really basic, run-of-the-mill tasks that come up all the time. If you can't even do them, you've got no business working here. Understood?" Lucinda nodded solemnly. "Good. Come with me."

Sara led Lucinda down an odd corridor full of doors. That is, even more full of doors than corridors usually are. It was more door than wall, and it seemed to go on and on. Sara stopped abruptly.

"I thought I'd start you off with something simple," she announced. "So today you're going to fight a dragon. Just remember not to get married," she added sternly, opening the door.

"I'm sorry?" Lucinda asked, not believing her ears and absolutely positive that not getting married was not what she was going to be worrying about.

"Don't worry, Gerda will look after you. She's a valkyrie, so you'll be fine I'm sure. Have a good day!" she said brightly, indicating that Lucinda should step through the door, which she did. "I'd leave it open, but I don't want to risk getting ash all over the hallway." There was a click as the door closed. Lucinda turned to ask what she meant by that, but Sara was gone. The door was gone. In fact, the whole building was gone. Lucinda found herself in a green meadow, being rapidly approached and shouted at by what first appeared to be a ball of metal on legs. As it got closer, Lucinda could make out it was a large woman in armour. There was a screech, and Lucinda looked up and saw a huge, green bird diving towards her, aiming for the yelling woman. It was carrying something blue, which it dropped on the ground as it swooped down low. The woman ducked and it flew up again. Lucinda stared in horror at it. It was huge, scaly and bright green, with leathery, bat-like wings. It had three horns on its lizard-like head. It was most definitely not a bird.

"Don't just stand there like a lemon!" the woman shouted at her, finally in hearing distance. "Get in there!" It swooped down to worry at the blue thing it had dropped, which, Lucinda realised with alarm, was a girl.

"Is that a dragon?!" Lucinda shouted back. "An actual, real dragon?!"

"Well it's not the bloomin' tooth fairy, is it?" the woman yelled. "Get it!"

Lucinda ran at the dragon without really thinking. This couldn't possibly be happening. The woman in armour had said it was real and it looked real but it couldn't possibly be real – could it? The dragon decided she was a threat; it turned round and hissed at her, giving her an excellent view of all its razor sharp teeth. It was real all right.

"Gerda, valkyrie, pleased to make your acquaintance!" the woman yelled.

"What do I do?!" Lucinda shouted, unsure if she should go for the dragon or the girl.

"What do you mean what do you do?" Gerda replied. "Get it!"

"But how do I do that?!" Lucinda yelled.

"Just get it!" Gerda yelled back, as if it was the easiest thing in the world.

"That is not a helpful instruction!" Lucinda screamed, as the dragon took a snap at her sword, driving her backwards. 'Excellent on-the-job training' Sara had said. That must translate to English as 'being yelled at by Gerda'.

"What's the matter with you, gi- boy?!" she bellowed, as the dragon almost tripped Lucinda with a swish from its tail as it turned around. "It's only a dragon, for crying out loud! I could have skewered it and fatally wounded several other nightmarish beasts by now! Come on, show 'im who's boss!"

"That's easy for you to say!" Lucinda yelled back. She'd lost her composure already. She was convinced that the only reason she wasn't dead was that the dragon seemed to be far more interested in the valkyrie than her, and it was increasingly irate at the way Lucinda was constantly dodging around to its back. It twisted itself around, first one way, then another, trying to keep them both in view. It hissed and spat fire at Lucinda. She ducked and felt the heat frazzle her hair. This was definitely not an acting job.

"Helpful tip: Dragons breathe fire!" Gerda bellowed, almost cheerfully. "Watch out for that!"

Gerda was one of nature's yellers. As the fight continued, Lucinda was yelled at for dodging, yelled at for not dodging, yelled at for trying to hit it, yelled at for not hitting it, yelled at for being almost burned, yelled at for falling over and yelled at for being a girl. She'd been called 'a great pansy' more times than she was willing to count. Gerda was one of those people who thought screaming at you that you were doing things wrong would somehow get you to do them right. Instead of say, explaining how to actually do it.

The dragon snarled threateningly and stamped around, trying to menace them both, whilst its hostage, a blonde princess who had quickly gotten out of the way once Lucinda had arrived, sat arranging her skirts a short distance away and looking bored. It was as if someone fighting a dragon was something she saw every day. She probably did. She was wearing a silky blue dress and more sparkly jewellery than Lucinda had seen in her life.

The dragon finally picked a target, and that target was Lucinda. It took a swipe at her, which she managed to dodge. But it was largely hissing and trying to bite the point of her sword as she waved it around. It was dawning on Lucinda that all it really wanted was for her to go away and leave it alone. It wasn't really attacking her, it was just trying to send her off. She backed away a little, lowering her sword. The dragon eyed her for several agonising seconds, before deciding she was no longer a threat and turning towards the bored princess. Gerda screamed a string of curse words, adding;

"Stop it, stop it before it takes off again!" Panicking,

Lucinda ran forward and tried to block it from getting to the princess.

"Bad dragon, shoo!" she shouted hopelessly, waving her arms about. This appeared to be the last straw. It reared up, and took a deep breath. This was no warning shot.

"What are you doing, you great pansy!" Gerda shouted, flinging her own sword to the ground in frustration. "Stab 'im!" Lucinda, having finally received an order she could actually follow, did as she was told, and managed to catch the dragon on its webbed toes as it rose up. She cut right through one of the webs.

To her surprise, it let out a cry like a distressed chick, curled up into a ball and refused to move. Lucinda approached it cautiously. She poked it. It hissed and curled up even further.

"I-is it supposed to do that?" Lucinda asked, looking around for Gerda, who had picked up her sword and was running towards them. The princess came wandering up too, looking a little bewildered. "Is it all right?" Lucinda asked Gerda as the valkyrie caught up.

"Oh, it's fine," Gerda replied, waving her sword around. It seemed like Gerda could barely talk without waving her sword around, as though it had replaced half her body language. Lucinda stepped back a little, out of slicing range. "They're right soft, are dragons. One little scratch and they think they've been killed!"

"Really?" Lucinda asked, giving it a cautious stroke. Its scales were hard and smooth, but oddly warm. She'd thought it would feel cold. Now that it wasn't spitting at her and trying to bite her, she was fascinated. She couldn't believe it was a real dragon. It uncurled its head, and she moved away hurriedly, but it just sulked at them all. It was smaller than she would have expected too; about twice the size of a large horse.

"Oh yeah," Gerda continued, patting the dragon on the nose. "Do y'know how that George bloke killed that dragon? It flew at him and he swung at it and nicked its wing," she demonstrated, slicing through the air and of course, by waving her sword about, "so it landed, and do you know what it did? Just stood there, shivering. Then he tied it up, using a scarf the girl he'd rescued was wearin', led it to the town square, quiet as a lamb, then chopped the poor thing's head off. It's a pity, they really keep the other nasty stuff down. Harpies and the like, you know."

"How horrible!" Lucinda screwed up her face in disgust. She looked at the sulking dragon. It was now lying with its head on its paws, like a scolded dog. She couldn't help but feel sorry for it. It had looked vicious before, but wouldn't any animal defend itself? Although it had been trying to carry off a princess-

"Horrible?" said the princess, pouting. "Isn't anyone going to ask if I'm unhurt?"

"No," replied the valkyrie.

"Are you hurt?" asked Lucinda.

"I'm fine," replied the princess sourly, indignant at her treatment so far. Both of them had completely ignored her up to this point, and princesses aren't accustomed to being ignored. Then she remembered who she was and who she was talking to and mentally switched gear. "I mean, Thank goodness you were here! Thank you so much, my hero, I am forever in your debt," she said sweetly, flashing Lucinda a smile. "Noble prince, you have rescued me from this terrible beast!" she indicated the dragon, which had uncurled completely and was tentatively trying to nibble Gerda's sword. "Oh, I was ever so frightened!

You shall surely be greatly rewarded!" She paused for a moment as if she was looking at some internal script. "My father shall offer you half the kingdom and my hand in marriage," she finished coyly. Gerda sniggered.

The princess gave the valkyrie a dirty look before saying to Lucinda;

"Art thou not pleased, my prince?"

"Er, no?" Lucinda replied, looking completely baffled. Seeing the princess's expression darken again she explained, "I'm not allowed to get married. It's in my contract."

"That's right," Gerda chipped in gleefully. "It's in his contract," she added, adding extra weight to the 'his' and nudging Lucinda, who remembered that she was supposed to be a prince.

"What's so special about it being in his contract?" the princess asked, frowning suspiciously.

"Well it ain't in mine," Gerda cut in before Lucinda could answer. "I can run off and get married any time I like." She winked at Lucinda. "Of course, I'm already married, so that'd be a bit of a problem." Then she looked pointedly at the princess. "Well?"

"Well what?" the princess snapped back.

"You've been rescued, 'aven't you? What you standin' round here for?" Gerda jerked her head towards a village a short distance away. "Push off." The princess drew herself up and it looked as if she would argue. But instead she stuck her chin in the air, and with as much dignity as she could manage, turned and headed towards the village. Then Gerda seemed to remember something. "Oh, wait a minute."

"Yes?" the princess turned back, looking hopeful.

"Chuck it a couple of bangles and take your crown

off, for goodness sake!" the valkyrie chided. "Else you'll only get carried off again." The princess made a face and angrily took off three of the dozens of golden bangles she was wearing. She threw them at Gerda and then stormed off to the village, muttering to herself. The valkyrie watched her go and shook her head.

"She still hasn't took her crown off, like I said," she tutted. She threw the bangles to the dragon, who sniffed them, picked them up delicately in its teeth and trotted off happily, though limping a little.

"Will she be okay?" Lucinda asked, watching the princess stride away. "She looked really upset. Shouldn't you have told her I'm really a girl?" She looked from the princess to the departing dragon and back again. "Sara really wasn't kidding about rescuing princesses." Lucinda would have pinched herself, in case she was dreaming again, but she was bruised and sore from the fight, so that was a pretty good indication of reality as she saw it. "Why should she take her crown off?"

"You know magpies? They like shiny things, right?" Lucinda nodded. "Dragons is the same. They like gold, rubies, diamonds, anythin' sparkly." She thumbed in the princess's direction. "With the amount of jewellery she had on, it's no wonder she got carried off. And it was probably on purpose too, not her though, she looked like she couldn't find her bum with a map. Probably Daddy heard a dragon knocking about and said 'Daughter dearest, why don't you put on your best jewellery and go have a walk in the garden, go on, the bit in the middle where there's no cover'." Lucinda was shocked;

"But why?" she asked. "Why would anyone do it on purpose?"

"To get her married off, of course."

"Oh, come on," Lucinda shook her head in disbelief. "There's no way!"

"Look, kings don't want any unmarried daughters about, they only cause trouble," Gerda explained. "If they don't get cursed when they're born, then they're like a ticking wossname. Better to cause your own trouble than wait for something to 'appen. Pick your poison, as it were. Dragons ain't so bad, you ain't even seen one before, and you managed all right. Better to get 'er carried off by a dragon and rescued in short order than end up enragin' some fairy who curses you too. Givin' up half the kingdom is worth it."

"Wouldn't you end up with a lot of tiny kingdoms if you did that?" Lucinda asked, puzzled.

"Oh, you do," Gerda replied. "Most of the kingdoms you get round here are little more than a castle with a town attached. Leads to a lot of fightin', particularly at the point when someone ends up with 'alf a castle."

"I still don't see why you couldn't tell her I'm a girl, though," Lucinda asked, still pretty confused.

"Of course you can't tell people! If it gets out that there's a girl doin' a prince's job, all Nifelheim will let loose."

"But why though?" Lucinda insisted.

"'Cause of what just happened, that's why. Sara wouldn't 'alf get some earache! Not enough princes to go around, you see. Hearing there's fake princes about, everyone'd be up in arms."

"But wh-"

"You ask me why one more time, and I'll give you a right ding round the ear 'ole! Try waitin' 'til I've finished explainin', why don't you?" Gerda gave Lucinda a stern look. "It's traditional to 'ave lots of daughters, in large numbers, sixes or twelves, each more lovely than the last and all that nonsense. But princes usually come in ones or threes. I'm sure you can do the maths."

"So there's really a shortage of princes?" Lucinda asked, picking up her sword and staggering as she put it back in the scabbard.

"Oh yeah. And it's made worse by deservin' poor girls, too." Lucinda waited patiently for her to explain. "You get some poor girl being treated badly by her step family, there's a ball at the local palace, but does the prince want to marry any of the eligible princesses thronging the hall, who would be an important political investment, oh no, he's got to marry the mysterious stranger who comes flouncing in late and then leaves her footwear where people can trip over 'em."

THE SECOND TEST

Gerda continued to complain about surplus princesses basically mucking things up for everybody all the way back to the office. Finally they came back through into the Rent-a-Leg building. Lucinda asked why it was called 'Rent-a-Leg' and was told that it wasn't. It was short for 'Rent-a-Legend', 'short for' in this case meaning 'the other letters are covered in rust'. The place was a honeycomb of corridors and little staircases and seemed to have a bad case of doors. There were doors absolutely everywhere; lining the corridors, at odd angles from the wall, there were some on the floor and Lucinda had even spotted one on the ceiling. There were doors within doors. And all of them went to different places. Lucinda was told by Gerda that she was not to go into any doors unsupervised, on pain of death, by order of Sara. Lucinda resolved to not even look at a door without permission. If Sara said 'on pain of death' Lucinda was willing to bet that she actually meant it. Sara looked up as they came into the office.

"And how was our first day?" she asked unnecessarily brightly. "I see you passed the first test." She was perched on the inside edge of the desk, doing some paperwork. It looked really uncomfortable. Maybe that was why she seemed so grumpy all the time.

"I did?" Lucinda frowned, feeling that there was a loop and she was out of it. "How can you tell?"

"You're still alive," Sara replied. Her nonchalance put Lucinda on edge.

"What exactly do you do here?" Lucinda asked, sounding more hostile than she had intended. "What kind of company hires people to fight dragons?"

"We rent people out," Sara replied. "Story people. We make stories."

"You make stories?" Lucinda replied. Sara shrugged.

"Somebody has to. Better than just letting any old thing happen." She leaned forward. "Is there a problem?" she asked pointedly, giving her the kind of look that teachers give students who haven't done their homework and are waiting for their excuse. It said 'this had better be good'.

"I'll just be off then," Gerda announced. "I expect you've got stuff to discuss." She paused before adding, "She's a good 'un, this one, Sara. Don't be too . . . you, y'know? I'm off." She did a sort of salute with her sword and strolled off down the corridor.

"Not a problem as such, no," Lucinda answered, trying not to sound ticked off. She fixed Sara with a defiant stare. "But some warning would have been nice! It's just that I was expecting a job holding a sign or delivering newspapers, and suddenly I'm thrown in front of a dragon!"

"Sounds like there's a problem to me," Sara asked, licking the end of her pen and returning to her paperwork. "It's not like I didn't tell you what you were going to be doing yesterday."

"Well, yes, but I didn't think you were serious," Lucinda answered, feeling slightly guilty.

"Now you know better," Sara replied. "We make stories. Stuff that happens in stories is going to happen to you. And it won't all be nice. Stories aren't nice. You want a job delivering newspapers, you go and get one. I won't stop you." She looked back down at her paperwork. Lucinda waited. After a minute Sara looked back up. "Still here, are you?" She gave her the teacher's look again. It looked like she was peering over a pair of invisible glasses.

"I can handle it," Lucinda said. 'I'm going to have to,' she thought to herself.

"When I say things won't be nice, I mean it," Sara replied. "You might be better cut out for newspapers. We aren't talking Mr. Bunny Goes to Market here." Lucinda hesitated.

"What sort of not nice stuff?"

"The kind that happens in stories," Sara replied tartly. "Worse than fighting dragons, certainly."

"Oh. Um." Was she really better suited to a normal job . . ? This was the sort of thing she dreamed about, the sort of thing she sought out every day. She hadn't thought dragons were real up until today, but she'd always kind of hoped. Could she really give this up, knowing it was here? Yesterday she would have laughed at the idea of actually fighting monsters. But now it all seemed so . . . easy. It had been the easiest thing in the world to go from 'dragons aren't real' to 'dragons are real and I have to beat this one'. She couldn't walk away and do something normal knowing about Rent-a-Legend. She just couldn't. She wouldn't be Lucinda if she chose normal over this.

She thought about stories. Sure, bad things happened in stories. But she was going to be the hero. So that would be all right, wouldn't it? Bad things happened to heroes, but they always came out of it okay. Otherwise, where was the justice in the world? Especially a world with dragons in it.

"You can walk away right now," Sara continued, "I won't blame you."

"No," Lucinda replied. Somehow, she must keep the job, and not just because of the money. The money was a pretty big motivator on its own. But something told her that this is where she was meant to be. "I'm not going to walk away." Sara gave her a good, long look.

"And you're sure?" Sara asked.

"Yes," Lucinda answered defiantly.

"Good," Sara smiled. "See you next week, then. Nine o' clock, Saturday." Lucinda nodded and walked towards the door, feeling odd. She wasn't sure if she was being bullied or if she'd just passed a test. Just as she had her hand on the doorknob, Sara spoke again;

"Cinders?"

"Yes?" Lucinda said, without turning round.

"Do you know why you got this job? Do you know how many people came here asking for it?"

"No." This time Lucinda did turn.

"Just you," Sara replied, quietly. She looked quite melancholy. "I had that paper specially enchanted so that only people who believed in stories could read it. You do believe in stories, don't you?" she asked. "Now that you've been in one, I mean." She fiddled with her pen.

"Sure?" Lucinda answered tentatively, caught off guard by such an odd question. Surely being in a story was even more reason to believe in them?

"Don't let me down, Cinders," Sara flashed her a sad smile, and returned to her paperwork. Lucinda let herself out.

She headed home feeling weird. She'd fought a dragon today. And won. But believe in stories? How was one supposed to believe in stories, exactly? She wondered what Sara had meant.

When she got home, she was accosted by her mother in the kitchen. Her father was reading the paper, as usual. He looked over the top of it, gave a snort of laughter on seeing her unusual attire and returned to the sports section.

"I hope they pay you enough, is all I can say," he remarked. Lucinda opened her mouth to retort, but realised that she had no idea what she was being paid and wisely shut it again. Her mother fussed and complained about 'the things they make young people do these days' and Lucinda was glad to retreat upstairs.

She immediately got onto her laptop and called Anna.

"What are you wearing? Is that for the video?" Anna asked her, peering at her screen, "'Cause if it is, you should've asked Pens first. He's designing all the costumes, you know."

"I know," Lucinda replied. "It's for work," she said, with a hint of pride.

"Oh man, you got a job?" Anna squealed and clapped her hands. "No way, where the heck do you work dressed like that?"

"It's like an acting job. Sort of." Lucinda scratched her head. It wasn't a lie, exactly. But she couldn't just outright say that it was a job fighting monsters and rescuing people. Even Anna would think she was crazy, and she wouldn't have blamed her.

"Anyway, congrats!" Anna gave her a double thumbs up. "Now you'll be able to get the money and we can all do this thing! Pens told me he has a job at a fast food place and don't ask me how, but Copper got a job in a fabric store. Like she even knows anything about that stuff. But it should be useful if she can get us cheap materials, though,"

Anna laughed. "Who knows, maybe she'll even learn something about sewing!"

"Yeah, I feel bad for Pens having to do most of the costume work," Lucinda agreed. She was quiet for a minute before adding, "You know, you really should stop lurking. I know you're there, you answered the conference call thingy!"

"And miss you girls gossiping about me?" came a third, male voice. Pens had no webcam, so there was no live feed, but there was an avatar of a boy with long, brown hair grinning back at them from his box instead. "Anyway, I wasn't here, Mum shouted me for something just as I picked up the call. Why, what did you say?"

"She says you're a terrible friend and she never liked you," Anna answered him, mockingly.

"Aww Cinders, I was gonna propose and everything!" he joked. "Hey, what did you do to your hair? I thought it was a wig, but it's not, huh?"

"Oh wow, me too. Gosh, I'm unobservant," Anna replied, hitting herself on the forehead.

"It's for work," Lucinda replied. "Hey guys . . . do you believe in stories?"

"What like, that mermaids are real and ghost stories and stuff?" Anna replied. "I guess some of them might be? I mean, scientists have only explored a bit of the ocean and you can't prove ghosts aren't real, right?"

"I think she means more like . . . that good should always win and the hero always gets the girl," Pens chipped in. "I guess so? It would be nice, but it doesn't always work out that way. All the guys with girlfriends around here are jerks, if you ask me," he complained. "They couldn't hero their way out of a paper bag!" The girls laughed;

"And you could?" they said in unison.

"Yeah, probably," Pens replied. "What kind of a question is that, anyway?"

"Oh, just something I was asked at work," Lucinda mused. "It seemed important . . . "

"It was probably one of those psychoanalysis questions, like what's your favourite colour and if you were an animal, what would it be and junk," Anna replied, shrugging. "I wouldn't take it too seriously. It's just a thing companies do."

"I guess so," Lucinda conceded.

"Seriously, don't worry about it," Anna reassured her. "Now, about this choreography, Pens-"

Lucinda spent most of the week being incredibly bored at school. She had made a few friends; Shu, a British-born Chinese girl, who seemed to know everyone on some level, had made her acquaintance, and she mostly hung out with her and her friends during class and break. But they didn't really share the same interests, and so her conversations with them were limited. Luckily she had Pens and the others to talk to after school about such things, although mostly how she was still getting the choreography wrong and how they weren't going to win the contest like that. It was great fun, but she couldn't wait until they could all be together.

When Saturday rolled around, Lucinda set off for the office early and arrived at about quarter to nine. She'd slept better this time around, but not much. Today at least, she was prepared. More prepared than last week, at any rate. Now she knew dragons liked shiny things, but didn't like actual fighting much, and particularly now that she knew they actually existed, rescuing princesses should be a doddle. She put on her prince outfit with a new found confidence.

It didn't last long.

"Take that off," Sara commanded, indicating her prince costume. "You won't be needing it today."

"But it's all I brought," Lucinda replied, dismayed. "What will I be needing?"

"This." Sara slid a package wrapped in brown paper over the desk. "It was finally delivered last night. Just in time. It's for your next test."

"I have another test?" Lucinda asked nervously, unwrapping the paper. Inside was a set of green clothes, similar to her prince outfit, but not so gaudy. There was also a pair of brown trousers, and some soft, brown leather boots. They came almost up to her knees.

"I told you the other day, you'll have three," Sara explained. "It's traditional." Lucinda felt her stomach lurch. She hated tests. It was bad enough worrying about what monster she was going to have to fight without worrying that she was being graded on it as well.

"Is it going to be worse than a dragon?" Lucinda quailed at the thought. What if it was a hydra? Or a gorgon, that could turn her to stone? What if it was a giant, who could just step on her or . . . She could barely think the thought.

"Definitely worse," Sara replied. "Dragons are easy. Dragons are dumb. Show them something shiny and they're no trouble. People aren't though. People are hard." That gave Lucinda a flicker of hope. It looked like she wasn't going to have to fight some terrifying beast she wasn't ready for today. "I didn't put that there for decoration," Sara scolded her, indicating the package of clothes. "Get dressed. They're waiting already."

"Who's waiting?" Lucinda paused as she lifted the package from the counter, looking baffled.

"The other eleven girls, of course," Sara replied.

Lucinda and the 'other eleven girls', all the same height, all in the same clothes and all, much to Lucinda's surprise, with the same hair had gathered in a forest. They were waiting for the leader girl and her father to explain why they were all here. Sara certainly hadn't. The girl and her father had walked around thanking them all for their participation and handing out equipment. Despite her identical apparel, the leader must have been a princess, because her father was clearly a king. Kings are hard to miss, especially when they're wearing crowns and ermine-trimmed robes.

Lucinda was worried. She'd been provided with a bow and arrows along with the hunter's costume, and hadn't the faintest idea how to use them. To take her mind of it, she tried to guess what sort of story this was. Given that all her companions looked the same, it was probably a clever ruse to trick somebody and win a bet or complete a terrible task. Perhaps they were going to cheat in a race. A really long race, if it needed twelve people. Or maybe someone had to pick their true love out of all these identical maidens. But then why were they dressed as men? It wasn't a big deal back home of course, but in stories it was always out of some dire need, and there would be terrible consequences if they were discovered. With a jolt, she realised the nature of the second test. She mustn't be found out. Right. That seemed easy enough . . . she was rather a tomboy, so she didn't need to worry about acting horribly girly. But she didn't think she acted particularly like a man either . . . She was running various scenarios through her head, largely involving having to pretend to shave or bathe discreetly in a pool when finally, they were called to pay attention.

"I'm so glad you've all agreed to help my daughter," the king boomed. "She came to me a few weeks ago and she was most distraught. So I said, daughter, whatever you desire, I shall get for you," he paused and a confused look flitted across his face, "and she said 'I want eleven girls who look like me, and twelve sets of huntsmen's clothes'." The princess nodded appreciatively. He continued, "That sounded like a damn funny request to me, but I did promise. Anyway, she's going to explain herself now, and I just hope all that trouble I went to was worth it, is all I can say."

"Dear comrades!" the princess began, "My fiancé promised to marry me when he became king, but now I hear he is engaged to another. This will not do!" There were murmurs of agreement from the girls. "We shall go to his palace, thus disguised, and shall enter his service as huntsmen! He shall not know us, though we be with him all the while! That should show him," she finished with an air of triumph. This met with some confusion.

"Er, dear," the king began, "are you sure this is the best course of action?"

"Yeah," agreed Lucinda, without thinking. "Isn't that a bit . . . a bit . . . crazy ex-girlfriend?"

"Well, that'll teach him for marrying someone else,

then won't it?" another girl argued.

"Indeed!" the princess stamped her foot. "If he doesn't want people sneaking into his palace in disguise, he shouldn't have left me to marry someone else when he'd already promised!"

"Yes dear, but isn't this a bit excessive?" the king persisted.

"Not in the slightest," the princess replied. "I want to see who this hussy is and what my future husband thinks he's up to. And of course I need a retinue. It's only proper." The king still looked unhappy. Lucinda could tell, because it was the face her father often wore when she was explaining why exactly she needed a long green wig and some tights with bats on and specifically why she needed him to pay for it now instead of saving up her pocket money. She could see his point though.

"Excuse me," she asked, putting her hand in the air. "Why don't you just go and ask this prince why he's marrying someone else? Maybe he's got a reasonable explanation?" There was silence as the group considered this idea. Some of them looked downright horrified, including the King;

"No, no that won't do," he replied, frowning at her. "That won't do at all. You can't just go around asking things." That was a new one on Lucinda.

"Why not?" she asked.

"Because you just don't," the princess replied in place of her father. "You have to turn up for three nights in a row in three different dresses and give them to the false bride in exchange for sleeping outside the king's bedroom, or get a job working in the kitchens and keep sneaking gold into his soup, you can't just ask things. I mean, you just, you just don't."

The king nodded in agreement. "You're absolutely right, my dear, you're absolutely right." He laid his hand on her shoulder. "I mean, I was worried that maybe you just needed three huntsmen or six, or if it wouldn't work out better if you were a goose-girl, but, I'm sure you have a plan in mind and we shall see how it goes. And if anyone gets injured, you've got lots of spares, right?"

"That's right father," the princess agreed earnestly. "You must leave now, we must be on our way." When she was quite sure the king had gone, she called out to Lucinda, "You there! At the back! The dissenting girl, yes you!" Lucinda stood up straight and almost saluted;

"Yes?" she started.

"Good show!" The princess went to clap genteelly, but then decided it would be more manly to punch the air instead. "That was brilliant, I thought Daddy was going to stop the plan then, phew!" There was a brief round of applause. "Ha ha, can you imagine if you were serious though? 'Why don't we just ask?' Oh, you are a clever one! What's your name?"

"Lucinda," Lucinda answered meekly.

"Ugh, that won't do. Do think of a boy's name to go by," the princess commanded. "That goes for all of you. Anyway, glad to have you aboard. Let's be off!" she added, leading the way out of the forest.

On the way, the girls had a go at practising walking like men, talking like men, and suitable manly topics for conversation. Lucinda had no idea at all, since her idea of 'manly' topics was limited to football and Call of Duty, neither of which she knew anything about and neither of which they would have here. Pens liked almost the exact same stuff that she did. She was the sort of girl who didn't get on with other girls, unless they themselves also didn't get on with girls. Her and Copper, an Australian friend of hers, had had a conversation on the topic, which had started off on the subject of Pens being the kind of boy who didn't hang out with other boys. As it was, the princess briefed them on the subject of hunting, which she had bothered to learn about by asking her father some questions. She could remember the information okay, but Lucinda had only ever fired a bow once, at a fair, and it had been a lot harder than it looked. Her arrow had gone about two feet, if that. Not that she was planning on hitting anything, but she was going to have to make it look like she was trying, surely?

It wasn't long before they arrived at the palace. The new king was quite happy to hire them all, and there was a short ceremony where they bowed to their new master and were presented with a token of their employment. There was a large lion sitting quietly right next to the king's throne. No-one even batted an eyelid at it. It was as if kings always had an untethered, man-eating beast next to them. Powerfully curious, she stayed behind a little as the other girls left for the courtyard leaving it and the king alone. She peeked around the doorway at it. She had the shock of her life.

It spoke.

"Dude," the lion said to the king in a mellow sort of tone, "those are girls, man." It had quite the wrong sort of voice for such an animal. It sounded like a hippie or a guru. Someone who had figured out the whole universe and was completely at peace with it. The king however, did not look at peace. He looked affronted.

"Oh come on, they're so not," he retorted. "They're huntsmen, you can tell, by how they're wearing huntsmen's clothes. I mean, why would they be dressed like that if they were girls, right?"

"I'm telling you man . . . " The lion shook his head as if he were laughing something off. " . . . they're totally girls. Trust me."

"Prove it then," the king said huffily, crossing his arms. "Prove to me that they're girls."

"Hmmmmm . . . " The lion closed his eyes. Lucinda realised she was holding her breath and let it out as quietly and slowly as she could. "How abooout . . . we spread peas on the floor?" he concluded after some deliberation.

" . . . Have you been at the catnip again?" the king said in an exasperated tone, raising both eyebrows. "How will that prove they're girls?"

"Princesses can feel a pea through many layers of mattresses, right?" the lion observed. "So like, they can totally feel one through one boot, easy." The king immediately spotted a flaw in this plan;

"What if they aren't princesses?" he pointed out.

"The chances of them being princesses is pretty high, man," the lion replied. "There's like, twelve of them." The king nodded thoughtfully.

"I'll have a servant bring peas from the kitchen and call them back," he said.

Lucinda crept away until she was sure she wouldn't be heard and ran as fast as she could to the courtyard, where the girls were waiting. Panting, she hurriedly explained the situation. The princess nodded.

"Very well. Now then-" She stood up to address the others, "-are any of you also princesses?" Four of the girls put their hands up. "Now, I know we all have very sensitive skin, but girls, you must step firmly on the peas. Just pretend they aren't there. We shall not be discovered."

The king called them back to the throne room, under the pretence that he wished to look upon his fine new employees once more. The girls stepped right over the peas without flinching. The lion appeared nonplussed.

"Such fine huntsmen you are!" the king exclaimed, putting the tiniest stress on the word men and throwing the lion a look as he did so.

"Is that all you wish of us, my liege?" the princess said, in one of the cringe-worthiest, fake, male voices Lucinda had ever heard.

"Yes, my dear huntsmen, that will be all," the king nodded graciously at them. Lucinda hung back once more.

"See?" the king told the lion smugly. "They didn't feel the peas, I told you they were men. Score one to me." Once more the lion looked thoughtful, insofar as a lion can.

"Somebody must have warned them, man," came his eventual reply. "You should like, give them another test."

The king scoffed. "Well this time, I'm picking the test," he answered haughtily. "Let's see . . . we should put spinning wheels at the side of the room there. Girls like spinning wheels. They'll be distracted by the spinning wheels and want to try them out. Men would never do that."

"That's sexist, man," the lion replied, sounding disappointed. "Just because girls do spinning a lot doesn't mean it's like, their hobby or something."

"Yes it does," The king replied. "Girls like spinning. They're always spinning straw into gold and all that. Or whatever you spin stuff from. I've never done it, because I'm not a girl. See? It's foolproof."

"Really, man?" the lion continued, obviously trying to keep the sarcasm out of his voice. "Maybe we should put some flowers on the spinning wheels, and some kittens, and like . . . what do modern ladies like . . . chocolate and some shoes," he said, "and a pony. Girls like ponies, too."

"Great idea, let's do that!" The king clapped his hands, while the lion rolled his eyes. "Footman!"

Once more Lucinda pelted to the courtyard to warn them of the plan, and once more the princess ordered the girls to ignore the trap. The king called for the huntsmen again. He really had had twelve spinning wheels brought out. He had also added flowers, chocolates, kittens, shoes and a very small pony, which was tethered to the last spinning wheel and was eating the other distractions in a gormless sort of way. The girls walked right past them and ignored them completely. The king sent them out again. Lucinda hung back once more.

"I told you so, dude. There's no way anyone would ignore all that stuff," the lion said, looking up at the king in disdain, "girls or not. Someone warned them they were gonna be tested, I'm telling you, man." The king looked over to the curious array of things on the other side of the throne room. The pony dislodged a fluffy white kitten from the top of a chocolate box and started to munch on the contents.

"I suppose so," The king agreed grudgingly, "but I still don't think they're girls. I think you just don't like huntsmen. You never like my huntsmen." The lion gave this due consideration;

"Call them back in here and I'll prove it to you once and for all," he stated confidently.

"How do we stop them preparing for it, if they really are being warned?" the king asked.

"Trust me, man," the lion replied, "they're not getting out of this one."

Lucinda ran back to the courtyard and told the others that they were to be tested again, but that she didn't know how and that it was something they wouldn't be able to fake. The footman came to get them immediately, what with not having some silly trap to prepare, so they had no time to think of a plan. As Lucinda waited in line, wondering what the lion had up his non-existent sleeve, it dawned on her what the test was . . .

"My huntsmen, my lion Aesop here has a request for you," the king announced. "Please do as he asks." The 'huntsmen' waited with baited breath.

"Take off your shirts," the lion commanded, smugly. There were shrieks of indignation and horror from the line of girls, as many of them instinctively covered their chests. The king leaned over and said to the lion;

" . . . Why didn't you just ask that for the first test?" The lion merely smiled.

"You gotta have three tests, man. It's traditional." The king smirked and looked back at the line of now silent huntsmen.

"Well? Remove your shirts, 'gentlemen'." The princess glared back at him. She narrowed her eyes.

"You'd like that, wouldn't you?" she scolded him. "Marrying any old hussy that comes to court you, I'll wager we're not the first girls you've asked, you promise-breaking charlatan!"

"Alana, is that you?" he asked. The girl stuck her tongue out at him.

"It's about time!" she berated him. "Honestly, why do I even want to marry you?"

The other girls were herded out of the room by the wise lion to let the couple sort out their differences. He explained that the king had promised his father on his deathbed that he would marry someone else and that he had been trying to think of an honourable way to get out of the unwanted betrothal. He hadn't been any cleverer with that, and so it had been taking them a while to sort out.

Lucinda headed back to Rent-A-Legend feeling odd. No-one had noticed they were girls except a talking, magical lion. Heck, the man hadn't even recognised his own fiancée until she shouted at him. So maybe this was going to be easier than she thought. She did wonder how Sara would react. But as she was thinking about that, another problem became alarmingly apparent. She didn't know how to get back to the offices. She had arrived back at the small clearing where she'd come from, but there was no door here, just like there had been no door when she'd been shoved in front of the dragon yesterday. Gerda had opened a door in the nearby village that led back to the offices then, but Gerda wasn't here. She took a few deep breaths, trying not to panic, when a door opened right in the air.

"She's back. Blimey, that didn't take long, did it?" Gerda had opened the door from the other side, and was stood holding it open. It was the strangest thing, a doorway just hanging there in the middle of nowhere. But Lucinda had seen stranger things today, and she merely stepped through gratefully. "I knew you wouldn't know 'ow to get back, so I kept checkin' through the door for you," Gerda explained. "'Ow did it go then?"

"I think I'd better tell Sara . . . " Lucinda made her way down the corridor to get her 'grade'.

Lucinda was a bundle of nerves, she'd expected the test to be based on if she was discovered or not, in which case she had surely failed.

"So only the lion noticed you were women, even after he told the king about you?" she summarised. Lucinda waited tensely for her response. "Hmm. That'll do." Sara looked back down to her papers and rifled through them, looking for something.

"So..?" Lucinda prompted, looking hopeful.

"You pass," Sara confirmed. Lucinda sagged with relief. "Be back here tomorrow at nine," Sara added. Lucinda nodded gratefully and left. She was elated at how well it had gone, but she couldn't help wonder what strange task awaited her next . . .

YOU'RE NOT DOING IT RIGHT

Lucinda arrived the next morning to find Sara sat on the edge of the desk, deep in conversation with the posh-looking woman from the other day. She felt like she shouldn't interrupt, so she closed the door quietly and hung back to wait for them to finish.

"It's much too early," Sara was saying, "I don't care what Gerda said about it being good training, I'm not sending someone I don't trust. So I'm sending you." It was hard to tell behind all the fur, but the woman looked doubtful.

"If it is too cold . . . " came the muffled response. Now it was Sara's turn to look doubtful.

"Freya," she said witheringly, as if she were a teacher addressing a particularly slow pupil, "it's sub-tropical down there-"

"But I cannot go in the water, and the villagers don't trust me-" the woman addressed as Freya replied.

"I don't have a choice. He's been missing for over a week and it's not like him. You know what Charmings are like. Something is wrong. If anything has happened to him, I . . . I . . . " Freya put a gloved hand on Sara's shoulder, and was about to say something, but then she caught sight of Lucinda.

"Good mornink," she greeted her loudly.

"Hmm?" Sara looked round sharply. "Oh, morning Cinders. There's no need to skulk by the door. This is

Freya," she said, gesturing to the furry woman. "She's one of my top employees."

"Pleased to meet you," Lucinda said, holding out her hand. Freya took it. Her hand was oddly cold for wearing such a thick glove.

"Pleased to meet you, also. Freya Fumikosdottir," she introduced herself. "Sara has told me you had a good first day. Well done. We had some princes, the trouble we had with them, you would not belief." She had an accent Lucinda couldn't quite place. She thought maybe it was Russian or Norwegian.

"Lucinda Martin," Lucinda responded. "That's an unusual name." Although she was painfully aware that the woman right next to her was Saharaleia something something something, Freya's name sounded like an Earth name with something out of place.

"I am Icelandic, but my grandmother came from Japan," Freya explained. "Many people remark on this, don't worry."

"Now you've been properly introduced, I think you should be going, Freya," Sara announced, shooing her away from the desk. "I'm not paying you to chat to the new girl. See if you can't find out about that thing."

"What thing?" Lucinda asked curiously as Freya's furry form disappeared into the corridor. It was a wonder she could fit through with all that stuff on. Then again, maybe it was all fur and if you chucked a bucket of water over her she'd shrink down in size. One of the shells above the desk started to make a weird, flapping noise.

"If I'd wanted you to know, I wouldn't have called it 'that thing'," replied Sara, giving Lucinda a stern look, before reaching over to grab the ringing shell. "Good morning, this is Rent-A-Legend." She listened intently to the shell, occasionally nodding. "Oh dear. No, that won't do." She glanced over at Lucinda. "No, no, we don't have any. And I don't think that would solve the problem, not like you want." She listened again. "Look, I've got a prince, will he do?" There was another pause. "That's all very well, but I'm afraid you're going to have to take it or leave it . . . Right then." Sara yanked on the shell's cord and it shot back upwards. "Well, that was your assignment for today. Possibly more than today. You might have to spend the night in a spooky castle."

"What?"

"You heard. Consider it your final test. I seem to recall we had a conversation about this not being all kittens and sparkles." Sara nodded towards the rightmost corridor. "Get going. It's the black door, about seven doors down on the left. You can't miss it, it's got bats carved in it." She rummaged around for some papers under the desk.

"Um . . . " Lucinda took a few steps towards the door but immediately shuffled back again.

"Problem?" Sara asked sharply, giving her what she had come to think of as 'the invisible glasses look'.

"It's just that I was told I've not to go through the doors unsupervised. You showed me through yesterday . . . " Lucinda trailed off.

"I've told you which door it is. You've been supervised enough," Sara replied. "From what they told me, there's nothing in there that will hurt you," she continued, adding, "which appears to be the problem."

"What is it I'm dealing with today? People? Monsters?" Lucinda asked, still unwilling to leave.

"You're going to a little place called Bad Schwartz," Sara explained. "Their vampire is broken. Go and fix him."

"I don't suppose you could tell me how to do that?"

Lucinda hazarded.

"Quests don't come with 'how to' instructions, Cinders," Sara replied, giving her the look again. "Heroes get told there's a problem and then they deal with it. So deal with it."

Once through the door, Lucinda found herself in a narrow, rocky cave. Once again, with no door. Gerda had picked her up both times so far, and Lucinda fervently wished she'd been paying attention. Would Gerda pick her up again this time? This might take much longer than the last test and Gerda's job was not limited to being a rookie chaperone. If only she knew how to find doors.

Lucinda was also concerned about spending the night. It was Sunday, and she had school tomorrow. Her parents would go *spare*. She couldn't take her mobile with her on quests, it would surely arouse suspicion and it wouldn't work anyway, so she had no way to contact them if she would be out late. She'd be grounded for life! There'd be no way she was allowed to go to America then. But it was early morning after all . . . at least she had plenty of time.

After poking at the walls for several minutes trying to suss out a return door, Lucinda decided that she may as well head into the town. She had a job to do, and in any case Sara knew where she was. If she didn't come back, Sara would be *bound* to send someone looking for her. Probably. A girl could dream.

With a final, hopeful glance at the rocks, Lucinda headed out of the cave. It came out on the side of a valley, where a narrow, winding path led steeply downwards towards the village. Both sides of the valley were covered thickly in trees, but Lucinda was so high up she could easily see the houses at the bottom of the valley and the other side, which was nowhere as steep. It also had a tall, forbidding castle, towering above the forest. That was unquestionably where she was supposed to spend the night. If you were in a strange place by yourself in a story, then it was inevitable that you would end up in the biggest, scariest and above all, most dangerous building around. She squinted at it, trying to make out if there were bodies hanging from the castle turrets or any other such worrying signs, but it was too far away. She set off down the path, trying not to slip. Once out of the forest, she came upon a villager, an old woman, drawing water from a stone well. The villager glanced round as she approached, looked back at her pail of water and then did a double take. She nearly spilled her water in her haste to put it down, and hobbled over to Lucinda as fast as she could.

"Welcome-" she spat the word, "-to Bad Schwartz," she hissed. "What sorry errand brings a young lord like yourself to our wretched town?" She was squinting furiously. Lucinda wondered if she had something wrong with her eye.

"Er, I'm not sure," she replied, "I think I'm here about a vampire."

"'Tis a terrible place for-" the old woman stopped abruptly. *"What?"*

"I said I think I'm here about a vampire," Lucinda repeated. The old woman looked as if she'd been stung.

"No, no, no!" she said crossly, in a much more normal voice. "You're doing it all wrong! You're here to see the Count on matters of business. You are most definitely *not* here to see about a vampire."

"But-"

51

"I expect you're here to see the Count on matters of business," the old woman said, going back to sounding like a snake in a sandpit. "Oh, you poor lad. So tragic." She shook her head sadly.

"Oh, er, yes," Lucinda agreed, deciding it was for the best to play along. "I have business with the Count."

"'Tis as I feared," the old woman whispered. She pointed up towards the hill, her finger shaking. "He lives in yonder castle."

"Thank you?" Lucinda replied tentatively, starting to head in that direction. The woman grabbed her arm.

"'Tis a terrible and unholy place! *Death* awaits all who enter!" the woman wailed. Then she added in a normal voice, "Now, if you just follow this road straight here, you'll come out the other side and there's a forest path, just go up there. Can't miss it. I'm so glad they sent someone."

"Right, thanks," replied Lucinda, pulling her arm away and heading in the direction the woman had pointed. She had just reached the first house when the woman came scurrying up shouting;

"Ooh, ooh! I forgot! You mustn't be out after sunset-" she paused, then added in a spooky voice, "-woe betide thee if thou linger out of doors after sunset . . . 'twould be a most grievous thing."

Lucinda looked around as she walked through the village. It was actually very nice, and not wretched at all. There were pretty window boxes full of flowers on every house and there was a splendid fountain in the village square. The houses all had very tall, pointy roofs and they were painted different colours. The streets were cobbled. The place was positively picturesque. The only thing that seemed out of place were the bars on the windows. The villagers themselves seemed to be the most dreadful thing about the place. A woman suddenly grabbed her wrist when she reached the fountain about halfway through the village.

"Good sir, are you going to the castle?" she enquired. Lucinda nodded. "Oh you poor creature! Do take this talisman!" she said earnestly, pressing a carved, wooden amulet into Lucinda's hand.

"Um, thank you?" Lucinda said.

"Much good it will do," the woman mumbled.

"Does . . . does it not work?" Lucinda asked nervously. "Is it not powerful enough?" The woman gave a snort.

"That'll be the day!" she scoffed. "I don't know why I even bother. I've got all these charms and things, and we never need them."

"You don't?" Lucinda was baffled.

"And don't even get me *started* on garlic," she complained. "Is it too much to ask for a little consideration for the small business owner?"

"No?" Lucinda tried.

"That's right, no!" the woman said. "You tell him from me. Oh, and make sure you're in before sunset." With that, she turned on her heel and left, muttering to herself.

Lucinda managed to get to the other side of town before she was stopped again, when a woodsman on the edge of the forest nearly chopped his own leg off trying to keep an eye on her and chop wood at the same time.

"My lord, hark-" he started, but Lucinda stopped him. It was hot and she was tired and she didn't know how to get back home and she just wanted to get wherever she was going without being yelled at.

"Yeah, yeah, everything is horrible, please punch that guy in the face," she said irritably. "How much longer before I get there?"

"About twenty minutes on foot," the woodsman replied in a perfectly sensible tone. "I suppose you've been told to be in before sunset?"

"Yes."

"Good. Do you know, the last three heroes I told actually turned around and *walked away?*" he said in a disgusted tone. "Actually *walked away!* One of them was muttering about health and safety! What's the world coming to, I ask you? And I heard tell some of them left after just *two* warnings!" he carried on. "Two! *Three* warnings is traditional and they *actually left* after two!" Lucinda nodded politely and made to carry on up the path, but the woodcutter stopped her. "I'm really glad you're going," he said, sounding genuinely relieved. "Please talk some sense into him, he's been just terrible, and I don't mean in a good way. He's got, listen to this, he's got a *girlfriend!*" he complained. "And she's normal! Well," he stopped ranting for a moment, "she's a witch, from what I heard. But that's another thing!" he carried on. "Does she have the decency to descend upon the town wearing black and cursing people? NO! She comes up here wearing *white* and she brings a *picnic basket!* And *singing!*"

"I expect it's not decent hauntingly beautiful, bewitching, 'come hither little children' singing either?" Lucinda asked, catching on. "I expect she sings to bluebirds, about princes and dreams and so on?"

"No, that would be better," the woodsman said, shaking his head. "I mean, at least that would be proper. If you're singing in the woods, that's what you're supposed to be singing. But she just sings sort of . . . normally. Just, you know, normal songs. Although, I thought I heard her singing about cats made of jelly once." He made an odd face, then shook his head as if dislodging a thought. "And she's not very good. I mean, she ought to be really good or really awful, but she's just . . . *normal,*" the woodsman tutted. "Young people today, I ask you! And that's *another* thing! *Young!* He's supposed to be an ancient evil that men are not meant to wot of! But he's only twenty-one! *Twenty-one!* Even I'm older than him!" He looked at Lucinda's face which had taken on the stony expression of people who are wishing they hadn't said something, and scratched his nose. "I do apologise sir, I've kept you for far too long," he said, looking embarrassed. "Anyway, I hope you can sort him out, m'lord. Good day to you." He turned back to his chopping.

Lucinda wasn't too sure what to make of that last warning. 'Please sort him out,' he'd said. And Sara had told her to 'fix their vampire' whatever that meant. Did she have to stake the guy? She had her sword with her, but she didn't know if that would work. Besides, that was killing somebody. She couldn't just go around killing people. Of course, if he was the traditional kind, then she wasn't going to have much choice. But somehow, she got the impression that him *not* being the traditional kind was the problem.

It was much cooler in the forest, and a great relief after walking all the way across town. But the forest was quite thick, and that made it gloomy. Lucinda thought she could see shapes moving in the darkness. She shivered. This place seemed a whole world away from the bright, little village, covered in flowers. It put her in mind of one of those scary video games, where there's nothing but creepy scenery and movements out of the corner of your eye, but then all of a sudden there's some horrible monster or ghost lurching out at you. She fiddled with the hilt of her sword. She wasn't very good at using it. When she'd been fighting the dragon, she realised with a horrible sinking feeling, the only reason she'd had such an easy time was that the dragon had been too interested in her shiny sword to really attack her properly.

The further she got into the forest, the more convinced she became that something was following her. She looked around nervously, jumping at every rustle of leaves and snap of twigs. The trees were starting to look like they had faces. When she thought she saw one of them wink at her, she looked straight ahead and strode up the path, determined to look as confident as possible. Nothing sensible would attack a confident swordsman, right?

There was a horrible growl from the bushes on her left.

Lucinda tore off up the path, as fast as her legs would carry her. But the path was gradually getting steeper and she wasn't the best runner in the world. There were panting and crashing noises coming from either side of the path now, and they were getting closer. She forced herself onwards, ignoring the burning pain in her legs. The castle was still nowhere in sight, and she had no way of knowing how far away it was.

Suddenly, she came to a fork in the road. Lucinda broke out into a cold sweat. She knew the castle was up here somewhere, but she didn't know if there was anything else. If she took the wrong road, she might end up even further away from it, heading towards who knows what. And she wouldn't know until it was too late. All around her, howls went up from the trees. Not having any time to stop and think, she ran straight up the left path. The trees thinned out here, and she could see black shapes following her on both sides. Three enormous wolves burst out of the undergrowth and stood snarling, right in the middle of the trail. She couldn't possibly run past them, so she stumbled to a halt, gasping for breath, and drew her sword. It was the only thing she could think of to do.

"Get back!" she screamed at the wolves, which were stood there growling and slavering. One of them took a step forward. "Get back, I said!" she shouted again, her sword shaking as she stood there trembling from fear and exhaustion. The wolves stayed were they were, but continued to snarl. An idea struck her, "I don't-" she gasped, trying to get the words out and get her breath back at the same time, "-I don't suppose you speak English?" The wolves merely growled louder. The leading wolf started to move forwards, this time followed by the other two on the path. Lucinda risked a backward glance to check none of them were sneaking up on her and was surprised to find that there were none barring her way down. Thanking her lucky stars, she hurtled back down the path, but her sword was now a hindrance, and it bit into her leg as she swung her arm downwards. Crying out in pain, she stumbled, letting go of the sword, and fell, rolling several feet down the path. Battered and bruised as she was, with blood now running down one leg, she dragged herself back up again. More wolves had appeared from the trees further down; she had nowhere to go. She looked around in panic, and saw the others bounding down the path the way she had come. But her heart leapt when she realised that she was at the fork in the road again, and the path to the right was free. Without waiting to see what the wolves would do, Lucinda forced her aching legs to propel her upwards. She'd never run so much in her life; her lungs felt like they were on fire. She ran almost blindly onwards, the wolves shadowing her on either side, until after what felt like an eternity, she saw the castle. It was tall and black, and it was surrounded by matching tall, black railings and an ornate gate. The gate was slightly ajar. She dredged up a last reserve of strength that she didn't know she had, and wrenched the gate open just enough so that she could fit through. Once through, she heaved on the other side of the gate until it clanged shut. She hurriedly removed her hands from the gate in case the wolves tried to bite them, but they were leaving. She looked along one length of the fence, then the other; there didn't seem to be anywhere that they could get through, and it was too high for them to jump. She'd expected them to mill about, or to snap at her through the fence or lie down patiently to wait. But they'd just given up, and were wandering off. Only one wolf remained. It had something white in its mouth. It walked towards Lucinda, causing her to scramble backwards over the loose dirt and stones. But instead of trying to bite at her like she expected, it merely pushed the white thing under the fence with its nose, then walked calmly away into the bushes.

She stared after the wolves, trying to get her breath back, until she realised with a start that it was going dark. Which was impossible. She couldn't have been in the village all day; she'd left the Rent-a-Legend office at 9:00am, and she'd only been two hours at most.

"And everyone warned me to be in before sunset," she said aloud. She shivered and picked herself up from the floor. After poking it with her foot to check it wasn't anything dangerous, she picked up what the wolf had dropped. It turned out to be a white rectangle of card. It was edged with silver, and in black ink were printed the words:

'Thank you for using our
Eldritch Castle Location Service.
We hope you have a pleasant stay
and will consider using us again!'

"'Eldritch Castle Location Service'?" Lucinda read out, creasing her forehead. She turned and looked at the castle. It was all tall, twisty, dark towers and grandiose balconies, hung with dark materials. It smacked of spider webs and coffins. It looked even worse than the forest did, and the forest was looking pretty darn eldritch as it was. No-one in their right mind would ever stay at a castle like this - it might as well have had a sign outside saying 'Hey, want to be murdered in your bed? Then come on in!'.

When she looked closer, she realised that there *was* a sign on it. But it didn't mention murder. It had bats on it. Exceedingly cute, stylised bats. It read 'Welcome to Castle Von Stollenheim' in an unreasonably cute font. She was debating about whether or not to take a closer look, lest her eyes be playing tricks on her, when she heard someone calling to her from the doorway.

"Excuse me?" a young man called, sticking his head out of the door and waving. "Hello there! Sorry, but are you coming in or not? You *were* told you had to be in before sunset, weren't you?"

"Lots of times, yes," Lucinda replied. The exhaustion must be getting to her. Why, in the middle of this horrible forest, with its horrible wolves, would there be a horrible castle with *cute* things on it? With a nice, sensible person telling her to come in? Or was he?

"Oh, er, I mean . . . blast it," cursed the youth. He cleared his throat and then said in a more foreboding tone, "Come my boy, you do not want to be standing about in the cold." Lucinda didn't know about cold, it was a warm night, and she'd just run enough to keep her warm all *week*;

"It's not very cold, really. It was very hot in the village," she replied.

"Won't you come in and er . . . partake of some . . . wine?" the man tried uncertainly.

"I can't have wine, I'm only fifteen," Lucinda replied without thinking, standing up and peering suspiciously at him.

'In this sort of situation,' she thought to herself, 'the weary traveller comes upon a spooky castle in the woods, and is apprehensive, but glad of any kind of shelter at all, and then regrets it when the seemingly friendly staff turn out to be luring guests in to be dinner for their evil master.'

"The children of the night- what?" the youth stopped suddenly, using his regular voice again. He seemed to be listening to something. "Chiltren? Look, I told you I'm not doing the stupid accent, okay? It's just not me." Intrigued despite herself, Lucinda moved closer.

"Look, you must be the servant, right?" she asked. "I'm not going to be tricked or get bitten by any vampires, okay? I'm a prince, I'll have you know," she added, sounding a lot more confident than she felt.

"Oh gosh, no!" the man replied, sounding genuinely shocked. "She'd kill me! I'd never hear the end of it. What?" He stopped again, listening. 'She'd kill me' he'd said, so perhaps the vampire here was a woman? She might be all right, then. From what she could remember, female vampires just tended to moon about looking pretty and being tragic. Or possibly sexy. Lucinda finally got close enough to see him properly. He certainly didn't look like a vampire. His hair was red, so red in fact, it was very nearly a bright orange, and his eyes were a startling blue. He wasn't particularly attractive, which should have been another dead give away, if more recent vampire stories were to be believed. He was wearing plain black trousers, a white shirt and a plain black waistcoat. There was something brown on his shoulder, which he appeared to be listening to. "Really . . ? Oh, you're right . . . " He peered back at her, trying to decide what to do. "Right, right, *shut up*, I'll handle it," he muttered. Lucinda realised the brown thing was in fact, a bat. "So are you coming in or not?" he asked her. "It's traditional to be in before sunset, so I'd appreciate it if you'd get on with it."

"Charming," said the bat on his shoulder in a slightly squeaky voice. "You have to be charming."

"No I don't," the youth argued. "Not to princes. In fact, I don't think there's even supposed to *be* a situation involving princes. That's not traditional *at all*."

"Oh, hark at Mr. Traditional!" the bat squeaked in disgust. "Like you're one to talk!"

"Anyway," said the boy irritably, cutting the bat off before it could raise any further objections, "let's get you inside, get you some food and find you a room. I trust you found the castle okay?" he asked, opening the door wider and gesturing into the hallway.

"Found the castle . . ?" Lucinda asked, or rather started to ask. A large wolf was padding down the very middle of the hall, along a long, red carpet. She shrieked in an incredibly un-princelike manner.

"Don't worry," the boy reassured her. "He's only one of my little wolfies. They lead travellers up to the castle. Isn't that right, Hans?" he crooned, reaching out to ruffle the fur on the wolf's head. The wolf licked his hand and wagged its tail.

"*Wolves* lead people to the castle?" Lucinda spluttered. "What for? And they didn't 'lead' me, they were going to eat me, I swear! I had to run for my life and I cut my leg, look!"

"Well, travellers aren't going to take shelter in a big, old, spooky castle by choice are they? It's traditional," he explained. "And no-one's . . . going to . . . eat you . . . " he trailed off. He was staring down at her leg with a wooden expression. "Oh dear," he swallowed, "I do wish Rosie was here."

"You've got to stop depending on that woman for everything," the bat chided. "Honestly, she's got you wrapped right around her little finger, it's *embarrassing*."

"Don't you call her 'that woman' and no it isn't," he snapped, avoiding the subject of fingers. "I can do this." He drew himself up haughtily. "I'll just . . . not look."

"Will that help?" asked the bat.

"Probably not," the youth admitted. He took a deep breath and held out his hand for Lucinda to shake. "I'm Count Johann von Stollenheim the Third. I'm the resident vampire around here."

"Ngh," said Lucinda, sinking to the floor as her legs finally gave out. Each waited to see if the other would make a move. "You don't *look* like a vampire," Lucinda said finally. "If you're a monster, you should have the decency to look like one. I was fighting a dragon last week, and I wasn't prepared or anything, but at least I knew what it *was*."

"I *told* you, you should do the accent," the bat complained from his shoulder. Johann merely shrugged, dislodging it. It flew up into the rafters and carried on mumbling to itself about 'kids these days'.

"Humans go around not looking like monsters all the time, and no-one complains about that," he retorted. "Anyway, you're one to talk, Princess Charming." Lucinda groaned and buried her face in her hands;

"I'm so fired," she moaned. "I'm *so* fired. And I really need this job! Why doesn't Sara *tell* me anything?" she complained. "But that's not going to matter, because I'm going to die aren't I? 'Horrible things happen in stories'," she finished bitterly. "Why didn't I listen?"

"You might try listening now," Johann chided. "You aren't going to die, that cut isn't deep enough. And if you mean me, I'd catch hell off Rosie if I bit you. She might be a witch, but she's still a human. And you can be assured that she's alive and well. It's hard to date someone who's dead. Now stop being a such a wimp and get up off the floor, so we can find you a room and fix up your leg," he finished, grabbing her arm to haul her to her feet. "You're supposed to be a man, so you'd better start acting like it." There was a "hah, says you" from the rafters. "Please excuse the sexism there, but you know what I mean." Lucinda staggered to her feet but snatched her arm away.

"I can stand on my own," she said defiantly.

"That's the spirit," Johann nodded. "This way then."

Lucinda was led up some stairs and along a corridor. The way was lit by long, dribbly candles in bat-themed candlesticks. They went through a pair of heavy double doors into what seemed like a separate bit of the castle, that looked more like an apartment. It was lighter in here. Lucinda looked up and saw what she could have sworn were the long electric lights they had at school. Johann waved her into a bedroom. There wasn't a coffin in sight. It had a little dressing table, scattered with bits and bobs;

cosmetics, a hair brush and a few hair pins. There was a fluffy dressing gown on the back of the door. The duvet had a colourful, artsy pattern on it, made up of lots of coloured squares.

"You can use Rosie's room," he informed her. "I'm not expecting her for a few days, and she won't mind anyway. Just wait there, all right?" He went out and then immediately came back in. "On second thoughts, you should come next door to the kitchen." Lucinda gave him a suspicious look. "I'm going to get us something to eat and also get some bandages for your leg, and I don't know about you, but in my opinion that sort of thing requires *clean hands,*" he finished pointedly. Lucinda looked down at her hands. They were covered in mud and scrapes from her fall on the path.

"All right then," she replied, and followed him into the kitchen feeling slightly guilty. She washed her hands at the sink. It was stainless steel, and it had a selection of soaps, washing up liquid and hand wash on a little shelf behind it. It looked quite modern, especially in contrast to the rest of the castle, which was all flickering candlelight and Gothic decor.

"Normally people aren't allowed in here, except me and Rosie," Johann explained, while he busied himself making something and pulling out what appeared to be a first aid kit, "but you don't seem to be a normal sort of person, so I suppose I can make an exception. Vampires aren't expected to have kitchens, you see. Not ones with a fridge and a microwave in them, anyway," he explained. Lucinda finished washing her hands and stood by the table. Johann glanced around at her and returned to whatever he was doing.

"If you don't want to go back to Rosie's room, you

can sit at the table," he said waving his free hand at it. "You'll be closer to the hot water anyway, so it'll be more convenient for me." He rummaged around in the fridge and suddenly stood upright. "You're not a vegetarian, are you?"

"No," Lucinda replied, sitting at the table. The kitchen may be modern, but the table wasn't. It was a huge, rough-hewn oaken one, and the heavy chair made a horrible rattling noise as she dragged it out to sit on it. A plate of ham salad sandwiches was put in the middle of the table.

"We'll see to your leg before we eat," he said, taking a length of bandage out of the first aid kit. He also took out a tube of antiseptic cream. "You'd better wash it," he commanded. "Here, I got you a clean cloth."

The cut didn't turn out to be nearly as bad as she'd thought. It felt like she'd sliced halfway through her leg in the forest, but she *had* been exhausted and running from wolves at the time. Once she'd cleaned it up, he handed her the ointment and bandages. Lucinda had never had to use any bandages before, so she just wrapped them around her leg until she could just about tie them up. What would her mother would say when she got home? On the bright side, maybe she could act suitably injured as to get a day off from school.

"Hey, it's Monday tomorrow!" Lucinda blurted out, standing up too quickly and wincing.

"That's generally the day that follows Sunday, yes," Johann answered, biting into a sandwich. "Is that a problem?"

"I have to be at school tomorrow!" she answered, starting to panic. "And my mum is going to kill me! What time is it?!" Johann glanced at a clock on the wall.

"It's about 10pm," he answered, taking a second bite. "You sure get worked up over nothing, don't you? Would you like a cup of tea? It'll calm you down." Lucinda gave him an annoyed look.

"It's not nothing! Do you have any idea how much trouble I'll get in?" She pursed her lips together. "And that's just at home! I don't even have any idea what Sara wanted me to do and you know I'm a girl, so I'm going to get fired! Not that it'll matter, 'cause I'm going to get grounded forever for staying out all night and they'll never let me buy that plane ticket!"

"That 'not listening' thing? You're doing it again," he said calmly. "It's 10pm here, but I have no idea what time it is in your world. How long ago did you get here?"

"I don't know!" she snapped. "About an hour and a half ago, maybe two hours?"

"Then it's an hour and a half maybe two hours later than when you left your world then," Johann said. Lucinda slumped back down into her chair. "Tea?" he asked brightly. She nodded mutely. "I never did ask your name," Johann asked her as he busied himself with the teapot. "It was most ungentlemanly of me, I do apologise."

"It's Lucinda," she answered taking one of the sandwiches.

"That's not a very good name for a prince," he said, setting the teapot on the stove and sitting back down. "You should change it. Or do you have a nickname?"

"Cinders," she replied.

"Even worse," he thoughtfully chewed his sandwich. "How about . . . Lucian? That sounds like a princely sort of name."

"I suppose so," Lucinda considered it for a moment. "Sounds better than 'Prince Lucinda' anyway." She took a bite of her own sandwich. "A lot of things sound better than 'Prince Lucinda' though, if you ask me." Johann laughed. She watched him eat half his sandwich. She gave him a critical look. Then she inspected her own sandwich.

"What?" he asked, noticing her expression.

"Are you *really* a vampire?" she asked sceptically.

"Yes," he replied simply.

"Really?" she asked again.

"Yes, really," he replied again.

"And you're sure about that, are you?" she asked him a third time.

"What do you want, a demonstration?"

"No," she said quickly. "It's just that I didn't know vampires could eat normal food."

"Yes, we eat normal food," he answered, "or as we like to call it around here, 'food'." The kettle whistled and he stood up to take it off the hob.

"So you don't drink blood then?" she asked, if a little timidly.

"Well . . . " now Johann hesitated, "yes, but it's not . . . I don't . . . not very often. It's not blood that's the problem, per se," he replied, struggling to find the right words. "Vampires don't work that way."

"Don't they?" Lucinda asked. "Everything here is a story, right? So it should work like it does in stories," she said, ignoring the fact that she was eating ham sandwiches with a vampire who owned a microwave.

"Not . . . exactly," he said awkwardly. "Stories happen here because they're good places for stories to happen. But they don't just happen. There's things behind them, you know? Mostly people I'd say, but there's causality and a bunch of other complicated stuff, too."

"People like Sara!" Lucinda exclaimed, catching on.

"But why? Why live according to stories?"

"It's more convenient, I suppose." Johann shrugged. "Not everyone is as fortunate as me. It's really no wonder the common folk have a tendency to go seeking their fortune. You can sit around at home being dirt poor and not having enough to eat or you can take a chance on getting wrapped up in a story and striking it rich."

"So . . . " she might regret it, but was going to have to ask anyway, "how come you aren't skulking about on balconies ambushing women or whatever?" Lucinda wasn't actually sure what vampires did all day, or all night rather, but she was sure it involved ambushing women. As far as she knew, it was *all* ambushing women.

"Well, it's the strangest thing," Johann began, with the exaggerated patience of someone who has had to explain this particular thing more times than they care to count, "if you go around skulking on boats murdering people, sneaking into young ladies' bedrooms and terrorizing villagers, people tend to come after you with pointy, pointy sticks and chop your head off. You might find it surprising that I don't like the end of the story, so I tend not to start it in the first place. Vampires aren't stupid, you know."

"Oh. Makes sense . . . " Lucinda trailed off. She was handed a mug of tea. "But still, if you don't like all this traditional stuff, why do you bother?" Lucinda was intrigued. "I mean, why the scary wolves and the spooky castle if you don't want to frighten people?"

"It's expected of me," he replied. "I don't want to disappoint people entirely. There's a balance to be kept. I do get rather lonely up here, though," he said. "It's so nice to have a sensible conversation with someone other than Rosie for once. People always seem to want to discuss wine. Then when I tell them which ones I like, they look disappointed."

"That must be annoying," Lucinda sympathised. "Wine sounds like a pretty boring topic."

"It is. Very much so. You know, I'd much rather have your job," Johann actually grinned, which was a little disconcerting.

"Oh?" Lucinda prompted.

"I'd much rather be a hero. Perhaps we could switch places. We do look a little alike, maybe no-one would notice," he laughed.

"I'd like to say I'd make a better vampire than I would a prince," Lucinda smiled back at him, "but I'd be a liar. I've been pretty terrible, so far."

"You're only a beginner," Johann pointed out, "you can't expect to become hero material overnight. It's the same for everybody, even vampires."

"I suppose so," Lucinda conceded.

"For one thing, you shouldn't panic so easily," he told her. "Panicking is for comedy sidekicks. Just try and deal calmly with the situation. Try and pay attention to things and get a handle on the situation before you rush in."

The two of them talked for a while longer, Johann giving her some pointers on being a hero, and finally she went to bed. She was woken up by a mob in the middle of the night, but all she heard from her room was Johann shouting at them, albeit politely, to go away, because people were trying to sleep.

FAMILY TROUBLES

Lucinda woke up feeling groggy. She hadn't been able to get much sleep, which wasn't surprising because it was only evening in her world, even now. It was strange having gone to sleep so early, but she had been exhausted from the chase in the woods. She still wasn't entirely sure what she was supposed to be doing here. She got the impression that she was meant to be talking Johann into being a more traditional vampire, which seemed like a stupid idea, because then she was unlikely to make it home again.

She left her room and headed for the stairs, but something made her hesitate. There was a feeling of tension in the air. She could hear a conversation . . . Johann was talking to someone. As she reached the end of the corridor, something in his voice made her stop. It sounded like he was being interrogated. Not daring to move out of the safety of the corridor, Lucinda pressed herself against the wall, stood as still as she could and listened.

"No father," came Johann's voice from the bottom of the stairs.

"I do not believe you," said the other voice mildly. It was a man's voice, and it sounded old . . . but not croaky and weak, as a feeble old man would sound, rather, old as stone, like a mountain, ancient and unfeeling. It hinted of graveyards and ancient tombs. This was a *real* vampire's voice. Lucinda risked a peek around the corner. Standing at the bottom of the stairs was unmistakably a traditional vampire. Luckily, he was facing away from Lucinda. All she could see was his black cape and black hair, which was thickly streaked with grey.

"There is someone here," the older vampire said. He sounded more amused than angry.

"There was a prince outside last night, but they didn't stay a prince for long." Johann didn't want to tell this other vampire about her, clearly. Lucinda tried not to breathe.

"Or outside for very long?" droned the older man. "Are you consorting with human boys now, as well?"

"I assure you father," Johann said earnestly, "there are no boys in the castle."

"Mmm." Johann's father did not seem convinced, but he changed the subject anyway. "And the villagers? They bar the windows and are in before sunset?"

"Yes, father," Johann answered.

"They know their place, still?" the older vampire pressed him.

"They certainly do, father," Johann answered tactfully.

"You are not answering my questions properly Johann," the older vampire remarked. "Yet there is the ring of truth in what you say." He paused. "I have taught you well," he added, with the merest hint of pride. "Remember that you walk a dangerous tightrope. Humans are fickle, you must keep them in check," he sniffed. "Are you getting enough blood?"

"Yes, father," Johann answered meekly.

"Hmph. Enough for *you*, perhaps," he scoffed. "From that woman of yours, no doubt. You must desist from seeing her, she's weak. I should find you a princess, it's a pity you refused to marry the one I had in mind-"

"I do not need a princess, father," Johann answered, remaining as obstinate as he dared. His father made a disapproving noise.

"You do not have enough power, Johann," he scolded. "You need to be more ambitious!"

"I told you father, we do not need power-" Johann said, a faint tremor in his voice.

"And *I* told you, you are *wrong*. If you would just come to Sheva and mix in royal circles-"

"I do not *want* to mix in royal circles father, especially not there, bad things happen to royalty-"

"As you please," the older vampire cut him off. Lucinda heard a rustle of cloth as the vampire moved across the room. She held her breath, in case he was headed for the stairs. She tensed up to run, but then he said, "I can see my advice falls on deaf ears, as usual. I shall take my leave, but you would do well to reflect on this." Lucinda heard the doors creak open.

"Mother said I should tell you she says hello!" Johann blurted out suddenly.

"Did she now?" the vampire said dismissively. "Good day, Johann." She heard the door bang shut. Lucinda waited. There was a chance that the vampire would come back, and her feet seemed to have glued themselves to the floor.

"Lucinda?" Johann's voice called up the stairs, "I know you're there. You can come out now."

"Are you sure?" Lucinda asked nervously, managing to get her legs back under control and peeking round the corner. "I thought you did very well," Lucinda complimented him, as she made her way down the steps.

"I don't think he knew I was here."

"*I* do," Johann said, narrowing his eyes. "It bothers me. It's like he *knew* someone would be here. *I* didn't know someone would be here. I'm not even expecting Rosie *and* he knew it wasn't Rosie. But the really weird thing is, I don't understand why he'd even care. It's odd that he would come all the way here just to lecture me about her . . . "

"It is?" Lucinda asked. Her parents sometimes went to great lengths to lecture *her*. Johann didn't seem to hear her.

"It wouldn't have hurt him to say hello back," he mumbled to himself. He stared into the distance for a moment before continuing in a louder voice, "You should leave as soon as you can. And you should stay away from my father. If you ever see him again, stay out of his way." Johann went to head up the stairs, clearly distracted. His easy-going, carefree manner had disappeared along with the older vampire.

"Wait!" Lucinda shouted. "I still don't know what I'm supposed to do here. And I don't know how to get home!"

"Hmm?" Johann turned around, though clearly still distracted by his own thoughts. "Oh, I think you were sent to see if I was terrorising the villagers properly and so on. I'm not sure who sent you, I presume it was the villagers who complained, but you can tell your boss that they're all very annoyed with me, and that that's the best they're ever going to get. I've got a spooky castle that people travelling through the woods are forced to stay at even though any sensible person would rather stay out in the cold and I wear appropriate clothes when there are guests." He seemed to be going through a mental check-list. "I offer reasonable hospitality, and young ladies often stay in the castle and moon about the balcony in their nightwear. They're usually the same young lady, but no-one needs to know that. There's bats in the castle and wolves in the forest. I don't know about them making 'vunderful musik'," he said, pulling his face at having to use the accent, "but they certainly make a racket. It's close enough."

"All right then," Lucinda agreed reluctantly, "but I still don't know how to get home."

"I'm afraid I can't help you with that," he replied. "I've never had to go to these offices of yours before, so I don't know where the door is. One of the villagers should be able to tell you. If they can contact it to complain, they can contact it to find the correct door." That was something that had Lucinda puzzled. Despite Johann's mood, she risked asking;

"Why do the villagers complain about you not bothering them, anyway? What's their problem? I don't get it." Johann paused on the stairs.

"Oh, various reasons," he explained. "For example, the rent for areas terrorised by things like vampires and werewolves is very low. If I don't keep up a suitable level of terror, they might actually have to pay some. Plus people sell garlic and things, you know. Also because it's *traditional*." He made a face again.

"So it's just about money?" she surmised. "They want monsters and things around just to save on the rent?"

"It's not *just* about money, but I'd wager it has a lot to do with it. You'd be surprised what people will put up with for money," he answered.

"No I wouldn't," Lucinda muttered to herself. Rather more loudly she asked hopefully, "Can't you come with me?" Johann shook his head.

"I'm afraid that wouldn't do," he explained. "I'm not

supposed to go out after sunrise, and in any case, I'd probably blow your cover. Sorry."

"I understand," Lucinda replied, sighing. "Well, thank you and goodbye then."

The sun's rays were just about piercing through the gloom of the forest as she set off back down the hill. She wondered if Sara would be angry. But on the other hand, she thought crossly, *she* was the one who should be angry. Sara never gave her any information, she just shoved her through a door and told her to get on with it. It wasn't her fault she couldn't do her job properly if she didn't know what she was actually supposed to be doing. Maybe she should tell Sara that Johann's father was sorting him out? Unless she'd misunderstood all that stuff about 'keeping the humans in their place' . . . Almost as she thought it, she heard his voice again. At first she thought she was imagining things, but it was definitely him. She sidled over into the undergrowth as quietly as possible in case he came back up the path. She crouched down behind the bushes and listened hard, praying that vampires didn't have any exaggerated senses like they did in films.

"Marissa, I told you to leave me alone," his voice floated up through the leaves. "I see you're wearing black again. It's ridiculous. As if you have reason to mourn."

"I'll have reason enough if you don't stop this," a woman's voice replied. "Just leave and come home, you're only making things worse-"

"Home, Marissa? I see you're still having trouble with the meaning of 'divorce'," he said. "I refuse to return to that wretched human town."

"Elves are clearly not doing you any more good than humans did," the woman addressed as Marissa replied. "I've never seen you look so old, and you're going grey already-"

"How I look is none of your business," he scoffed. "Why are you here? Were you waiting to ambush me in the woods? Get a life, woman."

"I was going to see Johann before he goes to bed," she replied. "I can't see my own son now?"

"Can't *I?*" he demanded. "I was just trying to give him some fatherly advice."

"You stopped being his father the day you married that elf," Marissa countered. "You'll never get him to marry for power. He isn't like you. Why do you even need it-"

"Don't you *dare* lecture me," he answered. "You humans don't know how lucky you are. You'll never understand what it's like to be born a vampire, Marissa."

"Johann is doing just fine, leave him alone and stop all this nonsense-" Marissa began.

"Johann is walking on a knife edge, and one day he will get cut," the vampire replied. "Vampires cannot win. Either they will turn on him because he is weak or they will turn on him because he is strong. Better he be strong than weak. Better he have power. I won't have us cower from humans like Lydia and Victor. Have you seen the state of him? They'll both be dead within five years."

"Heinrich's boy . . ?" Marissa gasped. "This-, this *is* about what happened to Heinrich, isn't it?"

"What this is about is none of your business, as I have told you again and again," he snapped.

"All this time . . . " Marissa sounded like she was almost crying, "I-I thought it was *my* fault-"

"Johann told me you said hello," the vampire said curtly, "I have only one word for you, Marissa – *Goodbye.*" There was a sound like a flock of birds taking off and Marissa called something Lucinda couldn't hear. She heard footsteps coming up the path. Lucinda tried not to breathe. But it wasn't Johann's father walking up the path – through a gap in the leaves Lucinda saw a woman in a black, lacy dress and matching veil make her way slowly past. Her face was hidden, but her hair was the same vivid red as her son's. She didn't think Johann's mother was a threat, but she didn't want to explain why she was hiding in the bushes eavesdropping on private conversations, either. She waited until the woman had gone and then continued downwards.

When she finally got to the village, she found Gerda waiting for her.

"I've come to get you!" the valkyrie shouted, as she waved her sword in the air. "Sara really needs to think these things through. I told her you still didn't know how to get back. She said it wasn't her problem."

"I'm starting to think that Sara isn't exactly the best boss in the world," Lucinda said as she came walking up to Gerda. "How did she expect me to get back then? I've got school tomorrow!"

"She don't suffer fools, our Sara," Gerda sniffed. "She's tryin' to teach you independence, I reckon, and I don't think it's a bad idea, neither. You just have to get used to her, is all. It's not like her other heroes get their 'ands 'eld."

"Are we going then?" Lucinda asked, pouting a little. She'd been hoping for some sympathy.

"No," Gerda replied. "Not 'til you find the door."

"I thought you said you came to get me?" Lucinda asked, annoyed now. This didn't seem fair. It was only her third day. How was she supposed to know how to do things if she hadn't been told how to do them?

"I came to get you, yeah," the valkyrie nodded, "but

only if you couldn't find the way back yourself. If you can't find one little door, you might as well quit now."

"No-one tells me anything and I'm expected to just do things perfectly the first time?" Lucinda complained.

"Not perfectly, no. But you're a hero now, and heroes don't get things handed to 'em on a plate," Gerda explained. "Heroes get themselves into sticky situations and then they get themselves out. Otherwise, they're just the idiot who came before the hero and failed. You know, the one who steps off the path or uses the wrong magic ladle, etcetera."

"Well yeah, sure heroes think themselves out of jams in stories, but I'm not one of them!" Lucinda pointed out.

"You are now," Gerda said. Lucinda stayed silent and thought. What had Johann said last night? He'd said a lot of things actually, but one thing in particular had stuck in her mind.

'Don't panic.' Lucinda thought, repeating Johann's advice to herself, 'Just think things through.'

"This is another test, isn't it?" Lucinda asked. Gerda nodded. "I thought Sara was only giving me three tests? Wouldn't it have been better to warn me?"

"Heroes don't get warned," was Gerda's reply. "And this ain't Sara's test, it's mine. Can't let 'er have all the fun, can I?"

"Fair enough," Lucinda replied. She stayed silent and thought. Gerda merely sat herself down on the edge of the fountain and waited. Eventually Lucinda said, "So – How do I find the door?"

"You can ask people about it," Gerda replied. Was that a smile Lucinda saw?

'This is like a computer game,' she thought to herself. 'You get to a village and there's someone you have to meet or something you have to find, so you ask around and one of the villagers knows about it.' She looked around at the village. If this really was like a computer game, she'd be able to just wander around people's houses, taking anything she fancied and no-one would blink an eye. She suspected that if she tried that here she was much more likely to get arrested or chucked in a river. There weren't any people about. It was only just getting light, and most of the villagers were still asleep, although she could see light coming from the bakery windows.

Heroes in games didn't have to deal with this sort of thing, she thought to herself irritably. If they needed to find something, everyone was always awake and it was always daytime. None of *them* had to face the problem of knocking on someone's door at 6am in the morning and trying to get a civil answer out of the irate villager they'd just woken up. But then, it wasn't as if games like that were *logical.* Like the monsters. How did people manage to live with monsters all over the place? Where did they carry their loot? And why were there only about seven towns in the whole world?

Then Lucinda was reminded of another game. A game that *did* use logic. There were a few of them; mystery games, comprised of puzzles and scenarios, where there *was* a logical answer to everything, instead of 'equip the blue flower and run backwards around the third cherry tree three times, then press X'.

It wasn't logical to bother all the villagers, no matter the time of day. And even if it was, why should they know where the door that led back to the Rent-A-Legend office was? But there was one person around who definitely knew.

"Gerda, can you tell me where the door is please?"

79

Lucinda asked. She held her breath.

"Oooh, I didn't even 'ave to say 'What's the magic word?'" Gerda laughed. "It's in the tumble-down house at the end. In the wardrobe. You 'ave to knock three times."

"Thank you," Lucinda breathed out.

"That was pretty good," Gerda said. "Pretty quick thinkin'." She got up and grabbed her sword from where she'd left it on the side of the fountain. "Maybe next time you'll bother to ask *before* you go runnin' off on a quest, eh?"

"Point taken," Lucinda agreed, feeling slightly guilty. After all, the first time she hadn't had time to ask, but there had been nothing stopping her the second and third times. She decided to change the subject. "Don't you have a scabbard for your sword?" Lucinda asked as they set off towards the ruined house. "Isn't it annoying carrying it around everywhere?"

"Got a scabbard somewhere, but I don't use it. What if I need it to stab somethin' in a hurry?" Gerda answered, waving it around. "Hey, what happened to yours?" Lucinda winced.

"I dropped it in the woods," she admitted, ashamed. "I was being chased by a pack of wolves and I panicked. Am I in trouble?"

"Nah," Gerda reassured her. "You can borrow one of mine." Lucinda breathed a sigh of relief. She'd already not done what she was really supposed to and losing her sword on top of that . . . it hadn't been a good day.

When the two of them got back, they found Sara hastily changing her clothes. She was wearing a purple dress, draped over with a red sari embroidered with golden birds, and she was adorning herself with bangles and other jewellery in the manner of a warrior girding herself for battle. She slid tens of bangles onto her wrists and shook her hair out, letting it fall in waves. There was a crown-like object on the counter, made of delicate golden chains and coins. She laid it almost reverentially on her head. She looked extremely regal and her outfit sparkled as she turned to look at them.

"Those are gorgeous," Lucinda said, a little awestruck. Sara smiled properly for once.

"They were my mother's," she replied.

"You goin' out Sara?" Gerda asked.

"There's a problem at Moonton-On-Sea," Sara explained.

"I thought you said they managed to find a hero without you?" Gerda started, sounding alarmed.

"They found a hero all right, but they don't have any virtuous maidens to offer as a sacrifice." Sara grimaced. "Apparently the maiden they had planned on using decided she'd rather be un-virtuous than to risk being eaten by a sea serpent. I told them she was no good in the first place if she pulled a stunt like that. So I volunteered. This is more proof that things are getting worse."

"Getting worse . . ?" Lucinda asked, mystified. "Are . . . are you really volunteering to be eaten by a serpent?"

"No," Sara told her. "I'm volunteering to be bait, yes. Eaten, I should hope not. Unless this hero they found is completely useless. But if there's no-one to lure out the serpent, then they'll never kill it and it'll ravage the place." She pursed her lips together. "It's exactly this sort of thing that I'm trying to fix. And speaking of fixing things, how about that vampire?"

Lucinda gave Sara her report. Her reaction put Lucinda strongly in mind of a kettle about to boil.

"So you basically had a ham sandwich, went to sleep, got up and came home?" Sara surmised. "You did not, in fact, fix their vampire like I asked you to?"

"He said he was being as traditional a vampire as he's going to get," Lucinda explained. "Besides, what do you mean by 'fix'? He seemed all right to me."

"He's supposed to be oppressing the villagers and getting his butt handed to him by some vampire hunter as a result," Sara snapped.

"He said that's the bit he doesn't like, so he isn't doing it," Lucinda explained, wishing that Johann was here to explain himself. She could understand why people not volunteering to help stop a serpent was bad, but surely a vampire choosing *not* to be a monster was a good thing?

"I don't *care*!" Sara shouted, actually slamming the desk, causing her bangles to rattle furiously. "That's how the story is *supposed* to go!"

"I don't know about that . . . " Lucinda responded, without thinking.

"Oh? And how are vampire stories supposed to go then, pray?" asked Sara coldly.

"Um, these days there seem to be more stories about friendly vampires than the traditional cape-wearing, bat-fancying kind," Lucinda explained. "Even if they're not friendly, they seem to keep themselves to themselves. I mean, there's still the other sort about, but it's all more complicated . . . they don't just go around oppressing people because that's what vampires *do*."

"Really?" Sara narrowed her eyes, as if she were trying to ascertain if Lucinda was lying. "That's how vampire stories go these days, is it?" Lucinda nodded. Sara looked down at the desk, lost in thought. "It figures. But, yes . . . " she mused. "A new kind of story . . . that might work . . . "

"What exactly is it that you're trying to do here?" Lucinda asked. Clearly this wasn't just about one vampire being a nuisance. "What is it that you want me to *do*?"

"I told you that we make stories, correct?" Sara asked. "Well we also fix them. If a story goes wrong, it needs to be fixed. And they seem to be breaking all the time, recently. It's gotten worse and worse. Villains are getting stronger, heroes are getting more timid, the whole world is falling out of balance. Just like Earth . . . " Sara trailed off momentarily before continuing, "The hero must win, evil must be vanquished and there must be a happy ending. These new kinds of stories . . . There's a problem with a story where *everyone* gets a happy ending. Tell me, in these new stories - Who's the bad guy?"

"In these new vampire ones, it's usually the traditional kind of vampires," Lucinda replied. "The ones that won't fit in and live a quiet life."

"I see," Sara mused. "So it's not a case of evil winning . . . At least that's something."

"Like that other vampire," Lucinda added. Both the older women turned on her stares like startled cats.

"*What other vampire?*" they said in unison.

Lucinda told them about her encounter with the older vampire. She told them about Johann's strange behaviour after talking with the older vampire who had been revealed to be his father, and how he'd told her to stay out of his way should she see him again.

"I got the impression they didn't like each other

much," Lucinda finished.

"Ha!" Sara scoffed. "I'm not surprised. Vampires are like tom cats, they're very territorial. No sense in sharing your prey after all. I don't suppose you caught his name?"

"He didn't mention it," Lucinda answered. "He was talking to his son after all. He was trying to talk Johann into something he didn't want to do. A marriage, it sounded like." Sara wrinkled her nose, and her voice was full of loathing;

"Marrying him off to some poor woman he can suck the blood and power from, no doubt. Human leeches, that's all they are."

"Why do you employ one then?" Lucinda asked before she could stop herself.

"*I* don't," Sara replied. "I told you we fix stories. I got a complaint from the villagers that theirs wasn't behaving properly and was asked to fix it." She gave Lucinda a pointed look. "And if I *did* I wouldn't put up with this nonsense." She ran a hand through her fringe in frustration. "A vampire is merely a cog in the machine that is a story, and if the cog spins the wrong way, the whole thing breaks down. I can't have that. It's got to work, they've *all* got to work . . . " Sara hid her face in her hands and massaged her forehead. Sara had been acting very strangely since Lucinda had come back from Bad Schwartz. Lucinda didn't know Sara very well yet, but it was clear that Gerda did, and Gerda was looking extremely worried. "Speaking of cogs that don't work-" Sara started, taking her hands away from her face.

"I promised Lucinda a look at my swords," Gerda announced suddenly. "We'll just 'ave a quick gander while you finish gettin' ready for this quest." She motioned Lucinda to follow her down the corridor on the right.

They went a little way along, and then through a door that went not into another world, but into a storage room. The corners of the room were dusty and the walls needed re-painting, but the racks of swords and armour that ranged the sides of the room *gleamed*.

Gerda shut the door carefully and listened. She waited for a few moments, then straightened up.

"Right," she said far more loudly than was necessary, "let's get you a sword then!" Gerda strode over to the nearest sword rack and picked up a sword. She slashed it about a bit. "Hmm," she said to herself and then put the sword back. She did this for a few other swords, finally throwing one to Lucinda. "Try that one, Cinders. Give it a wave."

"This better not be the twin sword to the sword of a dark lord whose name people fear to speak," Lucinda muttered, slashing the air.

"What?" Gerda asked, giving her a funny look.

"Nothing," Lucinda said quickly. "I think this one's all right . . . " This one was a lot lighter than the other sword she'd been given, but she had no idea what made a good sword. There was no response from Gerda. She was eyeing the door. Lucinda dropped her voice to a whisper. "So what are we doing in here exactly?"

"Givin' Sara a chance to cool off," Gerda replied. "You've given her an idea, but hearin' about that vampire has got her knickers in a twist. She can't stand 'em, and she *really* hates the modern ones-" She stopped abruptly as if she'd heard something, then sidled over to the door and listened intently. She heaved a sigh. Apparently not. "She says they should just stick to bein' monsters. She says we'd all be better off, cos at least we'd know 'em when we see 'em." Lucinda recalled her similar comment to Johann and his retort that you couldn't tell with humans, either. She felt he had a point, but there was something else here. Something she wasn't being told.

"This isn't about Johann, is it?" Lucinda observed.

"Who's Johann?" Gerda frowned.

"The vampire I met who won't scare the villagers," Lucinda explained. "It's not about him, is it?"

"It ain't for me to say," Gerda chided her. "It's Sara's business. She's a secretive person. She don't let her right 'and know what her left 'and's doin'."

"I kind of noticed," Lucinda replied, "what with the vague quest details and all."

"Yeah, well that's just hero stuff," Gerda explained. "Heroes are supposed to work things out for themselves. If someone says there's a chimera on the loose, you're not supposed to ask for a map and chimera-slayin' instructions, you're just supposed to get on with it."

"I bet if you guys had the internet I could get directions," Lucinda pointed out. "I bet you could just Google 'slay chimera' and it would come right up." Come to think of it, she would bet it would work at home, too.

"What?" Gerda gave her a puzzled look.

"Oh, nothing," Lucinda replied, lamenting the lack of existence of 'GoogleOtherworlds'.

"Anyway, I reckon it's safe to go out now," Gerda walked over to the door and opened it, letting Lucinda out before her. "I reckon you should leave it here and collect it when you come into work," Gerda said, faking nonchalance as they walked back down the corridor, "I think it'll suit you better than that other one. It's lighter, a lot better for a beginner." Sara was waiting for them.

"So, you have school on weekdays, is that correct?" Sara asked, as if the previous conversation hadn't happened. Without waiting for answer she added, "What time does it finish?"

"3:15, but I need to get home and change and stuff?" Lucinda hazarded. No matter what kind of question Sara was asking, it was always like maths – there was a right answer and a wrong answer.

"Be here at 3:45," Sara commanded. "Now if you'll excuse me, I have a serpent to bait." With that, she strode off down the corridor like a glittery warrior.

"And where have you been all day?" her mother interrogated Lucinda as she walked into the kitchen.

"I've been at work, remember?" Lucinda replied, as she raided the fridge.

"You were an awfully long time, weren't you?" her mother scolded. "And just look at your knees! You've got *bandages* on!"

"It was part of the job," Lucinda defended herself. She wasn't about to admit that she had fallen partway down a mountain and cut her leg open with a sword. Her mother would forbid her from going. And that was without mentioning that she'd been chased by wolves and spent the night at an older man's house.

"I hope you're being paid enough," she tutted. Lucinda wondered again how much she was actually getting paid. She made a mental note to ask Sara when the opportunity arose. So far she'd been concerned with not getting fired, but she'd have to bring it up at some point. Sara had asked her to come back, and that was a good sign. There was no guarantee, but she'd just have to find out tomorrow.

The next day, Lucinda hurried home from school, got changed into her now washed prince clothes and made her way to the little alley with the fire escape. A lot of people would have been incredibly embarrassed to walk down the street dressed like a red peacock, but Lucinda had done a lot of dressing up and filming amateur videos with her friends, back in Manchester. They filmed all over the place, whether there were people around or not, so she tended to forget that she was dressed unusually. Nevertheless, she got the feeling that the Rent-A-Legend offices were supposed to be a secret, so she pretended to be looking at the goods in the fancy dress shop window nearby until no-one was paying her any attention.

Feeling like an inappropriately-dressed ninja, she ducked into the alley and scurried along it. She ducked behind a skip whilst she waited for a passer-by to cross the gap outside the alley and then hurried up the stairs.

Sara glanced up as Lucinda entered, shutting the door carefully behind her. Clearly there was one less sea monster in the world. She was wearing a red, silky shirt and black leggings. There were no emergency princess supplies in sight, today.

"There you are, Cinders," she said, her quill pen busily scratching its way across her paperwork. Sara always seemed to be doing some kind of paperwork. Lucinda wondered what kind of work stories generated. Lists of characters? Wages for princes and princesses? For vampires and trolls? Well, okay definitely not vampires, given yesterday's reaction. She didn't quite have the courage to bring up her own yet.

"You failed the third test," Sara said, looking up as Lucinda approached the desk. Lucinda bit her lip. So she'd failed after all. "But I'm not stupid," Sara continued, much to her relief, "and believe it or not, I'm not completely heartless. You can have the job. You're not dead and no-one thought you were a girl, even when it was pointed out." Lucinda said nothing and tried to keep a straight face. "And you brought something to my attention. These new vampires. The old ones were dealt with by hunters and mobs with pitchforks and flaming torches. But it's not like that any more, you say."

"And that's a problem?" Lucinda hazarded.

"Yes," Sara was bent over, leaning her elbows on the desk with her hands clasped in front of her face. It would have looked so much better if only she'd had a chair to sit on. "Broken stories are always a problem. Do you believe in stories, Lucinda?"

"You asked me that the other day," Lucinda replied. "I think so. But what do you mean?"

"Do you believe that justice will prevail, that the good guys should win, etcetera?" Sara clarified.

"Of course," Lucinda replied. That was a much easier question than she'd expected. Of course she believed that. Did anyone not?

"Well, nothing is that simple any more, Cinders," Sara sighed. Her tone darkened, "Apparently the world doesn't work that way. But that's where I come in," she continued, "I'm not putting up with this nonsense. Earth can keep its shattered stories, but I don't want that broken causality leaking in here. I need to fight it." Lucinda thought she heard just the tiniest amount of stress on the 'need'.

"What do you want me to do, exactly?" Lucinda asked nervously. There was an edge to Sara's voice that she hadn't heard before, and Sara always seemed to be on the point of kicking something as it was.

"Well, today," Sara's voice brightened up unexpectedly, "I want you to talk to a witch."

"A witch?" Lucinda was caught off guard by Sara's sudden change in tone. "What for?"

"These new vampires. I don't know anything about them," Sara explained, "but I know of someone who does. Rosalind, the Silver Witch. I want you to ask her about them."

"Why do you hate vampires so much anyway?" Lucinda asked, unthinkingly. That was the wrong thing to ask. Sara stood up, her lips pursed, but before she could say anything;

"You'd best tell her, Sara." It was Gerda. She and Freya were standing in the hallway to the left.

"I think so also," Freya agreed. "It's only fair, if you going to drag her into this." Sara placed both hands on the desk and stared at it. For a moment, Lucinda thought she was going to argue, but;

"Very well," Sara conceded. "I told you we fix stories. And I didn't lie. It's important work. But I started fixing them because there is one particular story I am working up to - *mine*." Sara looked back up, and now her eyes burned. Lucinda had to stop herself taking a step backwards.

"Sara has 'er own vampire problem, you see," Gerda explained, walking across the room. Freya followed her. "Her step-father is one. Count Von Stollenheim. Well," Gerda snorted, "ol' Chalkface is *King* Stollenheim now."

"Stollenheim?" Lucinda frowned, trying to think. "That name sounds awfully familiar."

"Of course it does, it's *mine*," Sara said, grimacing. "When my real father died, my mother re-married that blood-sucking parasite, Stollenheim. I took his name so as not to upset her, but it wasn't that long after they were married that she died."

"From a 'mysterious illness'," Gerda added, "as if there was anything mysterious about it."

"I vowed not to change my name back until I bring him to justice," Sara continued. "There was no evidence, you see. I couldn't prove he'd killed the queen. So he took over the country, and I couldn't stop him. I tried, but then he banished me." There was a pause as the three women waited for Lucinda to work this information out.

"The queen . . . your mother? You're a *princess?*" she exclaimed. Even on Earth, princesses did not sit around in gloomy offices, doing paperwork and answering the phone.

"You really shouldn't be surprised," Freya put in. "This is story country. Princesses are everywhere. They get kicked out of kingdoms and go do housework for dwarves and things like this all the time."

"What do you think 'appened when she went back to challenge 'er wicked step-father who threw 'er out of 'er own kingdom?" Gerda asked. "Go on, guess. Bearin' in mind that this a story-friendly place, like Freya said."

"Well," Lucinda began, uncertainly, "she ought to have gone back with a rag tag band of misfit adventurers, who despite their differences, pulled together to restore the rightful heir to the throne. Probably there was a prince involved who did all the things girls aren't supposed to do, like fighting and shouting witty things and kicking in doors."

"That's what should have happened all right," Gerda said, "but it didn't."

"Our rebellion failed," Sara continued almost in a whisper. "We couldn't get the support. People said that wasn't how you were supposed to attack a vampire, and I had no chance regardless. Leave him well alone, they told me."

"The man has an impressive and loyal army too, not the shaved gorillas with the IQ of 'alf a turnip, like any decent evil overlord would hire," Gerda explained. "He's cheatin', is what he's doin'. It ain't right."

"I had a few rebels, that's all. And they wouldn't fight," Sara replied, through gritted teeth "'It's suicide' they said. 'You can't just turn up with a handful of people and overthrow someone, life doesn't work that way'. And that's when I knew something was wrong." She stood up and gestured at the office around them. "So I set up this office. Now I spend all day finding people heroes and fixing up other people's happy endings. So that I can have mine." The three of them looked at Lucinda expectantly.

"I don't quite understand," she said hopelessly. This was something way beyond pretending to be a prince.

"This office is a cover for my rebellion," Sara explained, playing absent-mindedly with one of the shells. "It was foolish of me to expect mere civilians to help me, perhaps. But this place allows me to gather heroes, and heroes are practically honour-bound to assist me," she paused and looked up at the ceiling with an odd smile on her face. "That bloodsucker won't know what hit him."

Sara gave Lucinda very specific instructions to the witch's house, which Lucinda was initially very suspicious about. Sara had never even given her basic instructions, heck, she sometimes had trouble managing to reach the clarity of 'vague'. However, the witch lived in a magical forest, and both witches and magical landscapes are very tricky. There were always rules in these situations, like never drink from *this* pool or never step off *that* path. She was told to look for the door with the unicorns on it and sent on her way. She found it easily. There were two unicorns on it in fact, rearing up and crossing their long horns.

According to the notes, this place was called the 'Blue Forest'. It was full of limpid pools, picturesque clearings and flowery hillocks. It seemed like every plant had flowers on it. The forest floor was the most noticeable feature; it was a sea of bluebells that waved gently in the breeze. Lucinda thought they looked like the waves of the sea. That must be how it got its name.

Following the instructions, she came across a large clearing where a few unicorns were grazing. They were terribly pretty. She stopped to watch them. She had an urge to call to them. The instructions didn't say anything against it, but it might not be the best idea. Could they speak? In some of the stories she knew, they could talk, and they were very wise. But she also had vague recollections of stories where the unicorn was alluded to as a fearful creature, safe only for maidens to approach. She was pretty darn sure that she qualified as a maiden, but those sorts of unicorns hadn't seemed particularly bright and she was dressed as a man. There were two unicorns drinking at a clear pool in the centre of the clearing, and two more, probably colts, play-fighting with one another. She'd always thought of unicorns as just white horses with horns, but these had goat's feet, their tails were similar to that of a lion and their heads were more like that of a deer. The colts were more well-built than the females. All of them positively shone in the sunlight. Perhaps they did it on purpose, either to show off or as some kind of dazzling defence mechanism. Their horns were quite long; perhaps half a metre in length. They looked like they could easily skewer any unfortunate animal – or person – foolish enough to upset them. Lucinda decided it would be best if she left them alone. If they were the wild and dangerous kind, they might not discriminate between a man and a woman dressed as one.

Reluctantly, she decided to press on. She backed carefully away . . . and trod on a twig. It was probably the only twig in the entire clearing and she had stepped on it. It made an infeasibly loud snap. The unicorns looked around like startled deer. But they didn't flee. They merely stared.

'What do I do, what do I *do?*' Lucinda thought to herself in a panic. 'If they're the vicious kind and I make the wrong move, I'm *dead!*' She tried to breathe normally and remembered Johann's advice 'Don't panic. Heroes don't panic, panicking is for comedy side-kicks'. Just back away slowly, that was the answer. Lucinda moved backwards as slowly and carefully as she could. Two of the unicorns started to walk towards her, while the other two turned their heads from one side to the other, as if deciding what angle she was best viewed at. She tried to back away faster, but immediately caught her foot on a small rock and fell over backwards. She swore.

All four unicorns closed in on her. She struggled upright and found her back against a large tree. The unicorns were far too close now, there was no help for it, she would have to try climbing it-

"Oh, not *another* one!" the nearest unicorn exclaimed, tossing her head back and shaking it.

"That's the second one *today,*" said one of the males.

"If it keeps up like this, we shall have to find somewhere to move," the second female agreed.

"I don't know," the fourth unicorn chipped in, "I hear it's like this all over. No decent ones anywhere any more, so they say." They all looked at her expectantly.

"So you *can* talk," Lucinda croaked. "I suppose you aren't going to gore me after all, then?"

"Maiden," said the first mare in an exasperated tone not unlike her mother's, "why are you wearing such strange attire? Why do you seek the appearance of a man?"

"I'm looking for a woman actually . . . " Lucinda replied, somewhat confused.

"I *meant*," she said testily, "why are you dressed like a boy?"

"Oooh," Lucinda slapped her forehead. "It's my job. I'm supposed to be a prince. I'm not doing very well so far though, it only seems to fool princesses, really dim kings and townsfolk."

"Women can be princes these days?" remarked the other colt. "Well, why don't we just paint ourselves green and say we're dragons?" his unexpectedly deep voice dripped with disdain.

"Why are you a prince, maiden?" asked the second female. She sounded younger than the leading unicorn, and kinder too.

"I need the money," Lucinda mumbled.

"Oh, money is it?" the second colt remarked. "Humans and their money. They certainly do some strange things for it."

"I don't suppose that many maidens are short of money, lately?" the younger mare enquired.

"Umm. I don't know, maybe?" Lucinda answered. "Why?"

"There are many . . . " the lead unicorn paused, picking her words carefully, " . . . *unusual* maidens about these days. Earlier we ran into a fairy girl who was acting bizarrely, and there is a witch living in a little cottage who grows flowers and sings songs. She moved here about two years ago. Her house isn't even made of confectionery! I mean, honestly-"

"Um, this witch," Lucinda cut in, "I think you might be talking about the one I'm looking for."

"Indeed?" the lead unicorn answered, pricking up her ears. "Why do you seek the Silver Witch?"

"Because she knows a lot about vampires," Lucinda explained. "We're looking to fight one. He's an evil tyrant, and we want to restore the rightful heir to the throne. She was cast out of the kingdom by her step-father when her mother died." The unicorns' manner changed immediately. They started chattering excitedly;

"Did you hear that?"

"A proper quest!"

"It's supposed to be an evil step-mother, but that's good enough for me."

"We can help in a real quest! It'll be my first real one!"

"So you'll help me then?" Lucinda asked. It was a pointless question. The unicorns were now radiating helpfulness like a sales assistant who only gets paid commission. There was a brief argument over who would get to carry Lucinda, and the winner, the younger mare, knelt down so that Lucinda could get on. Lucinda looked at the proffered back blankly.

"I shall carry you to the witch's house," the unicorn explained. "It *is* allowed, regardless of your attire, you *are* a maiden."

"Er . . . " Lucinda hesitated, "I've never ridden a horse before. I live in a town," she added by way of explanation. "In fact, I don't think I've even *seen* a real horse before." The unicorn looked offended, which is quite hard to do with a head like a sparkly, white deer.

"We are *not* horses," she replied haughtily, "we are *unicorns*. We do not spook at silly things, go flirting with the opposite sex at every opportunity,"-one of the colts tried to look like butter wouldn't melt at this, which unlike looking annoyed, is *very* easy for a unicorn to do-"or let maidens fall off and crack their heads on a rock or any other such nonsense," the unicorn finished.

"Just climb on and hold on to her mane," the lead mare encouraged, giving Lucinda a little shove with her nose. Lucinda got on reluctantly and grabbed two good handfuls of the unicorn's thick, silky mane. It felt a lot like she imagined that strands of silk would feel like, and she was afraid that she would pull it out. She said so.

"Do not worry, maiden," the filly answered, "our manes are as gleipnir, you can do no harm. If you fall off, you can take my alicorn and scatter it to the four winds!" Lucinda had no idea what any of that meant, but she assumed it was supposed to be reassuring.

Only the younger female accompanied Lucinda through the forest to the witch's house. The other three stayed behind in the clearing to do whatever it was that unicorns did all day. The filly pointed out sites of interest, and the various magical properties of the plants and pools they passed. Many of them did quite horrible things; there was a small purple flower that turned people to stone should they eat it, and should some unlucky soul decide to stop and inhale the scent of an otherwise harmless looking white lily, with a bright red stamen, they would drop down dead. There were pools that granted youth for a short time but then caused you to die, or showed you the best and worst thing that would happen in your future when gazed at under the full moon. Lucinda was surprised that anything could live here without going bonkers, and that was if they even lived long enough. But there were as many beneficial plants as there were dreadful ones, and a few pools that would cure illness or grant the drinker some magical ability *without* giving them something crippling in return. Lucinda got the impression there weren't actually any flora, fauna or water features that *didn't* do anything, and after being told about an innocent looking yellow flower that turned your skin an unpleasant shade of purple if it got trod on, she asked the unicorn about it.

"Is there anything *normal* here?" she asked, aware that she was in fact a girl dressed as a man, riding a unicorn, which didn't count as normal even in a fairytale. The unicorn tilted her head to one side and then turned to look back at Lucinda and replied;

"I do not understand. What is normal? This *is* normal, is it not?"

"You know." Lucinda gestured at the scenery, unnerved herself and then redoubled her grip on the unicorn's mane. "Is there anything here that's just . . . you know, a flower, or a pool? Is there anything here that doesn't actually do anything?" The unicorn looked puzzled and then looked back ahead.

"Such a thing would be unusual indeed," she replied. "What use is a flower that is merely a flower?"

"Umm, it's useful to other flowers, I suppose? And bees?" Lucinda replied uncertainly. The unicorn had a point really. What use was a flower that didn't do anything? But then again, with that logic, what use was a flower that killed you if you trod on it? Other than flowers, who was it supposed to make itself useful *to*? And not to put too fine a point on it, but what use was a unicorn? Or humans? Out loud she said, "What use is a magical flower?"

"More useful than an unmagical one," the unicorn replied. "We unicorns could not live here without the magical plants around."

"Why's that?" Lucinda asked.

"Magical creatures need magic to live," the unicorn explained. "This forest grows on a wellspring of magic, and that is why we unicorns can live here. Without it, we would die, as you die without water." Just then, they emerged into a clearing and the witch's cottage came into view. Lucinda had expected something forbidding and gloomy like Johann's castle, but it was anything but. It had stone walls, the kind that would be called dry stone wall were it not that the cracks had been filled with plaster and the edges of the rocks smoothed down so that they were nearly flat. The roof was thatched; it should have looked like a scarecrow having a bad hair day, but someone had re-thatched it immaculately, and there were flowers growing in it. The chimney at least looked as expected of a proper witch's cottage; it looked like you could open bottles with it. There were all manner of flowers growing around the house too, in all the colours of the rainbow and some the *rainbow* had never even thought of. Lucinda wondered what horrible things they would do if she smelled them, ate them or in some cases the unicorn had described, just looked at them funny.

"I will leave you here," the filly told Lucinda, leaning down so that she could get off safely. "Should you need us, call us, and we will be there." Lucinda dismounted, wobbling slightly as she hit the ground. She turned to ask the unicorn exactly how she might call them, but the filly was gone. Completely gone. Lucinda wrote it off as a unicorn thing, and headed towards the cottage.

There was a winding path, scattered with white sand and, Lucinda could swear as she crouched down for a closer look, that multi-coloured gravel that you can get for fish tanks. It was like someone had gone out of their way to make the place look as little like a witch's house as possible. Maybe it was a trap? If people weren't expecting a wicked witch, then they'd be easier to trick. After all, Hansel and Gretel might have fallen for it, but there wasn't a kid these days that would go near a gingerbread cottage. Okay, they *would*, but they'd make darn sure that the witch wasn't in, or at least that they were armed with a shovel or something.

Lucinda made her way cautiously up the path, eyeing the assorted flora with deep suspicion. The plants here were even weirder than the ones in the forest; at least the ones in the forest *looked* innocent, some of these looked as if they'd committed murder already, not least the black and white spiky, curly vine thing growing up a pole near the door. It looked like a convicted burglar.

Still keeping one eye on what she presumed was the garden, merely because it happened to be growing in front of the house, Lucinda knocked timidly at the door. There was some muffled swearing from inside and a hasty "Just a minute!" followed by a tinkle of glass and some *more* muffled swearing. Finally there was the click of a latch, and the door was opened by a tall woman in her mid-twenties, wearing a pale grey, hooded robe and, under that, a heavy looking apron with a large red and green stain on it. She wasn't old or ugly, she wasn't wearing a pointy hat, or black, and there were no cats in sight. Oddly enough, this pretty much confirmed for Lucinda that she was a witch. The unicorns aside, Lucinda had started to think that if you didn't look like what you were supposed to look like, that's what you probably were. On this basis, the woman at the door could also have been a fireman, a gorgon or a small, scented candle, but Lucinda was expecting a witch, and so this must be she.

"Hello, my name's Lucian," Lucinda introduced herself. "I'm looking for a witch?"

"That might just be the most pointless thing I've ever heard anyone say," the probable witch replied. "If you weren't looking for a witch, why on Earth would you come all the way out here, to what is clearly a witch's cottage-"

"It's covered in flowers!" 'Lucian' protested.

"-a witch's cottage that's covered in flowers, and just knock on the door?" the very-likely-a-witch continued, unperturbed. "Witches are quite notorious for creative unpleasantness to wayward travellers that happen upon their cottages. If you weren't looking for a witch, that would have been a very stupid thing to do."

"I think it might have been a very stupid thing to do anyway," Lucinda countered, "considering the lecture you've just given me. I might have been in a desperate battle against time."

"You might, but you aren't, or you'd have been yelling at me by now," the probably-a-witch shrugged. "Since we have more or less established that I'm a witch and you're dangerously new at this would you like to come in?"

"Yes, please," Lucinda said. "Maybe you should give

me some tips."

"Maybe I should," the witch replied, studying her for a moment. "I'll put the kettle on, then." The witch waved her inside and then shut the door. "I've dropped a vial somewhere, don't step on it, okay? It had some potion in it and it wasn't finished. A finished potion, even a dangerous one, is easily reversible, but there's no telling what an unfinished one will do."

"Sounds like a good tip," Lucinda said, gluing herself to the top of a stool and inspecting the floor.

"Speaking of potions-" the woman raised her voice so she could be heard from the other room, "-I hope you don't want any, because I'm swamped with requests and since I broke that one, I'm behind. Luckily it won't take too long to fix up another batch-" the witch mumbled away to herself as she bustled about in the other room, which appeared to be a kitchen, from what little Lucinda could see through the door. The front room also looked like a kitchen at first glance, but although the walls were ranged with cutlery, there were shelves filled with strange jars and bottles, full of different coloured liquids; some bright, some dark, some were even striped. There was a cauldron in a fireplace at the other side of the room. There were flowers and herbs tied in bunches all along the walls, the freshest of them over the fireplace. There were plenty of live plants as well, lined up on every windowsill. They made the air a little stuffy, but the myriad of fragrances that filled the room were not unpleasant.

The witch returned from the other room and shoved a large mug of hot tea into Lucinda's hand. She moved a pot full of purple and yellow spotted flowers onto an already crowded windowsill, moved the small table they had been on into reach and pulled up a stool for herself.

"So, why have you sought out the Silver Witch?" the woman asked, taking a sip of tea. "Sorry, I'd be more mysterious, but I'm having a trying day. The name's Rosalind." She had discarded the hooded robe and apron whilst she was in the other room, and now her face was fully visible. Her eyes were grey, and her hair white; it shone like the coats of the unicorns. She was wearing a blue, silk scarf around her neck.

"I need to know about vampires," Lucinda explained. The witch took a leisurely sip of her tea before asking;

"What for?"

"We need to defeat one," Lucinda replied. "I'm on a quest."

"'We'?" the witch repeated. She paused again. "Are you going to kill him?"

"What? No!" Lucinda replied automatically.

"No . . ?" Rosalind raised an eyebrow. "You're sure about that, are you?"

"Well . . . " Lucinda shifted uncomfortably. She hadn't thought about it. In stories, villains didn't get killed, they got 'defeated'. Her quest didn't sound so noble when it boiled down to killing someone, whether he was a vampire or not.

"I don't know," Lucinda admitted, feeling like this was the wrong answer. "I certainly don't want to kill anyone. But I guess realistically we might have no choice."

"Indeed," the witch gave an approving nod and continued, "So, you think you don't know how to battle a vampire? Are you sure you need my advice?" Lucinda gave a start. Put like that, it did seem amazing that she, or Sara, or in fact, *anyone* should need advice on how to fight a vampire, even if he *was* cheating. *Everyone* knows how to fight vampires. This was surely another test. Why would

Sara send her to ask about something that everyone knew?

"I think . . . " she began slowly, "I think that I don't know anything about vampires. I think what everyone thinks they know about vampires isn't . . . quite right?"

"And I think you just earned yourself a cookie," the witch replied, putting down her mug of tea and leaving the room. She returned with a tupperware box, which was indeed filled with cookies. "They're for my boyfriend, but we might be having a long and involved chat and no client of mine is having a long, involved chat with no biscuits."

"I wasn't your client before then?" Lucinda asked, taking one from the box. It had brightly coloured bits of leaves in it. It tasted of cinnamon and something she couldn't quite identify.

"Not if you were going to kill someone just for being a vampire or to be so stupid as to think that what everyone knows is actually right," the witch replied. "So who is this vampire?"

"Count Von . . . something," Lucinda struggled. "It begins with s and sounds like a German Christmas cake."

"Not Stollenheim?" the witch replied, her face falling. She'd gone almost white.

"Yes, that's it," Lucinda said, worried by Rosalind's reaction.

"*Why?*" she demanded. "What has he done? He can't possibly have done anything!" She sounded alarmed, but then her tone changed, "I'm going to kill him next time I see him."

"He threw my boss out of her kingdom," Lucinda explained, despite her confusion. "He married her mother, the queen, but then the queen died, and he banished Sara from the country. So we want to restore her to the throne." Colour returned to the witch's face.

"Oh, you mean *King* Stollenheim," she practically spat the name that time. "You can chop his head off and put it on a spike for me. In fact, take me with you and I'll even do it myself," she added. "I can't stand him. He just uses people, all the time, even his own family - in fact, *especially* his own family. He treats them like pawns."

"Are you Rosie by any chance?" Lucinda asked her.

"How did you know that?" the witch asked back.

"I met your boyfriend, Johann," Lucinda explained, "I *knew* there was something bugging me about that name, I *knew* I'd heard it somewhere else. It *wasn't* Sara that I remembered it from at all! That means she's his step-sister . . . oh dear."

"Why 'oh dear'?" Rosie asked suspiciously.

"Sara hates vampires, because of her step-father . . . for obvious reasons," Lucinda replied. "I get the impression that she isn't someone you want to hate you."

"There's no reason for her to hate my Johann though," Rosie argued, "he's as untypical a vampire as you could hope to meet, and he hates his father, even though he won't admit it to himself."

"I suppose so," Lucinda conceded, deciding not to mention that Sara had been very upset that Johann wasn't being hunted down with pitchforks and flaming torches.

"Well, I couldn't be happier to help you take *him* down," Rosie announced, "so let me start by telling you that everything you know about vampires is wrong, particularly in the weaknesses department." She took a deep breath. "They don't care one way or another about garlic, they're nocturnal because it's easier to hunt humans at night and not because sunlight causes them to crumble into dust, incidentally that was never a thing anyway, and religion is unlikely to have any effect on them unless they suddenly decide to repent. And water is just water to them, no matter how holy it is."

"This is sounding awfully unfair," Lucinda complained. "How is anyone supposed to have a chance?"

"That's the thing. In a story, the brave heroes are *supposed* to have a chance," Rosie explained. "That's what weaknesses are *for*. I mean, by that logic, tigers are unfair because they've evolved to be bigger and deadlier than you."

"Then what are we supposed to do?" Lucinda demanded, feeling swamped.

"Well, they aren't actually undead. Not Stollenheim's sort, anyway," Rosie pointed out, "so all that business with the cutting off heads and staking them in the chest *will* work. They can also get sick or weak. Very weak, in fact, if they're suffering from severe mana deprivation. I suggest you try some biological warfare and possibly some politics to back it up. Get the kingdom on your side."

"What's mana deprivation?" Lucinda asked, frowning. "Mana . . . like . . . magic?"

"Exactly." Rosie nodded firmly. "Vampires, like unicorns and fairies and so on, need magic to survive. If you can deprive him of magic, *that* is when he will crumble into dust."

"And how do we do that exactly?" Lucinda asked, reeling from the comparison of the beautiful, shining unicorns to the terrifying vampire she had seen in Bad Schwartz.

"Stopping him from drinking blood'd be favourite," Rosie answered, "and getting him to use up what he's already got. Vampires are just pointy-toothed humans if they run out of magic. I'd suggest taking him on with a team of people, with some means to prevent him biting them. All that other stuff might be nonsense, but there's a reason people go after vampires in a mob."

"So, blood has magic in it?" Lucinda guessed, leaving well alone the problem of where she was going to find a mob for now. "I suppose that explains why you always need it in spells."

"Yes and no," Rosie gave her an annoyed look, presumably because it had just been implied that she had a gruesome collection of blood somewhere for use in spell-casting. "All living things have magic in them, some more than others. Humans have quite a bit, but they don't usually harness it, so it builds up . . . animals constantly use the little they have. Like cats. Always getting where they shouldn't," she added. "This place is full of magic, so the plants are chock full of it too, that's why the unicorns are able to live here. But you won't find any self-respecting vampire within twenty miles of a shiny, twinkly place like this, so they drain it from humans . . . via their blood." Her hand crept up to touch her neck, and Lucinda realised why she wore a scarf.

"I see," Lucinda replied. "Oh, hey . . . speaking of magic-" Lucinda started, as an idea hit her, "-is there a spell you can use against vampires? Why don't we just use magic to beat him? You could turn him into a frog or . . . or just a normal human, maybe?" Rosie snorted.

"Oh yes, let's use *magic* to fix everything, that'll work," she replied, her words dripping with sarcasm. "Magic will make *everything* better." Lucinda was taken aback;

"Did I say something wrong?" she asked.

"I'm sorry, it's just you hit a nerve there," Rosie apologised. "Everyone who doesn't use magic thinks it's easy and, well, *magic*," she muttered crossly, putting her hands on her hips. "Like you can just wave a wand or mutter some words and make everything better. Well you can't, and it doesn't. Besides, I don't do magic any more." Lucinda gestured at the vials and bottles around them;

"Is this not magic, then?" she asked, puzzled. "I always thought mixing up magical brews and things was what witches did."

"I do mix up a lot of potions and things, but I don't use magic to do it," said Rosie. "It's more like cooking or alchemy. Anyone could do it with the right tools and ingredients and the sense not to do stupid things like pull up mandragoras." She thought for a moment. "All right, so not *anyone* exactly, given the stupidity of the human race, but anyone sensible who got the right training."

"Could *I* do it?" Lucinda asked, powerfully curious. "I'm learning to be a hero, so it might be useful." Rosie gave her an appraising look.

"I suppose," she mused. "Heroes are usually more concerned with swinging their swords around and yelling when anyone with sense would be trying some stealth, but I could teach you some if you like."

"What about magic?" Lucinda asked eagerly. "Can anyone learn that?"

"Anyone can learn to juggle swords on a tightrope, it doesn't mean anyone *should*," Rosie replied, sarcasm creeping back into her voice. "I told you, I don't do magic any more."

"Why not? I'd be a really good student, I swear!" Lucinda insisted. "If *you* won't use magic, then isn't it a good idea for someone else to?"

"No, it absolutely is not!" Rosie scolded. "And I won't teach you about potions if you carry on."

"Okay," Lucinda relented, "but why won't you use

magic any more?"

"None of your business," Rosie replied curtly, "now if you've finished your tea, I really must get on with some work." She held her hand out for Lucinda's cup and strode quickly into the kitchen. There was a clatter as she dropped it into the sink, and then she was back. She coughed, indicated the door, and waited. Lucinda took this as her cue to leave, and reluctantly vacated her stool. She walked through the door and Rosie shut it behind her. Out in the cool, green forest, Lucinda stood still and felt her face burning. She'd just blown it. She'd gotten some good advice about vampires, but Rosie could have been a valuable ally. If only she'd kept her mouth shut. Heroes didn't have to deal with this in stories and games, they just got help wherever they asked and no-one got cross at them for being curious. She waited for her legs to feel like moving as the shock wore off. Just as she took a step forward, she heard the door creak open and heard something hit the path behind her. She looked down to see what it was. It was a small bundle, wrapped in a pretty handkerchief and tied up with ribbon.

"Deliver that to Johann for me." Lucinda turned around to see the witch leaning on the door. Lucinda was relieved to see that she was looking more upset than angry now. "I'm too busy this week to go myself. Don't you forget, because it's important!" she warned. "I'm free on Thursday afternoons. I'll teach you alchemy, but that's all. . . . I can't sit idly by and let you end up like me and if you're taking on Stollenheim you need all the help you can get."

"Th-thank you!" Lucinda stuttered, picking up the little package. "Look, I'm sorry I offended yo-"

"Just don't ask me about magic," Rosie cut her off.

109

"I've got my reasons. Can I ask *you* something? It's been bugging me since you knocked at the door, but *I* don't ask strangers personal questions."

"What is it?" Lucinda asked, a little apprehensively.

"Why on Earth is a *girl* walking around claiming to be a prince?" she asked curiously. "Ran out of boys, did they? Or is it for your father? Then again, you aren't from round here . . . I can tell."

"Yes, actually," Lucinda admitted. "They keep running off and getting married. I'm not allowed - it's in my contract."

"Is that so?" Rosie mused. "Are you supposed to look like a girl?"

"Not as such, no," Lucinda replied, feeling horrible. If Sara heard about this, she'd be fired on the spot. So far, it seemed like she'd only fooled extremely unobservant people. It was not encouraging, but at least there seemed to be a surplus of those.

"I should work on that then, if I were you," Rosie advised. Finally she said, "Go on then, what's your real name?"

"Lucinda," she answered. "My friends call me Cinders," she added, hoping that Rosie would get the hint.

"Well then Cinders-" Rosie replied, giving her a little nod, "-I'll see you on Thursday. Your homework is to learn about plants. See you then."

"See you," Lucinda replied, feeling relieved. As long as she left the subject of magic well alone it seemed, the two of them would get on. She was still worried that several people could clearly see that she was a girl, but she didn't have to worry about that *right* now. It could wait.

A NEW RECRUIT

Lucinda wandered back through the forest with mixed feelings. She hadn't realised how far it was from the witch's cottage back to the clearing where the unicorns had been, and without a unicorn to escort her it seemed to be taking forever. Not that she minded. The forest was cool, and pretty to look at, and there was a pleasant breeze blowing through the trees. As long as she remembered not to tread on any flowers, drink from any pools or breathe too deeply, she would be fine. So she hoped. She had looked at the instructions, to see if they could be followed backwards, but it didn't quite work. Nothing terrible had happened so far, though. It was quiet, and there was nothing to hear other than snatches of birdsong and her own thoughts.

Her own thoughts were becoming dark and troubled, despite the light and airy atmosphere of the forest. Rosie's question kept coming back to haunt her - 'Are you going to kill him?'. Lucinda had embarked on a quest that was, in essence, an assassination. That would sound very exciting and noble in a story - 'And so our plucky heroes defeated the despicable tyrant, and everyone lived happily ever after'. But did they? 'Defeat' was such a deceptive word. Villains who take over kingdoms and play political games got killed, not like super villains in comic books that got sent to jail, to break out and wreak havoc another day. Evil royals couldn't magically become someone *else's* wicked uncle. You were either in line for the throne, or you weren't. On the other hand, King Stollenheim had been married twice, and he'd even had a child. So perhaps you could. That bothered Lucinda as well. If they didn't kill him – and she'd much rather they didn't, whether he was the scary kind of vampire or not – maybe he would just go and find some other princess or queen to marry, and come back. His family was another consideration. Wouldn't Johann be upset if his father was killed, even if they didn't get along? What about his wives? Why did they marry him if he was such a horrible person? Were they tricked, or did he have redeeming features too? Was it really right to kill him, even if he didn't? Lucinda mentally swore at generations of heroes. They never had to worry about the morality of *their* jobs. They could just waltz into places and steal things and wreck the place, killing any bad guys that got in the way. But it was okay, because they were *bad* guys. And heroes stealing was perfectly fine, because it was *them* doing it, even though stealing and wrecking stuff up was what had got the bad guys in trouble in the first place.

She was brought out of her thoughts by the sound of someone singing. It was faint at first, but the further along the path she walked, the louder it got. She came to a pool, and saw that it was coming from there. Peeking around the corner, she saw a girl, naked, bathing in the pool and singing to herself. There was something feathery hanging from a tree on the near side of the bank. Not wanting to intrude, Lucinda crept past, and moved quietly on.

She heard the singing stop only a few minutes later, but paid it no mind and carried on down the path. She was sure that this was the path the unicorn had taken her down – she remembered the clearing that was full of poisonous flowers, and held her breath for as long as she could after running past it. As she stood gasping for air in what she hoped was a safe place, she heard the singing start again. It seemed closer, and louder. Lucinda carried on past another pool, another one she thought the unicorn had pointed out to her as curing people who had been turned to stone or otherwise altered. There was another girl there, singing louder than the last one. Or was it was the same girl . . ? She didn't want to look too closely. Again, Lucinda crept past.

Another ten minutes of walking, and Lucinda heard the singing a third time. The girl appeared to be singing at the top of her lungs, and perhaps she was imagining it, but she thought the singing sounded quite determined.

Again, she came to a pool, with a maiden bathing in it. This time, Lucinda stopped to consider the situation. Wasn't there a fairytale about this? A man comes across a group of beautiful women bathing in a pool, and he steals one of the piles of clothes or robes from the edge. The unfortunate girl who has her clothes stolen, instead of kicking the little punk where it hurts, asking what the heck is wrong with him or screaming for the aid of her sisters who, admittedly, have rather selfishly left her all alone with no clothes, does what is apparently the only option left and marries the jerk. Years later, from the nursery rhymes her children are singing, she figures out where the magical fairy robe is hidden, takes it, and gets the heck out of there. Lucinda scanned the clearing. There was only one girl, but there was indeed a feathery robe hanging from a tree on the nearest bank. She thought for a moment. Sure, there were lots of stories about fairy maidens, but didn't mermaids also do this sort of thing to lure men to their deaths?

'I'm not some idiot who's lured by naked women,' Lucinda thought to herself, 'and I'm not a prat who goes around stealing innocent girls' clothing, so I'll just move on . . . ' She got about ten paces away when the singing stopped abruptly, to be replaced by running footsteps.

"Excuse me!" the girl shouted, running after Lucinda. She was dripping wet and clutching her hastily grabbed robe to cover her modesty. "Excuse me, my lord?"

"Yes?" Lucinda asked, cursing the fact that this was one time she would have liked to be seen as a girl.

"Please . . . " the girl started. "Please take this!" she thrust the robe towards Lucinda, completely forgetting or perhaps not caring about her modesty.

"*Why*?" Lucinda was aghast. Luring her to the pool, she would understand, but this must be a fairy's robe and what was the point in giving it away? Luckily the fairy did not make her wait for an answer.

"Oh *please* take it," the fairy begged. "Then we can get married and have children." Lucinda goggled.

"I . . . I honestly didn't think I was that attractive," she said, holding up her hands as if trying to ward the fairy off. "I don't even know you and anyway, I can't get married, it's in my contract."

"Contract, my lord?" the girl asked, her brow wrinkling.

"Yes, my contract," Lucinda explained. "If I get married, I'm fired. And I really need the money."

"Princes need money?" The fairy girl tilted her head to one side. "If we get married, I could make money. I bet there's lots of things I could do. I could learn to spin straw into gold perhaps." Lucinda waited. After a few moments the fairy added, "So, can we get married now?"

"Look, I really can't marry you," Lucinda told her, "I'm sorry."

"Why not?" the fairy demanded, pouting. "You can

get another job, can you not? I still do not understand why you need money. Is there a ransom you need to pay?"

"No, it's nothing like that!" Lucinda turned to leave. "I have to go, sorry." She set off down the path again hoping that the girl would take the hint, but she followed her, still insistent that they get married. This went on for several minutes.

"I can always wait until you get a new job," the girl persisted.

"I really, *really* can't marry you!" Lucinda said desperately. "I'm not supposed to tell you this-" she continued when nothing seemed to deter the fairy, "-but I'm a girl. Okay? I can't marry you because I'm a girl! Plus all the other stuff I said!" she added. The fairy considered this;

"I don't mind," she replied simply.

"*What?*" Lucinda shouted.

"I don't mind if you're a girl," the fairy repeated, "I'll still marry you."

"That- That's not the point!" Lucinda protested. "It doesn't matter whether you mind or not, we absolutely cannot get married under any circumstances. *Ever,*" she added for good measure. To her horror, the girl began to beg;

"Please take me with you!" she cried. "*Please!* I don't want to go home. I *can't* go home . . . "

"Why?" Lucinda asked, feeling a twinge of pity despite the fact that she was annoyed and slightly creeped out.

"I'm to be married to the prince from the next Realm, and I do not want to marry him. So I thought I'd run away and be in a story for a while," the fairy explained. Lucinda repeated that sentence to herself.

"Wait, wait, wait." She held up a hand. "You're telling me you're running away from home to get married . . . because you *don't want* to get married?"

"Naturally," the fairy replied. "When a princess does not want to get married, they run away and marry the first person that is nice to them. It is traditional."

"Did you grow up in a Disney movie? I don't see why you have to get married," Lucinda said. "Anyway, weren't you just waiting to have your robe stolen? That's not remotely nice!"

"That is traditional for fairies like me, so that would be acceptable too," the fairy explained. There was an expectant silence. Lucinda decided to try a different angle of attack;

"But, but, I didn't rescue you, so it doesn't count, surely?"

"You will have rescued me from boredom," the fairy sulked. "I should think it will suffice."

"Can't you just tell this prince no?" Lucinda was getting frustrated now.

"Our parents arranged it, I don't think they care if I say no."

"Isn't there something else you can do? Like, another story you could be in?" Lucinda asked in desperation. "I mean, fairies must do lots of other stuff besides getting married, right?" The girl considered this.

"Well, some kinds of fairies help people for saucers of milk, I think . . . " she ventured, "or there's the kind that steal children or lure men away to Fairyland." Lucinda went very quiet. She didn't remember any stories like that from when she was little. There was the bad fairy in Sleeping Beauty who was touchy enough to curse people because she didn't get an invite to a royal party. But if Lucinda had been the only one not invited to something important, she'd be pretty upset, too. Perhaps that was how good fairies became bad fairies in the first place. And whoever the poor girl was supposed to marry must be pretty awful for her to run away like this.

"I'm probably going to get in trouble for this-" Lucinda began. The girl perked up and listened intently. "-but I work for an agency that makes stories. Maybe my boss will hire you. If she doesn't, we're on a quest. Maybe she'll let you join, I don't know. BUT," Lucinda said, holding up a finger, "I can't promise you anything. My boss isn't exactly Mrs. Helpful."

When they got back to the clearing where the return door was Lucinda pushed on the area where it was supposed to be. There was no resistance at all; no invisible wall, no shimmer in the air. She just pushed on the spot where she could see a large knot whilst standing by the tree stump in the clearing, as her instructions said and a slit opened in the air. She let the fairy girl through first. The door was at an odd, slanted angle and when she stepped through herself, she found they were in a different corridor than when she'd gone in. She wondered why they hadn't taken this door to the forest in the first place. She quickly saw why – the door shut behind her, but when she opened it again it was nothing but blank wall. She prodded it experimentally before shrugging and heading up the corridor. Sara didn't look up when she came in.

"Er-" she began.

"I don't like the sound of that," Sara said, glancing up. Lucinda had the pleasure of seeing Sara do a double take. "Cinders, what have I told you about bringing half-naked girls back to the office?" Lucinda hesitated;

"I, er, I don't think you told me anything." Sara smiled briefly.

"Not in a joking mood today, I see," Sara replied, looking back down at her work and scribbling something. "All jokes aside, in future please don't."

"I didn't know you did jokes," Lucinda actually grinned. This was a pleasant surprise. Sara didn't seem angry. But then, vampires not terrorizing the villagers was a broken story, princes bringing home mysterious, beautiful maidens was not. The fairy had long, wavy blonde hair down to the middle of her back and big, sparkling, green eyes. She was about a head shorter than Lucinda, with a petite frame. Her robe was covered in a variety of feathers, and was made of a semi-translucent material which shone gold when it moved.

"I see you have acquired a fairy," Sara observed. "It's most unusual to see one this young outside of Fairyland," she paused and laid down her pen, "isn't it, princess?" Both girls jumped. Sara continued, "I don't recognise *you* as such, but you're almost the spitting image of Queen Maia." Sara folded her arms and looked expectant. The fairy girl looked down at the floor and at first Lucinda thought she had started to cry, but the sharp intake of breath was followed by a declaration, not a sob;

"I am Princess Erlina Halfenna of the Light Realm of Fairyland." She puffed out her chest and drew herself up to her full height, such as it was. "How do you know Mother?"

"I come from the country of Sheva. Our countries share a border. Before I was exiled I met her a few times," Sara explained. "She and mother used to take tea together once in a while," Sara sighed. "I'm in no position to criticise a princess who's been forced to leave her kingdom. I hear

118

the situation is becoming somewhat unstable." The fairy frowned. Lucinda thought she looked confused at the remark, but Sara must have read something else. "So why are you here? What do you want?"

"I merely wish to be of some assistance to my lord," the girl replied meekly, inclining her head to indicate Lucinda.

"Very well," Sara replied, albeit raising an eyebrow at 'my lord'.

"And when I have been of some assistance, my lord and I shall be married," the girl added confidently, earning her stares from both Lucinda and Sara, who transferred her gaze to Lucinda. Lucinda tried to sum up in a single facial expression how that wasn't what they had agreed at all, quite the opposite. It didn't work. As Sara opened her mouth to reprimand Lucinda however, Erlina added, "Once my lord's contract runs out, of course."

"I see. Very good then," Sara nodded, ignoring Lucinda's now frantic 'that wasn't what I said, don't do this to me' pantomime behind Erlina's back. "I shall add you to the staff list. As it happens, I've got a few jobs you'd be perfect for."

"Wonderful!" Erlina beamed and turned to Lucinda, clasping her hands. "Isn't that wonderful, my lord? Now we can work together and make lots of money for you!"

"Yes. Terrific," Lucinda gave up. She could sort this out later and maybe find someone nice for Erlina to marry while she was working at other stuff. She sighed inwardly. She felt like she was in a computer game and that she had a list of side quests to do before she could complete the main one. Speaking of which-

"Sara, speaking of money and everything," she asked. "When do I get paid and how much?"

"Hmm?" Sara looked up from her paperwork again, where she had industriously been writing out what appeared to be Erlina's contract. "Paid?" There was that look again.

"Yes?" Lucinda asked hopefully, sensing an answer she wasn't going to like on the horizon.

"Hmm. Paid," Sara repeated. "You want paying, do you?" she asked, as if it was a novel idea.

"Yes please," Lucinda asked, trying to keep the pleading out of her voice. "I took this job so I could afford to go see my friends next summer-" Sara waved a hand irritably.

"What you do outside of work is none of my business," she said, "but I suppose . . . " She looked up at the ceiling. "I suppose we should pay you *something*. Princes normally do quests that net them some treasure, usually via a wife or similar . . . but you can't do that . . . Still, it's most un-hero-like to want paying, Cinders. Ask me again in a month or so," she continued, "but I'm not promising you anything. For goodness sake, if I went around *paying* everyone, the world would be in a worse state than it already is." Lucinda was crestfallen. Finally she had a job, an awesome job so far, despite the leg wound and the unwanted fiancée, but she might not get paid anything?

"Right, well . . . I'll be going then . . . " she said. She left Erlina discussing possible stories she could participate in and went home.

Once home, Lucinda had gone straight to her room and now lay on her back, still in her prince clothes, staring

120

straight up at the ceiling. She'd been thinking about it the whole way home. 'I can't promise you anything,' Sara had said. 'It's most un-hero-like to want paying'. While she had to admit that it was indeed un-hero-like to want paying, that wasn't really her problem right now. What was she going to do? Everyone else had a normal job, and they might only be getting minimum wage, but at least they were getting *something*. Was she going to have to quit and get a new job? Could she even go and do a normal job after working at Rent-A-Legend? Could she serve coffee or answer phones, knowing full well that she could be fighting dragons and learning how to make magic potions? There was no way. This was what she looked for every day, something different, something exciting. She couldn't possibly give it up for *money*. But she still badly wanted to see her friends . . . She'd turned her laptop on, and she looked over as her instant messenger dinged. It was probably Pens. She got up and sat at her desk. It *was* Pens.

'Hey, you there? Put me on voice call if you are,' he'd typed. Pens would cheer her up, surely. He always did. But there was another problem. Lucinda looked at the laptop feeling increasingly guilty.

'How can I tell Pens and the others 'Sorry, I'm not coming to meet you all, I like my job better than you'?' she thought to herself. 'I just can't. What am I going to do?' Reluctantly, she switched the conversation to a voice call.

"Hey Pens," she said, trying not to sound gloomy. She failed miserably.

"What's up?" he asked, sounding concerned.

"Oh, not much really," she replied quickly. "How are the costumes coming along?"

"If you talk about it, you'll feel better," he coaxed. Lucinda sighed. It was impossible for her to say no to Pens.

"I don't think I'm going to get much money out of this job, if any," Lucinda confessed. "I don't know if I'm going to make enough money for a ticket."

"So just wait 'til a better job comes along and then quit?" Pens suggested. "What's the big deal?"

"I really like it and I get to do some awesome stuff and we're working on something kinda important . . . " Lucinda trailed off.

"Sooo . . . you actually don't want to quit, even though the money sucks . . ?" Pens surmised. "That's kinda awesome! I wish my job was like that! Maybe you can make stuff and sell it on eBay? Or sell some of your costumes?"

"No way, they're all right for us, but I couldn't sell them, they suck!" Lucinda protested.

"SO? Learn to make better stuff, then. You can do it!" There was a pause. "Man I need a webcam, already. I was giving you a thumbs up. Anyway, heck, I'd buy some off you. I know loads of people. You could do other stuff too, like custom plushies."

"I wish I still lived in Didsbury," Lucinda blurted out, "I miss you so much."

"Come on now, you've met some new people right?" he replied. "And we talk online every day."

Lucinda was frustrated that he seemed to have missed the point, but she pressed on, "It's boring around here and no-one really gets me," she complained, sulking. "Everyone's just so . . . dull. And distant. There's no-one I can really talk to. I wish we'd never moved here."

"All the more reason to hang on to your job then, right?" Pens encouraged her. "Tell you what, I'll come visit you when I get paid, okay?"

"Do you have enough money for that?" Lucinda sat

bolt upright in her chair.

"Yeah, sure," Pens shrugged. "It's not *that* expensive. Plus I got a lot of overtime this month. I'll see if I can bring you some cloth and stuff too. We'll get you sorted out. Heck, if the worst comes to the worst, we can all chuck in for your ticket."

"I can't do that!" she protested. "Besides, I promised my parents-"

"That's an interesting magic mirror," came a musical voice from above Lucinda's head, "I've never seen one like that before." Lucinda whipped her head round to find Erlina standing behind her chair, on her tiptoes. Lucinda froze. She was only wearing her feathered robe. It was lucky Erlina was so short.

"Hello, new person! I didn't know you had a friend over?" Pens asked cheerfully. "Ooooh, 'No-one understands me Pens, I'm sooo alone'," he mocked, "but you've got a new friend you didn't bother to tell me about?" he laughed. "Maybe I don't need to come visit after all, huh?"

"Ah, no, that's not it!" Lucinda protested. "She's from work, I only met her today!"

"My lord, are you not going to introduce me to the noble in the mirror?" Erlina asked politely.

"No!" Lucinda answered without thinking. "I mean, later! Um, I'm gonna have to go Pens, sorry, it's a work thing!" She frantically signed out of her IM. "What was your name again? Erline?"

"Erlina," the fairy corrected. "You have a strange magic mirror. Why was that boy's face so still? This doesn't look like a prince's room at all . . . " she trailed off and stared around at Lucinda's room. She poked a little wind chime hanging from the ceiling. It made a tinkling noise.

"Does this call your servants?" she asked, giving the string a shake. It clanged like an alarm bell. Lucinda pounced on her, hissing;

"Don't do that! My mother will hear and she'll-" Lucinda's face went pale as she heard footsteps coming up the stairs.

"Lucinda Martin!" her mother shouted. "Stop making all that racket! And where on Earth have you been, your tea was ready an hour ago!" As the footsteps reached the top of the stairs Lucinda threw her bed covers over Erlina and lunged for the door. But she was too late. Her mother burst in with a face like thunder.

"You come down and get your tea this minute," she demanded, "and I'll bin those wind chimes if I hear you doing that again!"

"Just hang on, I was at work and-" Lucinda started, but to her horror, Erlina had pulled the covers back over her head;

"You didn't need to do that, my lord," she complained. "Do all your servants talk to you like this?" Lucinda's mother glared at the fairy girl before coming to terms with what she was seeing.

"Oh, I didn't realise you had a friend over," she said in a calmer voice. "Hello, I'm Lulu's mum. And you are?"

"My name is Erlina. I'm a fairy princess," she replied, "Lucinda and I are going to be married." She beamed. It was for all the world as if fairy princesses showed up to marry people's daughters every day. Lucinda's mother just blinked. Then she said;

"Oh, you're from Lulu's workplace! A princess, eh? I wish I was. Goodness knows, this one isn't," she indicated Lucinda. "Well, make yourself at home. Would you like a drink?" she offered. Erlina nodded and asked for a glass of water. Whilst her mother went to fetch the water and a cup of tea for Lucinda "while you're going" to buy her some time, she confronted Erlina.

"What are you doing here?" she demanded. "You aren't wearing any clothes! You can't walk around like that, you'll get arrested!" Erlina considered this;

"I am wearing my cloak," she declared, in the manner of one winning an argument, "so I am too wearing clothes," before Lucinda could respond to this she continued, "and I flew here, of course."

"You *flew* here?" Lucinda repeated, her curiosity temporarily overriding her shock.

"With my feathered cloak," the fairy explained patiently, "I can use it to fly. That's what it's *for*."

"Wait, but how did you know where I live?" Lucinda asked.

"Sara said she knows where you live," Erlina replied, "so I asked her how to get here."

"And, *and* how did you get in, if my mother didn't see you?" Lucinda frowned, still puzzled at everything else and a bit worried at 'Sara knows where you live'.

"With magic," Erlina explained, sounding rather puzzled herself. "How else should I get in?"

"Why are you here?" Lucinda pressed on, despite Erlina's infuriatingly acceptable answers, even if they were only acceptable because she was a fairy.

"I don't have anywhere to stay," she explained, "so I asked Sara did she know where you live and she said yes," she continued. "If we're going to be married, then we should live together."

"You can't stay with me, my mother will go mad!" Lucinda argued. "And stop telling people we're getting married. Are you even old enough to get married?"

"I'll be fifteen in a few months," Erlina answered. "It's not unusual for fairies to get married around my age."

"Well, I'm not a fairy," Lucinda said firmly. "There's laws and things."

"Your mother didn't seem to mind," Erlina pointed out.

"My mother thinks you're a princess from work!"

"I *am* a princess from work," Erlina pointed out. "We now work at the same place do we not? And I'm a princess. So is there still a problem?"

"*Yes.* I *don't want* to get married!"

"I don't see why you have to make such a big fuss about it," Erlina complained. Lucinda gave up and took refuge in the law;

"Look, you can't get married here until both people are sixteen," she said, "so we couldn't get married for over a year anyway, even if I wanted to."   Erlina looked thoughtful.

"I suppose so," she conceded.

"Why do you want to get married so badly? Isn't that what you ran away from?" Lucinda asked, rifling around in her drawers. Planning to get married wasn't against the law, but walking around half-naked definitely was. If nothing else, it was against the Law of Mum, against which resistance was futile.

"It's my duty. I have to get married and have a child. I'm the sole heir to the Light Realm," Erlina explained. "Mother was very firm about it. She was never married and she says she regrets it . . . " she trailed off. Lucinda now understood better her determination to marry, but she was amazed that Erlina hadn't spotted a giant flaw in her reasoning.

"Do they teach biology in Fairyland?" she asked.

126

"What is that?"

"Didn't think so," That pretty much explained that, but there was still something that seemed off. "Are you sure you're fourteen?"

"You are saying I am immature for running away from home?" The fairy pouted. "I just do not want to marry Tyr, so I must marry someone else. It's a perfectly logical course of action in the circumstances." Were all fairies this adept at missing the point?

"You just seem a bit . . . younger than you should," Lucinda said, picking her words carefully.

"We fairies live for some two-hundred years, so we age slower than you humans," Erlina replied. "It's only natural that I should look younger than you expect. We retain our youth well into our one-hundred-and-forties."

Lucinda gave up on that particular topic and continued looking for some clothes. She kept a few of her old clothes for costuming purposes. She dug out an old summer dress, plain white with blue edging around the hem and neckline. She handed it to Erlina.

"Here, try this. You can't walk around with your cloak on here. You'll get in big trouble."

"I suppose this place is nothing like Fairyland." Erlina sighed. "Do you use no magic at all? It feels terribly dry here . . . " She paused and stared curiously at Lucinda's laptop. "Why did you not just use your magic mirror to talk to that boy instead of that contraption? Surely a mirror is easier?"

"We don't have magic mirrors here," Lucinda explained. "Is everything magic in Fairyland?" That might explain Erlina's temperament. When you were a child, almost everything in the world seemed like magic - if your world really *was* magic, a childlike outlook on life would persist for longer. If you could use magic to fix everything, what use was logic?

"Of course," Erlina replied, puffing her chest out proudly, "fairies are one of the earliest and greatest magical races." Lucinda was struck by an idea.

"Could you teach me magic?" she asked eagerly. "Anyone can learn it, right? You don't have to be special or anything?"

"I can teach you magic no problem!" Erlina beamed and clapped her hands together. "I should be happy to!"

They were interrupted by Lucinda's mother, who elbowed the door open. She was carrying a tray with the girls' drinks, and had thoughtfully included a plate of sandwiches.

"I made you some butties since your dinner is pretty much ruined and you haven't eaten," she explained, doing a good job of keeping the annoyance out of her voice. "I made you some as well dear, I hope you like beef."

"That was very kind of you," Erlina thanked her.

"We, er . . . we have to practice, so-" said Lucinda, getting up to take the tray.

"I'll get out of your way, then," her mother replied, taking the hint.

"Oh er . . . Mum," Lucinda hesitated, knowing this was going to be awkward.

"What?"

"Can Erlina stay over tonight?" Lucinda asked, putting on her best puppydog face.

"It's a school night!" her mother objected.

"But Erlina doesn't have school tomorrow!" Lucinda argued. "Her school is having one of those teacher training day thingies," she carried on, before her mother could object. "She can always go home tomorrow morning when

I go to school."

"Oh all right, I suppose so," her mother agreed grudgingly, "but don't you two be staying up late. And you make sure to ask her mother," she ordered, before shutting the door.

"Why does your mother bring you food? Don't you have servants for that?" Erlina asked. "What's this about a school?"

"I'm not really a prince. And I have to go to school. Everyone does," Lucinda explained, quite amazed that Erlina hadn't figured these things out yet. She wondered if all fairies were this naive. Perhaps it wasn't naiveté. Maybe Erlina was one of those people who thought that believing in something hard enough made it true.

"I see," Erlina replied thoughtfully. "So you're only a prince at work."

"Right," Lucinda replied, grateful for some understanding at last, "now get dressed already. You can stay for tonight, but we're going to have to think of something . . . there's no way you can keep staying here."

"Why not?" Erlina asked. This was slightly muffled, because she was currently trying to find the armholes in the dress.

"My mother for one thing," Lucinda explained. "It's a miracle she let you stay tonight! I bet she would've said no if you weren't actually here." She made a face. "She wonders why I don't bring friends round, but she says no if I actually try to."

"So you're alone," Erlina concluded. That was a worryingly accurate observation. Lucinda was starting to suspect that Erlina was not the pretty princess she appeared to be. There was something sharp under that sugary coating of blonde airheadedness. Maybe she was the offspring of the twinkly kind of fairies that are happy and joyful all the livelong day and care about flowers, and the other sort that curse princesses and are touchy. But the nasty ones were often pretty too, so how were you supposed to tell who was the twinkly, princess kind and who was the nasty, vindictive kind? Johann had made a very good point that it was completely impossible to tell which humans were good or bad from their looks, so why should other races be any different? And then there was the princess/queen dilemma. Beautiful queens were almost certainly evil. For some reason, virtuous princesses became dreadful and bitter the second they got married. She wondered if Sara had ever been married. It would explain a lot.

Lucinda realised she had zoned out when Erlina touched her on the arm.

"Are you listening?" she reprimanded Lucinda. "We're not married yet you know, you should listen to me."

"Sorry, you reminded me of something," Lucinda apologised. "What were you saying?"

"I said I can stay hidden using my magic," Erlina repeated, "and that way I can teach you at the same time. You want to learn, do you not?"

"I'm not so sure that it's a good idea, but if you can stay hidden with your magic then I guess you can stay for a bit until we find you somewhere else. But I do need to find you somewhere else, okay?" Lucinda told her. "This isn't an anime, I can't have magical girls living in my room. I'm not some college guy whose parents have infinite patience and space for a ton of girls who show up and like me for no reason."

It turned out that fairies were great hiders, with many spells for it, a few of which Erlina tried to teach Lucinda, who had very little success. Erlina was concerned; fairies had no trouble mastering magic. When Lucinda pointed out that she was a human, Erlina said that it was largely a case of getting the hand movements right and wishing hard enough, which humans seemed to be pretty good at.

"I do not understand this at all," Erlina complained. "There are many human mages in Fairyland. Are Earth humans any different, do you suppose?"

"I doubt it. Maybe I'm just tired," Lucinda replied, yawning.

"I am tired also," Erlina said.

"Let's get some sleep then," Lucinda replied.

Lucinda let Erlina have the bed as she was the guest, and got out her sleeping bag and roll up mat. They were for going camping, although she'd never been. There was something about sleeping outside practically on the ground with all those insects under a thin veil of canvas at the mercy of the weather and with absolutely no security that just didn't appeal to her at all.

Lucinda made her way once more through Bad Schwartz to deliver Rosie's package. She would have taken Erlina with her, but Sara had wasted no time in putting the fairy to work. She was currently off being a lady of the lake somewhere, handing out magic swords. It was the early hours of the morning here. Lucinda picked her way carefully down the moonlit mountainside. The town was silent. Like this, she could easily believe this place was haunted by a vampire. It was made even easier when he

131

scared the pants off her by walking right out of the trees when she was halfway up the forest path.

"Oh. Hello again," he greeted her, brushing some leaf mould off his waistcoat. "Been sent to tell me off again, have you?"

"No, actually," Lucinda replied. "Rosie sent me to deliver this." She fished out the handkerchief. "What's in it? It feels like it's full of peas."

"Medicine," he replied, tucking it into his pocket.

"For what?" Lucinda asked. "I didn't know vampires could get sick." Johann seemed reluctant to answer, but after a pause he said;

"Vampires are technically always sick. It's . . . " he paused; he seemed unsure if he should continue. "It's what Rosie is researching. I help her out by testing things. It's how we met, actually."

"What's she researching vampires for?" Lucinda asked. "Seems like a weird thing to research."

"Look, shall we continue this discussion in the castle?" Johann suggested, a hint of reluctance in his voice. "I was only out here checking on one of my wolves. She's due to have cubs and she won't come back in the castle, it's most annoying. I'm covered in leaves and I'd rather not be."

The two of them retreated to the castle kitchen. Johann cleaned himself up and made them tea. It seemed to be both his and Rosie's default reaction to visitors. She got the impression that Rosie's research itself was not up for discussion, but there was something else she was interested in;

"So you met through Rosie's research?" she asked. "How did that work? Did she put an ad out? 'Vampire wanted, must be available on weekends'?" Johann laughed.

"No, it was nothing like that," he replied. "It could have been quite romantic. She was skipping through the forest, singing. Quite loudly, too, I could hear her from my balcony." Come to think of it, one of the villagers *had* complained about Rosie's singing. "You might have noticed that this isn't the sort of forest where people sing duets with nature, so I went to see who it was."

"Did you want to see who was singing so prettily?" Lucinda couldn't help smiling at the idea of a typical, soppy princess scenario involving these two. Rosie didn't seem the type.

"I was actually going to tell her to stop it." He rested his chin on one hand as he continued, "I thought the villagers would complain. And I wanted to see what weirdo thought a dark, dreary place like this was for singing in."

"Yeah, that's definitely not epic romance material," Lucinda giggled. "Prince Charming came upon a maiden singing in the forest, and as he looked upon her lovely face he proclaimed 'Knock it off would you, people are trying to sleep'."

"I'm afraid so, yes," Johann admitted. "That was certainly my intention, but her lovely face gave me quite a shock."

"Oh?" Lucinda prompted, guessing that it wasn't her *face* that had distracted him so.

"She looked like my grandmother," Johann continued. "I didn't say so, of course, she would have got the wrong impression. My grandmother also has white hair like that," he added, since it was clear that Lucinda *had* got the wrong impression.

"It wouldn't have been the most romantic dialogue,"

Lucinda agreed.

"It only got worse," he continued, smiling, "I made the mistake of saying I lived in the castle, which gave the game right away. She knew there was a vampire living there, and she was looking for one. I mean, she'd come to look for ingredients that night - there are some plants that won't grow in a sparkly, twinkly place like the Blue Forest on principle," he explained, "but she needed a willing volunteer to test out her potions and we're not the easiest species to get close to."

"So you volunteered?" Lucinda guessed.

"Actually I tried not to," he told her. "She was looking at me like I was a specimen and I didn't like it much. So in an attempt to dissuade her, I told her I'd do it in exchange for blood,"-Lucinda fought the urge to clamp her hand to her neck-"Much to my surprise, she agreed, albeit reluctantly. It just sort of went from there."

"Oh . . . " something struck Lucinda. She'd misunderstood something, somewhere.

"Hmm?" Johann lifted his head up. "Something wrong?"

"She's not researching vampires because of your father then?" she asked.

"What's this?" Johann blinked. "What does my father have to do with it?"

"He sort of came up in our conversation, and I get the impression she doesn't like him much," Lucinda was unwilling to tell Johann that his father was the target of her boss's rebellion. "I thought maybe it was something to do with him. But I guess she was researching vampires before she even met you. So why *is* she-"

"If you want to know, you'll have to ask her yourself," Johann cut her off and his brow creased " . . . How did you meet her again?"

"My boss wanted some information and she wants to order some potions too, I think," Lucinda explained, hoping he wouldn't pry further. Her loyalties were split on this one. Johann was very nice, but his father wasn't - both according to Sara, and by Johann's own admission. Telling him about Sara's plans would be a terrible thing to do, but she couldn't help feeling she was being dishonest with him and it irked her. Johann seemed to be as keen on avoiding the topic of Rosie's work as she was though, and she didn't stay much longer.

Two days later, and Lucinda arrived for her potions lesson, once more sans Erlina. She had spent the two days researching as much about plants as she could, as Rosie had asked. Very little of it had stuck. She suspected that most of the plants she would be using wouldn't appear in any Earth textbook anyway.

She was quite wrong.

"You want me to make tea?" Lucinda asked. She'd been expecting to make draughts that made the drinker invisible or would paralyse its victim or bend the laws of chance.

"Did you think you were going to walk in here and make ice bombs or something?" Rosie put her hands on her hips. "You have to start with basic, safe plants first, or you'd kill yourself trying to use this stuff," she said, gesturing at the assortment of botany on the windowsill. "They tend to do horrible things if they're prepared wrong, like the Japanese blow fish." Lucinda recalled some of the nastier things the unicorn had pointed out to her. Maybe it *was* better to start off making tea.

Lucinda was shown which bits of the leaf she needed, how best to dry them, how to steep them, how hot the water should be. Rosie pointed out a plant in the kitchen or outside occasionally, saying it was prepared in the same way, and telling her to note it down. They had plenty of time to talk, and although she was loathe to ask Rosie about her research given Johann's reaction, there were plenty of other things she was dying to ask.

"How come you're living in this forest?" she hazarded, as she helped Rosie tie something with blue and red flowers in bundles. "You *are* from Earth, aren't you?"

"How did you know that?" Rosie quizzed her, tossing a finished bundle onto the little heap by the wall.

"Your bookshelf. It's got a lot of familiar books on it," Lucinda tilted her head towards the bookcase. It was filled with a lot of Earth literature, mostly fiction, but there were quite a few factual books too, largely on plants and medical topics.

"Very observant." There was a hint of approval in Rosie's voice. "Yes, I am. And prompting your next question, I stumbled on a door when I was off on a gap year. I was in Iceland and I saw a fairy, who I followed. It was a pretty stupid thing to do, but I was just as interested in magic as I was in medicine."

"You just came across an Otherworld door by accident?" Lucinda gasped. "How did you get back?"

"I didn't," Rosie replied, "it shut behind me and I got stuck. I was on a gap year anyway, and it seemed like this fantastic opportunity, so I didn't worry too much about it at first. But as the time came for me to go home, I started to search desperately for a return door. I was supposed to study to be a doctor."

"So you became a witch instead?" Lucinda guessed. She was very, very glad that she had help with the Otherworld doors. If she'd been in Rosie's situation, she'd probably be dead.

"Once I realised I couldn't get back from the world I was in, I started to do research on other places." Rosie continued, "And I discovered that Fairyland had lots of doors to Earth. It was also where my mentor said any witch worth their salt went to study, so to Fairyland I went."

"Didn't you find one? How long have you been looking?" Lucinda asked, feeling a strange mixture of sadness and excitement. She certainly knew where a door back to Earth was if Rosie didn't, but if Rosie had been trapped all this time, her family must think she was dead-

"Oh, I found one," Rosie said, "but it was too late . . . " Before Lucinda could respond she added, "I don't want to talk about it. I was able to get back and see my mother, tell her I wasn't dead and I was living abroad permanently. It was around then that I met Johann. That was two years ago. It's been four years since I found that first door." She sighed wistfully. "Sometimes I wonder what life would be like if I hadn't taken the risk and gone through. But it's pretty pointless, I suppose. What's done is done." Lucinda glanced over at the witch. Her eyes were downcast and she was staring right through an unbundled bunch of flowers. Perhaps it was time for a topic change.

"Can I ask you something else?" Lucinda tried. "Can I ask you about . . . Johann's father?" Rosie's unfocussed look disappeared, to be replaced by a look of disgust.

"Must you?" she replied. "I can't stand the man. Between you and me, I really don't like vampires, as a species. Johann is different but his father . . . he represents everything I hate about them."

"I can see why Johann wouldn't get along with him, but what do *you* have against him exactly?"

"That's the thing, really," Rosie seemed to be struggling with her answer, "I almost hate that Johann doesn't hate him. He doesn't *like* him you understand, but . . . ugh. He spends his time trying to please his father, when all his father does is use him." She screwed up her face.

"How?"

"In all kinds of little ways. He's just using him to keep that area under his thumb. He married Johann's mother Marissa for the power. She was a Countess in her own right. The Stollenheims are attracted to power, but the family wasn't born with it. They married into power. So on his courtly rounds he comes across this elf queen and she's dying anyway, recently lost her husband, and so he took advantage. He ditched Countess Marissa and married her instead." She threw another bundle at the wall harder than necessary. "Then his new wife dies and he has a kingdom all to himself. And he *still* won't return to his first wife or pay any real attention to his son, even though it wouldn't affect his *precious* royal title. It makes me *sick*. Treating people like accessories, that's what it is," she tutted, "and would you believe, Johann and Countess Marissa are *worried* about him?"

"Why?" Lucinda asked, bundling up the last of the herbs.

"They say he's not the same man any more, that he's going down a dark path." She rolled her eyes. "'Being a selfish jerk' is how I'd describe it. Apparently he's been getting all secretive and cryptic and doing things that story karma is going to bite him in the butt for. He'll deserve everything he gets if you ask me, it frustrates me that *he* doesn't seem to care if they live or die and they still- *Ugh.*" She stared at the empty table and appeared to recover her senses. "You can't choose your family, I suppose." There were several things about Rosie's rant that Lucinda would like to ask more about, but she didn't dare. There was one safe topic though-

"Story karma?" she asked.

"Hmm?" Rosie looked up from the empty table. "Oh it's . . . I believe it's a combination of coincidence, magical forces and folk belief, but basically you reap what you sow here in the Otherworlds."

"What?"

"It's . . . " Rosie paused, " . . . you know how people are always whining that things are supposed to be done this way or that way and that vampires had better damn well lurk in castles not drinking wine or society will fall apart?"

"I've noticed that, yes."

"Well that's because they believe in 'story karma'," Rosie explained. "There are things that you're supposed to do and not do depending on your species, gender, status and so on. If you deviate from those things, or if you're a bad person, they think story karma will punish you for it."

"That explains a lot," Lucinda replied. "You don't seem to pay it much attention though."

"I think it's mostly driven by the people themselves," said Rosie. "There are areas where people have very different ideas of how stories should go. You don't find the same expectations in Fairyland as you do in human dominated regions, for example."

"You're not exactly a typical witch," Lucinda said. "Has anyone complained about you?"

"I might not wear black or have a pointy hat and a broomstick, but I look unusual and I live in a cottage in the woods by myself," Rosie replied, "and it's amazing how tolerant being unwell enough to seek out a witch makes people." They tidied up the chopping boards and any errant plants and then Lucinda said goodbye to Rosie. She was less uneasy about siding with Sara over Johann's father after hearing what Rosie had to say, but something was still amiss and she couldn't figure out what it was.

When Lucinda got home, she managed to make her magic teacher just as grumpy.

"You're a terrible student, Lucinda," Erlina berated her, "honestly, I mastered this spell when I was five." Erlina was starting to get to grips with contracted speech and had finally, after a suitable number of tellings off, stopped calling Lucinda 'my lord'.

"Maybe you're a terrible teacher!" Lucinda stuck her tongue out. "I'm doing my best! I just don't seem to be able to do anything much." The two of them had been trying a variety of spells for well over an hour. Lucinda was currently trying to change the colour of her teacup.

"It's like I told you, put your hands around it and visualise it as a different colour," Erlina instructed. "It's very simple. You *are* visualising it?" Lucinda tried to imagine the most neon cup she could. It was so bright in her mind's eye, but the cup remained its original pale blue. If she squinted a bit, it looked a tiny bit darker, but she suspected that was just wishful thinking.

"I give up," Lucinda let herself fall backwards onto the bed.

"Are all Earth humans this inept at magic?" Erlina complained. "All this effort for nothing is *exhausting*."

Lucinda sat up again. She felt like she should defend her species. Rosie must have learned magic just fine and she was an Earthling too. Plus, Erlina really did look exhausted. Perhaps she needed a break.

"You can't expect me to be good at something the first time I try it," she defended herself. "You're not telling me fairies are good at everything right away."

"We are talented at most arts," Erlina replied. "We are second in magic only to unicorns and they don't even have fingers. And I am a princess. I am *expected* to be good at things."

"Oh yeah? We'll just see about that shall we?" Erlina watched as Lucinda got up walked over to her desk, where she switched on her Playstation. "Let's see how good you are at this then, princess." She was willing to bet that fairies didn't have Playstations. Maybe seeing how it was difficult to learn something completely new and alien would help her understand the trouble Lucinda was having. Lucinda wasn't sure if her attitude was outright arrogance or some sort of fairy-human culture clash, but perhaps it would do her good to be taken down a peg.

"What is that? Oh!" Erlina leaned away from the television as it blared into life. "A different kind of computer, is it?" Erlina was used to Lucinda's laptop now, although she still didn't show the slightest interest in using it.

"Yes, actually," Lucinda rummaged around under the bed, trying to locate her second controller, "specifically one for games." She found the controller and switched the game. The fairy watched with quiet awe. Technology seemed to leave her spellbound. Lucinda handed Erlina the controller and the fairy almost hit her head on the bookcase in her haste to back away.

"I-is it safe?" Erlina eyed the black thing being handed to her.

"Of course it is," Lucinda reassured her. Erlina took it gingerly. Seeing the fairy's boundless confidence melt away was a new experience and her reaction was kind of cute. "Don't worry, this is a perfect game for a beginner. It's a lot of simple, little games. Mini-games they're called." The fairy jumped as the game started and again when the game announcer started blaring out instructions.

"What do I do?" she squeaked, visibly stiffening up with panic. "What does he mean buttons? I am not wearing any!" Lucinda pointed to the screen where an image of the controller was indicating which buttons did what and then down to Erlina's controller.

"You just press these, see?" Lucinda explained. "Don't worry, it's not like anything bad will happen if you lose." Erlina looked doubtful of this, but then she took a deep breath and stared hard at the screen with her chin stuck out in grim determination. The game started and Erlina was still at a loss.

"What do I do?" Erlina asked again. "What is happening?" Lucinda pointed to her own avatar and moved it around a little, and then to Erlina's and told her to push various buttons. Erlina started a little as her avatar moved.

"Now you have to move around and push all these guys off the cliff," Lucinda pointed to the screen again and demonstrated. All the games on this collection were sightly mad but this one involved using a man on an elephant to push as many people off a cliff as possible. They were all riding different animals and the different animals moved at different speeds and had different strengths. The hardest ones to knock off were worth the most points, plus you got bonus points for knocking the other player off. With several false starts and a few shrieks of both terror and delight Erlina started getting the hang of it.

"Ah!" she screamed. "I fell off! I fell off, what do I do?!" Before Lucinda could answer Erlina's avatar re-appeared and she breathed a sigh of relief. After she'd sent a few more beasts off the edge to the screams of the riders, she asked, "I say, those aren't real people in there, are they?"

"You ask me this *after* you've knocked six of them off a cliff?" Lucinda giggled.

"Well I didn't think they were, but the people in your laptop are real people, are they not?" Erlina pouted, but cringed again as her inattention caused her avatar to fall screaming over the edge.

"They're just little pictures, that's all," Lucinda reassured her, " . . . What if I'd said they were real?"

"I should have a new outlook on human entertainment," the fairy giggled, "but of course they cannot be real, why should they be riding such silly creatures all the way up there? It does not make sense. Everyone knows griffins make the best steeds and there's not a single one there." Lucinda suppressed a grin.

"Yes, if only everything could make as much sense as the Otherworlds," she joked.

"Are you making fun of me?" Erlina gasped in mock outrage. "I shall knock you off next!"

"Not if I knock you off first!" Lucinda didn't bother trying not to grin this time. They continued playing until Lucinda's mother came and told them it was time for Erlina to go home.

THE ATTACK

The next few weeks seemed to fly by. Erlina continued to stay in Lucinda's room, remaining concealed on weekdays, using her magic to stay hidden and only allowing herself to be seen by Lucinda's parents after school. On weekends they became inseparable, whether at Rent-A-Legend or Lucinda's house, with Erlina masquerading as a visiting friend. Lucinda continued to visit Rosie for potion-making lessons on Thursdays. She avoided bringing Erlina - she was worried one of them might let slip that they were practising magic.

Erlina was learning fast. She came and went to the Rent-A-Legend office on her own. The two of them had been on various quests; Lucinda had rescued a few more princesses and scraped her way through a few more monster fights – under the instruction of Gerda still, from whom she was taking fencing lessons - and Erlina had been a damsel in distress, the cure for a terrible plague and a stand-in valkyrie. Erlina also accompanied her on various quests as a guide or assistant.

In between all this, Erlina was still trying to teach Lucinda magic. Despite the fact that their video game sessions had taught Erlina some patience and understanding, Lucinda still wasn't getting anywhere. Even during half term, when they had whole days to practice, Lucinda couldn't manage the simplest of spells. Lucinda considered asking Johann about magic; he'd be a safer bet than Rosie, but Rosie had chosen now to take a break and stay at Johann's for a few weeks. She wasn't even coming back to teach Lucinda potions. Lucinda supposed that even

144

witches needed holidays.

By the Friday, when half-term was almost over, Lucinda was becoming worried about the fairy's health rather than her own lousy progress. Erlina was tired and irritable and her face was pale.

"I think maybe you should stay home," Lucinda suggested, as she got ready for work. "I can do whatever quest I get by myself. You worked really hard this week, I think maybe you're overdoing it." This wasn't the first time Erlina had seemed overtired either; Lucinda had noticed it before, like the time she couldn't do the colour-change spell. She'd brushed it off as Erlina being mentally tired from lessons and frustrated with Lucinda's lack of progress, but they hadn't been practising this morning. A thought occurred to Lucinda. "Are you homesick . . ?" she asked hesitantly. Erlina shook her head furiously.

"No!" she snapped. "I'm just a little out of sorts. The atmosphere is so dry here on Earth, it's uncomfortable," she complained. "I'll be fine. I suppose this is why no-one moves away from Fairyland for long."

When they got to the office, there was no-one manning the desk. One of the horns began to ring. It was curly and brown and it made a noise like a barking dog.

"Someone get that!" Freya shouted from down one of the corridors. Lucinda took hold of the thing and pulled, wondering how exactly you were supposed to answer it. She looked for a button or switch, but there were none. It seemed to have stopped ringing though, so she put it to her ear;

"-in your little office, don't you Sara?" came the tail end of a sentence. It was a man's voice, old, and it sounded horribly familiar. Lucinda drew a breath to speak but the next words froze her to the spot. "Well you aren't, and don't think you're ever going to see that prince of yours again. It seems plan A didn't work and I had a promising plan B, but it looks like I'm going to have to resort to plan 'C' after all. Such a pity."

"Who is this?" Lucinda managed to answer, sounding anything but brave. Was it really who she thought it was? Was he talking about *her*?

"Is that the little prince girl?" the voice replied, sounding amused. "Go home Earth girl, the sooner you stop playing hero the better off you'll be."

"Lucinda . . ?" Erlina gently touched her arm. "You've gone pale." The horn had gone silent.

"Hello?" Lucinda said, anger giving her courage. "What's that supposed to mean?" There was no answer.

"Lucinda?" Erlina tried again. Gerda came running in from the corridor to the left.

"Sorry Freya, I missed it!" she called down the opposite corridor. "Cinders got it though! 'Ere, what did they want? They still there?"

"There was a man on the phone," Lucinda replied, trying to keep her composure. "He started off saying something I missed and then he said you're never going to see that prince of yours again."

"*What?*" Freya had emerged from the corridor on the right, and she and Gerda exchanged a look.

"What exactly did he say, Cinders?" Gerda asked her urgently. "Tell us *exactly*."

"He said something, he thought he was talking to Sara. He said she thought she was something, I didn't catch the beginning of the sentence," Lucinda told them. She bit the end of her thumb in frustration. "Whatever it was, he said she isn't. I'm sorry, I didn't know how to answer the

146

phone!"

"Don't fret," Gerda reassured her. "Take your time. What else did he say?" Both women were listening intently, and Erlina looked from one to the other, looking increasingly worried.

"He said 'You'll never see that prince again'," Lucinda continued shakily, "he said he'd tried a few plans and they didn't work, so he's going to try something else. Plan C, he said." She suppressed a shudder. "Does he mean me?"

"No," Freya replied firmly, "we know this for sure." The two women visibly relaxed – they even started to smile. Gerda had a big grin on her face and Freya's mouth may not have been visible, but her eyes positively shone with joy. Lucinda had never seen anyone so happy to have had a threatening phone call.

"He's *alive!*" Gerda shouted, punching the air. "He's *alive*, Freya!" Freya exclaimed something in Icelandic; Lucinda didn't understand the words, but it was clear she was just as ecstatic.

"It's definitely not me, then," Lucinda observed, feeling out of the loop.

"No. He ain't talking about you," Gerda said, still smiling. "We do have real princes 'ere too."

"He means Charming," Freya explained. "We think we lost him, weeks ago. He is still lost, but we were afraid he was dead. Now we know he is not."

"He knows about me though." Lucinda couldn't help shuddering this time. "He said 'Is that the little prince girl?'" The two women didn't appear to hear her.

"What if he's lyin' though?" Gerda stopped smiling. "This is obviously a trap for Sara."

"Too bad for him, she is not here," Freya scoffed. "We will handle this. But we need to tell her as soon as possible. If he does something and we didn't-"

"Excuse me," Lucinda tried to keep her voice level, "is 'he' who I think he is? How does he know about me? How does he know my voice?"

"Sorry Cinders," Gerda apologised. "It ain't that we don't care you're rattled, it's just we thought a friend of ours was probably dead, and now he probably isn't. Let us have a little moment, all right?" Lucinda's anger was replaced by shame. She might feel out of the loop, but if she'd thought something had happened to Pens and then she heard he was safe . . . she felt Erlina take her hand and give it a squeeze.

"Lucinda has a point, though," Freya interjected. "How *does* Stollenheim know about her? Does anyone else know about you, Cinders?" So it *was* King Stollenheim that she'd heard.

"Just Johann and Rosie," Lucinda felt safe enough admitting to Gerda and Freya that her secret was out. "That's the Silver Witch and her boyfriend."

"The Silver Witch is all fine and dandy, but who's this boyfriend of 'ers?" Gerda asked. "Wasn't Johann . . . the name rings a bell."

"Isn't he the vampire you went to see?" said Freya. "They say vampires are all related . . . He is related to Stollenheim perhaps?" Lucinda cringed, and Freya gave her a look worthy of Sara. "He is, isn't he? You have been sharing information with him, maybe?" Gerda opened her mouth, but before she could start telling her off Lucinda tried to explain;

"It's not like that! Rosie is dating Johann, right? She agreed to help us with vampire advice! She *hates* Stollenheim and she says Johann doesn't like him either!" Gerda crossed her arms but said nothing, as if to say 'go on'. "I don't talk about rebellion stuff as such in my potion lessons anyway, I mostly talk about them and how they met and what they do."

"You don't talk about rebellion stuff 'as such'?" Gerda asked, still with her arms crossed.

"Well, no," Lucinda continued, "Johann gives me advice on hero-ing and Rosie is teaching me about potions and vampires. Even a bit about King Stollenheim himself. Which is *good*, right? They wouldn't tell me stuff like that if they were going to double cross us, would they?"

"Hmm." Gerda still looked unconvinced. "They tell you anythin' *useful*?"

"Not particularly. Look, it's not them," Lucinda protested. "The first night I was there his father was trying to get Johann to tell him there was someone in the castle, someone who wasn't Rosie. Johann wouldn't answer him properly and he went away. Then Johann said to stay away from his father if I saw him again. He's not passing him information, I'm telling you."

"I suppose," Gerda conceded. "I still ain't one hundred percent convinced. You be careful what you say around those people from now on. I ain't sure you should even keep seein' 'em." Lucinda chose not to answer. "If Sara were here, she'd ban you from goin'-"

"This missing prince then," Erlina piped up. "What are you going to do about him?"

"Yeah," Lucinda added, grateful to Erlina for changing the subject, "and how come he was targeted and yet all Stollenheim told me to do was go home?"

"That is your quest for today," Freya answered, taking a scroll from a pocket in her jacket. Lucinda shivered at a sudden chill, but then it was gone. "Sara has left instructions for you to scout out the town where Charming

went missing. See if you find clue to his whereabouts."
Freya headed off down the middle corridor. Gerda
indicated that they should follow her. Freya had stopped at
a door with a pretty, stained glass window in it. It was a
circle, with a design made of interlocking fish. Freya was
scribbling something on the scroll, using the wall to write
on.

"If we're being threatened, wouldn't it be better if
one of you went?" Lucinda pointed out. "I mean, I'm not
saying I won't do it, it's just if he turns up, I'm not going to
be much use, am I?"

"To answer both your questions, that's sort of the
point," Gerda explained. "I'm sure Stollenheim is wonderin'
what use you are too, and that means he'll probably leave
you alone. He don't see you as a threat, see? Just a spare
prince to keep the other stories goin'. And he don't
recognise you. I reckon he'd know us, so we'd be spotted
as soon as we set foot out the door."

"Besides, why do you think we send Lina with you?"
Freya cut in. "One fairy is worth about ten princes. If
something goes wrong, she can help you. You'll be fine."

"I'm not so sure about that," Lucinda argued. "I
don't think Erlina should go, she doesn't seem well." The
two women both turned and peered at Erlina, who was
now looking daggers at her.

"They say fairies never leave Fairyland for long,"
Freya mused, "perhaps it is like yuki onna and snowy
mountains? Perhaps you feel homesick?"

"I'm *not* homesick!" Erlina actually stamped her
foot. "I'm just tired because we were practising magic all
week, and Lucinda is *hopeless* at it."

"Yes, all right, we believe you," Gerda said. "Under
the circumstances, we don't 'ave much choice, there ain't

150

any point in arguing. If you're feelin' up to it then you go with Lucinda."

"But if there's trouble, you come back, you understand?" Freya instructed. She handed over the scroll she'd been writing on. "I wrote down some instructions for you. It will be nice to have proper instructions, yes? Now off you go."

Lucinda read the instructions from Freya as they walked through the pretty seaside town that was the location of their assignment. She was worried, but Freya's notes indicated the return door was very close and she could just disappear through it if there was trouble. She reassured herself that all she was doing was asking for information. She looked around. This place was called Polvan according to the notes, and belonged to a country under the control of Stollenheim's kingdom of Sheva. The townspeople had asked for a hero. Sara had sent them Charming, her most capable prince, who had pledged not to get married until her rebellion was over. He'd never returned. The town didn't seem to be in any kind of danger, though. It was quiet and picturesque. It reminded Lucinda of Bad Schwartz, although here there was no-one warning her to stay away from the castle or be in before sunset. Not that there was a castle. There wasn't much of anything, just rows of wooden houses lining a natural sea-front. There was a nice beach, the weather was warm and there were even palm trees dotted here and there. Lucinda didn't trust it for a second.

"Any moment now the peace is going to be shattered by an ear-splitting shriek and a dragon with eyes the size of soup tureens will come screaming out of the sky and start kidnapping people," Lucinda remarked, inspecting a pretty window box and then looking suspiciously up at the sky. "You just watch."

"I thought that was dogs?" Erlina remarked, skipping alongside Lucinda. She stopped to sniff at the flowers. "Dogs with eyes the size of soup tureens."

"Fine, dogs with eyes the size of soup tureens will come swooping out of the sky and start kidnapping people." Lucinda shrugged.

"When I was little, my mother would tell me that story often," Erlina said, "about the soldier and the tinder box. I always thought they were such silly dogs, with huge eyes like that on their little heads. But I suppose it meant that the dogs were very big."

"So you get told the same stories in Fairyland?" Lucinda frowned. "That's weird. What do you call them, 'human tales'?"

"Oh no," Erlina replied. "We call them history."

"Makes sense . . . " Lucinda was worried about the town being so quiet. What had happened to this Charming of Sara's? If an accomplished prince like him couldn't handle it, then how was she supposed to? She looked over at Erlina, who had started skipping again. She certainly wasn't worrying about it. Gerda and Freya had acted like she was some kind of trump card, but Lucinda had no idea why. She was certainly clever and sure, she could do magic, but she wasn't very strong, and that was before she'd started with this . . . whatever it was. It really was amazing how she seemed to have perked up once through the door. She looked like a different person than the irritable girl who'd been complaining about Lucinda's lack of magical prowess all week. Perhaps it was the sea air. It smelled strongly of salt, as sea air does, and it reminded Lucinda of holidays she took with her grandparents by the seaside. She last went about three years ago, before her grandmother passed away, and she remembered looking out to sea as they drove away in the car, longing to swim in that sparkling sea as a mermaid . . .

This could have been that sea. It was calm, but further out it glimmered in the sunlight. There was an island out there, just visible on the horizon. It looked quite mysterious. It was shrouded in mist, although with the warm weather here, she couldn't understand how. It was probably doing it on purpose.

They had no idea where exactly they should be going. Freya's instructions, whilst infinitely more useful than Sara's, were lamentably lacking in that area. Not that it mattered terribly. Generally, whoever they were supposed to see came to them, usually screaming. A woman walking along the street opposite them stopped and stared in amazement. She looked puzzled for a moment and then made her way over;

"My lord, how fortuitous that you have chosen to visit our humble village today!" she greeted them. "Please, won't you join us at our feast? 'Tis our yearly fishing festival!"

'Here we go,' thought Lucinda. Odd though, they really ought to have been asked if they would sort out the town's problem.

The two of them were ushered into a side room in the town hall. The woman who had brought them in, though smiling broadly, had more-or-less forbidden them to enter the main hall or go anywhere else until they were called. Lucinda took the opportunity to get out the scroll again. Freya hadn't had time to write down everything; it was mostly details of Charming and where he'd disappeared. There was something scribbled in the corner, and all she could make out were the words 'disagreement' and 'mermaids'. Lucinda sighed. At least this didn't look like the kind of place any self-respecting, traditional vampire would turn up. And like Gerda had said, she wasn't a threat, she was some girl in a costume. Strange as it was, she found herself relieved that Stollenheim was the traditional sort for once.

"What do you think the problem is here, anyway?" she asked Erlina, determined to get her mind off the subject for a bit. "Maybe their sea-monster isn't rampaging and demanding sacrifices like it's supposed to?" Erlina made a non-committal noise. She was too busy looking around the room. There was a bookshelf along the opposite wall, a polished, engraved table in the middle and a thick, red carpet, edged with gold covering most of the floor. This was clearly where they left visitors they wanted to impress.

Just as the two of them were getting bored, the woman from before returned, and beckoned Lucinda to come into the main hall. She had a curious expression on her face; she was looking just behind Lucinda's shoulder and she looked like she was trying to eat a lemon without anyone noticing. Lucinda instinctively turned to see what the problem was, but there was only Erlina, who was pouting a little, and fidgeting with the edge of her cloak. Lucinda looked back at the woman, who forced a smile and beckoned again.

The main hall had the trappings and furnishings of the first room, but the centre piece within did not. It was a great slab of a table, designed for meetings, not fine dining. Neither was the 'feast' displayed on it. There was a small selection of fish and a much smaller selection of cheese

154

and meat, some of which looked to be on the point of achieving sentience. Although what there was mostly, was lettuce. It had been used like backing paper. It was on every plate. It looked like they'd used it to replace anything they didn't have, which was practically everything.

"Please my lord, help yourself," the woman said, bowing and gesturing towards the table. There were about twenty other women on the other side of the table, watching them nervously. There was no way that the food was sufficient for them all, even without Lucinda and Erlina, who had politely but firmly been kept back from the table. The women were throwing the fairy dirty looks and the one who had waved them in was now trying to glare at her sideways.

"Don't worry about us, my lord," the first woman said, "Please, eat." People asking you to eat when they clearly weren't going to was never a good sign. Lucinda glanced sideways at Erlina. She wasn't paying the slightest attention to the food - her eyes were scanning the room and its occupants.

"Aren't *you* going to eat?" Lucinda asked them. "It's your feast, isn't it?"

"It would be most rude to eat before the guest of honour did, my lord," the woman replied. She seemed to be the one in charge. There was a general murmur of agreement.

"Where I come from," said Lucinda, "it's rude to eat before everyone else does. *Especially* when everyone else is standing pretty far away from the table," Lucinda paused, as the women exchanged worried glances. "You know, like they're waiting to see what will happen?"

"M-my lord, I do not understand-" the head woman began.

"Well we do," Lucinda replied, folding her arms. "I'm not sure if this is an attempt to poison us or what,"-she indicated the lettuce-riddled banquet-"but I'm not falling for it. What have you done with Charming? Where is he?"

"We - what?" The woman's eyes widened and she leaned forward. "Could you repeat that?"

"I said we're looking for a man named Charming," Lucinda hesitated as she realised who she was asking after. She pulled the parchment out again to check she wasn't off her rocker. "A prince. Called Charming. Prince Charming. Er, yeah, that's what it says." It hadn't yet occurred to her that they were looking for 'Prince Charming' and now that she came to say it out loud, it sounded silly. The women's bitter stares vanished, and they turned to each other, clasping one another's hands and uttering little gasps of excitement;

"There's a Charming about?"

"We're saved!"

"Oh thank goodness!"

"I guess you didn't take him then?" Lucinda asked, cursing inwardly that the situation had just got more complicated.

"Of course not!" The head woman put her hands on her hips and stuck her chin out. "We would never!"

"So if you weren't trying to feed us poison or sleeping pills, what was all this about?" Lucinda gestured at the paltry feast.

"Well . . . " A guilty look flitted across the woman's face. "We were hoping if you stopped a while, we might bring up the problem of the mermaids . . . It's gotten so difficult."

"Mermaids?" Lucinda thought back to Freya's scribbles . . . 'disagreement' it had said.

"They took all our men!" a young blonde woman burst out. "They stole them away, and we cannot fish!"

"The mermaids have taken all the men from the village," the head woman explained. "Without them to man the fishing boats, we cannot fish enough to support ourselves. There's only so much farming we can do . . . when winter comes, we'll starve."

"Also we would quite like them back," one woman added.

"Most of them anyway," another said.

"A hero came to sort them out, but they wouldn't come and face him!" the blonde woman shouted. "What kind of behaviour is that?" So this town wasn't that different to Bad Schwartz after all.

"Yes, how dare they not come out of their element to face an able swordsman on land," Lucinda said, doing a mental facepalm. "It's like they just don't know how to behave." Not that she approved of kidnapping men, but something was off here. Troubled townsfolk didn't usually try to trick people into helping.

"Exactly!" the woman replied hotly, not detecting the sarcasm. "They should have come out of the sea, tried to tempt him and got skewered like . . . like . . . skewered fish," the woman finished lamely. "What kind of villain doesn't face a hero when they find one?"

"The kind that wants to live?" Lucinda said. This was like the vampires again. Why would the mermaids stupidly come out to face a hero prepared for them? But why were they causing trouble when they knew what it would get them? Mermaids didn't *have* to kidnap people. They had a *choice*, unlike with vampires and blood.

"He sat on the shore for a long time, but they never came," the head woman said. "We told him maybe he should give up, but he refused. When we came back to check on him, he was gone."

"So who was this hero?" Lucinda asked.

"We never asked his name," the head woman replied. "Half of them never tell us anyway. It's all 'Oh, just a noble traveller ma'am, nothing to see here'," she tutted.

"'Half of them'?" Lucinda repeated. There was that guilty look again.

"He wasn't the only hero to come and try to sort them out," the woman admitted, looking down at the floor. "The mermaids took them all. No man can resist their singing. We didn't want to say, because, well, heroes nowadays, you tell them that many have failed and on they go. Anyway, all they want is the boat. All they ever want is the damn boat."

"'Damn boat'?" Lucinda asked, but Erlina cut her off;

"Why did no women try their luck against these mermaids?" she asked tapping her foot. "That would be the obvious solution, would it not?"

"It's not for us mere townsfolk to do such a thing," the head woman replied.

"Is it not?" Erlina glared from one end of the line to the other. "If there was a vampire problem in this village, what would the 'mere townsfolk' do? They would take up their weapons and fight." There was an uncomfortable silence. As one woman, the townsfolk turned to glower at Erlina. "If your man is taken by someone, is it not your duty to get them back? If a mermaid took my lord, I should march into the very sea to get him back." Erlina crossed her arms, returning their stares.

"Well you'd know all about that, wouldn't you, you little witch!" the blonde woman snapped. "Don't think we don't know what you are, I see your cloak of feathers!"

158

Lucinda had no idea what was going on all of a sudden, but the tension between Erlina and these women had been growing since the minute they'd walked into the hall. Now she fancied she could cut it with a knife, and it looked like knives might be imminent for other things, too.

"A mermaid is naught but a fairy with a tail! You're in league with them, I suppose?" The head woman drew herself up to her full height. "I ought never to have let you in, fairies cause nothing but trouble! I should throw you in the cellar-" The woman made to grab Erlina, but Lucinda stepped in her way.

"Hey, Erlina hasn't done anything to you!" she shouted. "Don't you dare touch her!"

"In the absence of the mayor I am in charge and if I say I'm going to throw a fairy in the cellar-" the woman began, making a signal for the other women to move forward. A few of the braver ones did, but most of them were eyeing either Erlina or the door. Lucinda drew her sword.

"Are we going to have a problem?" she said quietly, hoping her bravado would suffice to get the woman to back off. She stepped backwards and reached out her free hand for Erlina.

"I dunno what you'd defend one of those things for-" The woman was wearing a look of disgust.

"Look, I came here looking for someone," Lucinda explained. "It doesn't look like you can help me. I might be able to help you, but I'm not going to feel like it if you lock up my friend here just because she's a fairy, am I?"

"I dunno where you grew up, but it must have been a very strange place if you're happy to consort with the Fair Folk." The woman shook her head in disbelief. "Do what you want, I'm sure."

Lucinda led Erlina out of the hall, keeping her sword drawn and an eye on the women, who stared at them resentfully as they left. Lucinda heard the clunk of bolts sliding across after the town hall door shut.

"Well, that didn't go like I expected," she complained, sheathing her sword again and heading for the beach. She was glad she hadn't actually had to test her fencing skills. Gerda had been giving her lessons, but she still wasn't very good. The sword was largely for show. Princes had to have swords. Erlina had gone quiet. She seemed to be thinking about something. She wasn't alone. Lucinda was shocked at the townswomen's reaction; she'd always thought of fairies as small, twinkly things until she'd met Erlina. Erlina had largely only changed her opinion as to their size, but she'd still seemed *fairly* twinkly, apart from the occasional worrying remark or story. But these people were treating her like a demon. She was reminded of the day they'd first met, when she'd mentioned fairies kidnapping people and luring men away. Evidently, fairies weren't as harmless as she'd grown up thinking. She settled herself down on the beach, close to the water, looking out to sea. Erlina followed suit.

"Lucinda . . . " said Erlina, "thank you for protecting me."

"You're welcome," Lucinda replied. She still couldn't believe her ruse had worked. "I'm just glad they backed off when they did, or we would have been in trouble. If they'd really kicked off, I wouldn't have been much use."

"At least you would have tried!" Erlina screwed up her face. "Imagine, them just waiting for someone to come along, when the solution is right under their noses. That isn't how stories work!"

"I guess so," Lucinda said. That must have been why

Sara had sent Charming here. "Why do they hate fairies so much? They acted like you were some kind of monster. I've heard of the odd 'bad fairy' but . . . "

"I suppose they don't meet many modern fairies," Erlina replied. "We don't move about much, so they don't know we've changed. And there are still a lot of fairies who stick to the old ways. It's the same everywhere."

"What do you mean 'changed'?" Lucinda asked.

"It's like with the vampires and everything else," Erlina explained. "Many of us don't do things like kidnap children or play time tricks on people any more. But there are still fairies about who do, and these people grew up being told the old tales in any case."

"So you're saying fairies have gotten nicer like vampires and other mo-" Lucinda stopped herself saying 'monsters', "-and other races? But no-one has noticed, because you don't leave Fairyland very often?"

"Don't call me a monster, Lucinda," Erlina sulked. She shifted her position on the sand, hugging her knees and resting her chin on them.

"I'm sorry," Lucinda apologised, "I just never thought I'd have to put 'vampire' and 'fairy' in the same bracket, if you know what I mean?" Erlina actually laughed. "What?" Lucinda asked.

"Oh, nothing," Erlina replied, "you just reminded me of someone. . . . We're waiting for these mermaids, correct?" she asked, changing the subject.

"Yep," Lucinda replied, imitating her position. "They'll show up sooner or later, right?"

"I should think so," Erlina replied. "You want to ask them if they took Prince Charming?" Erlina normally gave Lucinda advice, but this time she'd been pre-empted. The two of them stared out at the sea. After a while Erlina asked, "What stories did you grow up with, Lucinda?"

"If you mean stories about fairies, mostly the sort that wear flowers and are tiny," Lucinda replied.

"What about heroes? And damsels?" Erlina pressed her. "Did they just wait around to rescued, like these townsfolk? Is that what you grew up with?"

"I think there were a lot of . . . of 'silly princesses' when I was little . . . " Lucinda began thoughtfully, "but there's a lot of stories about these days where it's the princess who's the hero. Nowadays all the princesses know kung-fu or have swans that fire lasers." Erlina blinked.

"I've never heard of princesses like that," she said bemusedly. "What fairytale are they from?"

"We have movies and cartoons these days as well as fairy tales and books," Lucinda answered her. "Games, too. Like I say, when I was a kid it was like, most princesses were just there to look pretty and get kidnapped. But now that sort of thing is looked down on. So maybe the stories got broken, but now they've mended again . . . in a different way? Like with the vampires. They're not broken, they're just different-"

"I think we have company," Erlina interrupted. She sat up. She was looking intently at three bumps on the water, a little way out. They were the tops of three heads, with just the eyes peeking out over the surface.

"Hello?" Lucinda called out, standing up and shading her eyes against the sun. "We don't want any trouble, we're just looking for someone. Can we talk, maybe?" The three heads vanished. "No, then," Lucinda's heart sank. How was she going to find this missing prince now, if the mermaids wouldn't talk?

There was a splash, and one of the mermaids rose out of the water closer to land. She was dark-skinned, with long, curly, jet black hair. It was partly braided, decorated with golden coins and beads. The same coins adorned a bikini-like top she was wearing to cover her chest; it was made of a stiff, red material patterned with white flowers.

"You want to talk?" The mermaid nodded once to show her approval. "Let's talk."

"I'm looking for someone," Lucinda repeated. "I think maybe he wanted to talk too." The mermaid gave her a curious stare.

"Come closer," she commanded, "step into the water." Lucinda considered this.

"Why don't *you* come closer?" Lucinda asked. "It's hard to hear you over there." Lucinda could hear her fine, but she wasn't an idiot. These mermaids had been taking people.

"I see we are at a stalemate," the mermaid responded, "I do not want to come out of my element and neither do you. It is understandable. However if you want to talk, I must insist you to step into the water. I see your companion."

"And that is the problem, is it not?" Erlina countered. "We don't see yours." The mermaid made an upward sweeping gesture with her right hand and was immediately flanked by two others. One of them was what Lucinda thought of as a typical mermaid; she had long, blonde hair, blue eyes and a bra made from pink shells. The other was brown-skinned, had mid-length brown hair and brown eyes. She wasn't wearing clothes as such; she had a large band of material wrapped round and round her chest, almost like a bandage. It was tied in a bow at the back.

"There,"-the mermaid gave a single nod again-"I promise you there is no-one else. Will you step into the water, now?" Now Lucinda had no excuse. She had to step

163

into the water or lose the lead. She looked back at Erlina for reassurance, who came forward to join her. She walked to the edge of the water and hesitated. She looked at the mermaids. They weren't too far away; she'd be able to put her feet on the floor where they were. She could move back if there was trouble. Besides, Erlina wouldn't let her or them do anything potentially fatal, surely?

"Just so you know, my friend here is a fairy," she warned them, sounding a lot more nervous than she'd meant to. "Okay?" The townswomen had seemed afraid of fairies, so maybe it would work on mermaids too. It didn't. All three of them sniggered.

"As you wish," the lead mermaid bit her lip, trying not to laugh. Lucinda stepped into the water. Before the mermaids could move, Erlina added;

"Much as my lord sounds *very silly* right now,"-she sounded as though she'd never been so embarrassed in her entire life-"he is correct that I will not take it lightly if you try anything." The water was only up to her knees, so Lucinda risked looking back at Erlina and to the mermaids again. They were sharing a look that said 'Humans, what can you do?'. Oddly enough, that little display of camaraderie was reassuring. If Erlina and they could relate, then they probably weren't *too* bad. Lucinda waded out as far as she could feel the sand solidly under her feet. The water came up to her elbows.

"Oh, how cunning," the lead mermaid remarked. "It finally occurred to them, did it?"

"Took them long enough, didn't it Nerissa?" the blonde mermaid chuckled.

Lucinda could see where this was going. "Yes, yes, I'm a girl," she admitted. "Can we get past all the laughing about it and cut to the chase, please? I'm looking for a prince who went missing around here about a month ago. Did you take him?" The three mermaids exchanged looks.

"Looks like there's no help for it," the mermaid addressed as Nerissa sighed. "I'm afraid we have to kidnap you." Lucinda opened her mouth to object, but was cut off;

"I don't know, Nerissa," the blonde mermaid piped up, "how do you know we can trust these people?" Erlina was wading into the sea to join Lucinda. Apparently she hadn't much liked the sound of Lucinda being kidnapped either.

"Bubbles, have you never heard the saying 'the enemy of my enemy is my friend'?" Nerissa answered.

"Yes," Bubbles agreed, "but my enemy is *also* my enemy. These people came to rescue the men after all." She looked accusingly at the girls. "*Didn't* you?"

"Not exactly, but it's not like we can ignore the situation, even if those women *are* jerks," Lucinda replied, figuring that she may as well be honest. "Do we get a say in being kidnapped or what?" Nerissa sighed impatiently.

"Do you want to find this prince of yours or don't you?"

The two girls were escorted to the mystery island, which despite being covered in mist from the shore, was actually bathed in sunshine.

"What's all that mist about?" Lucinda asked as they clambered onto the beach. "Shouldn't it evaporate?"

"It's a barrier to keep out prying eyes and scrying spells," Nerissa explained. "Your missing prince asked us to make it."

The island was quite big, and filled with tropical plants, trees, brightly coloured birds, and, most notably, men. They were everywhere; some sunbathing on the

165

beach, some cooking fish on little fires, some napping in the shade of the trees. The nearest of them looked up as the group arrived. The mermaids came onto the land too, they moved almost like seals, although of course they had the luxury of arms. Now that they were out of the water, their tails were visible. They were all differently coloured; Nerissa's was a pale green with splashes of silver, Bubbles' was various shades of pink and the brown-haired mermaid had a dark, purple tail.

"Nerissa is back!" one of the men called out. "And she's brought new people!" There was practically an uproar as the rest of the men looked up.

"Oh hey, and they're girls! Er, I think?"

"Real ones?" The two of them were soon surrounded by a large crowd of men. There seemed to be some disappointment as they got a look at the new 'captives'.

"That one's a boy and that one's a fairy!" one man complained. "They ain't real girls any more'n mermaids."

"Hey!" complained Bubbles. "We are *too* real girls! You've been surrounded by girls this whole time, don't be such drama queens!" A chestnut-haired boy at the front of the crowd complained;

"Everyone knows mermaids aren't real girls."

"Yeah, they're made of sea foam, right?" said a blonde-haired boy next to him.

"You speak for yourself, lad!" an older man complained. "I'll take an attractive woman with a fish tail made of sea foam over my lemon-faced wife any day."

"At least you've got a wife!" another man complained.

"Wife?" scoffed another man. "Who wants one of those? I just want some-"

"Silence, boys," Nerissa scolded them. "You'll find out how real I am if I smack you on the head!"

"Such a violent woman," chided a man sitting nearby a little way from the crowd. He had short, thick, black hair. He was dressed in a blue tunic, tied at the middle with a brown belt, and baggy, white trousers. He also had a blue cape, lined with white, which he was currently using like a beach towel. Unlike the other men, he hadn't moved when the girls had dragged themselves ashore. It wasn't too difficult to work out who he was. He had 'prince' written all over him.

"It's all right, I'm only made of sea foam," Nerissa replied sarcastically. The man just laughed.

"They're like this every time we bring someone new, don't worry," the purple-tailed mermaid reassured the girls, "I think they get sick of each other pretty easily."

"Honestly, these people are guests, not a circus attraction!" Bubbles snapped at the men. "Back off, will you?"

"Indeed, off with you," Nerissa commanded, waving them away. "We have business to discuss."

There was a general muttering and the crowd dispersed, going back to their fires, blankets or trees. The mermaids made themselves comfortable and bade the girls do the same. Nerissa had a hurried conversation with the prince, who dragged his cape over so he could sit with them.

"I believe you're looking for me?" he addressed this to Lucinda, holding out his hand. "Prince Charming, at your service. Sara is upset, I take it?"

"Well, she sent me here to find you," Lucinda answered, realising she had no idea how Sara felt about it. "Gerda and Freya were relieved to hear you were all right.

They were ecstatic."

"Oh dear, they must have been so worried," he said, "I did try to send word back, but I suppose nothing reached them." Lucinda had other things to ask, but there was something she just had to get out of the way or explode;

"You're really Prince Charming then?" she asked. "*The* Prince Charming?" Lucinda had heard of a lot of Prince Charmings and she had wondered as a child if they were all the same one. If they were, he must be married to about six different princesses. It would be handy she supposed, since Gerda had said kingdoms were getting smaller and smaller. But most un-herolike.

"*A* Prince Charming, certainly," the prince replied. "The name runs in the family and I have a lot of uncles and cousins."

"Ah."

"What's this about hearing I was safe?" he asked curiously. "Did you get my messages?" The girls looked at each other.

"No," Lucinda replied. "It was a nasty phone call we got. Saying we'd never see you again. I guess it wasn't exactly hearing you were 'all right' but . . . "

"It is as I feared then . . . " he looked upwards, where the merest wisp of the barrier could be seen.

"And what is that exactly?" Erlina asked him.

"We are being *watched,*" the prince replied grimly, looking back down. "Stollenheim knows what we're doing somehow, I'm not sure how *exactly*, but he does. I suspect he's been spying on us for a good while now. That's why I had the mermaids erect the scrying barrier. What else can you tell me about this call?"

"He said . . . he said plan A and B had failed, so he was resorting to plan C," Lucinda answered him. She shuddered at the memory. "Then he said I should go home and stop playing hero. He knew all about me. Outside Rent-A-Legend, only Rosie and Johann know about me." Erlina sat up.

"That's good news then, isn't it Lucinda?" she said happily.

"What is?" Lucinda asked, bemused.

"If Prince Charming knows we're being watched and he went missing before you even started working for Sara, then it can't be Rosie and Johann passing on information." Lucinda's heart skipped a beat. *It wasn't them*. She *knew* it wasn't them anyway, but now she could argue her case!

"I'm not sure when he started keeping tabs on Sara, but it must have been months and months ago." Charming folded his arms and stared up at the sky again. "We were *almost* ready to strike, and then *this* happened,"-he gestured around him-"and it's not the only convenient story that's taken Sara's staff away. I'm sure you know we're short on heroes?"

"I kind of noticed," Lucinda replied, waving a hand at her uniform. "What with being hired and all. But what do you mean 'this happened'?"

"This situation," he explained. "I'm sure this disagreement between the mermaids and the townsfolk has been engineered, along with several other stories to keep us busy. It's a *trap*."

Charming explained that he had come to Polvan to sort out a fairly routine mermaid problem. But something had been wrong. Normally it was a single mermaid stealing away a particular man or a few people, but this was a whole clan – made up of local and foreign mermaids alike - and they were abducting the entire male population. The townspeople, having failed to solve the problem, were relying on passing heroes to do it for them, but the mermaids ignored them.

"They were such fools. Standing on the shore, demanding we come out, calling us such names . . . " said Nerissa, "but then Charming came along. All he did was wait quietly on the shore, like you did. It turned out he wanted to talk."

"I wanted to know why they had taken part in such a broken story," Charming explained. "Those other heroes had only listened to the townspeople's version of things. I wanted to hear both sides."

"So there's a reason you kidnapped all these men and are keeping them here, then?" Lucinda asked. This earned her a condescending look from Bubbles.

"No kidding," the mermaid snorted, "because we always just do things for no reason."

"Sorry," Lucinda apologised. "The Otherworlds are still kind of confusing to me. As far as I can tell, sometimes people do stuff here just because that's what whatever they are always did."

"I used to rescue people from ships and laugh and sing and comb my hair in coves where humans might steal a glance at me, because that's what mermaids always did," Bubbles said, scowling. "But not any more." The brown-haired mermaid laughed;

"Mermaids never 'always' did that, they used to laugh and sing and drag people under water."

"Not where I come from, Pearl," Bubbles complained. "My clan is the rescuing sort. But it's hard to rescue anyone on an empty stomach."

"The townspeople were taking your food?" Erlina gasped. "That's terrible!"

"Isn't it?" Bubbles agreed. "It's that *stupid* one-boat

rule." Lucinda asked the obvious question;

"What the heck is the 'one-boat rule'?"

"You know," Charming answered her, "it's when heroes come along to a fishing town, and need a boat for their quest-"

"-and there's only one boat," Lucinda finished for him, rolling her eyes. "The heroes come to a *fishing* village or a *port* town, need a boat, and there's only *one* available! In a town by the *sea!*" she tutted. "And the one boat always ends up getting set on fire or stolen or sinks. I *hate* that!"

"It's most annoying, isn't it?" Charming agreed earnestly. "I tried to buy my own boat once and they said that would be unethical. I'm not sure that the guy understood what unethical meant though, to be honest."

"It's only been a tradition up until now though," Nerissa explained. "If a hero came along and the people had more than one boat, which they usually did, well, they just fibbed and said there was only one left, which the heroes couldn't have."

"I asked a fisherman I was dating once why they did that, and he said it was because they got sick of heroes coming along and pinching all their boats," Pearl added.

"Recently in Sheva, it's not just a tradition any more. It's become an actual law, and people come checking," Nerissa explained. "In many towns along the coast, they're always out fishing, so that there's only ever one boat in the harbour."

"They've been over-fishing like crazy *everywhere!*" Bubbles complained, slamming a fist down onto the sand. "We were reduced to a seaweed-only diet! We had to do *something*."

"But drowning people isn't done any more, plus it's

171

not their fault," Nerissa said, "so our clans came together and we came up with an alternate plan. We had to kidnap everyone instead. But that left us with another problem-" Nerissa stopped. She stared at the ground as if it had dealt her a personal insult. "Do you feel that?" she demanded of the other mermaids. She looked sharply towards the shore. The others followed her gaze. Prince Charming stood up;

"Something isn't right," he said. "Look at the sea." They looked.

"It's terribly choppy, isn't it?" Erlina stood up and shielded her eyes to squint across the waves.

"But there's no wind," the prince observed.

"The ground is shaking . . . " Nerissa added, having placed her palms flat on the floor. "It might be a seaquake. But we never get them here!" All over the beach and along the shoreline, the village men were getting up, emerging from the trees with concerned looks on their faces.

"Queen Nerissa, what's happening?" an older man asked. "Is it your mermaids doing this?"

"No, we-" Nerissa began, but was cut off as a group of mermaids came crawling up the beach at an alarming speed. Lucinda would never have thought people with no legs could move that fast.

"My queen!" the leading mermaid shouted as she drew close enough. "The- The serpents!" She panted for a moment as she got her breath back.

"Calm down," Nerissa commanded. "What's happening? Is this a quake?"

"No, my queen," the mermaid replied, still gasping for breath, "the serpents . . . there . . . there's a pod of serpents, going crazy! We can't stop them, there's too many!"

"Serpents?" Nerissa said, frowning. "What upset them?"

"We don't know!" The woman shook her head desperately. "But my lady, they're going to cause a tidal wave at this rate! We came to warn you!"

"A tidal wave?" gasped one of the onlookers. "Lady Nerissa, what should we do?"

"I'm not sure . . . we've never had to deal with a tidal wave before," Nerissa closed her eyes briefly as she thought.

"It's no problem for us," Pearl shrugged, "as long as we don't get impaled on anything."

"Not a problem?!" shouted one of the older men. "What about us? What are *we* supposed to do?"

"Maybe you should have thought of that before you started stealing all our fish!" Bubbles snapped. "The way I see it, this will be the perfect solution to all our problems!"

"I know you don't like humans Bubbles, but that's *not* the answer," Pearl intervened.

"Pearl is right," Nerissa agreed. "If we let the town be destroyed and its people die, new humans will move in, and we will be nothing more than dangerous monsters. Monsters who stole away their men and flooded their town."

"We *didn't* flood the town!" Bubbles protested.

"They won't see it like that," Charming answered. "It'll be all too easy for them to blame anything they don't like on the mermaids if we let this tragedy happen."

"Right," Nerissa said, setting her jaw and turning to head to the ocean, "let's do what mermaids do best!" There was a muttering from the crowd.

"Drown sailors?" one man suggested.

"Sing enchanting and beguiling songs?" suggested

another.

"Get naked?" suggested one of the younger men hopefully.

"I was talking about rescuing drowning people in storms," Nerissa replied icily, before continuing down to the sea.

Lucinda stood up, at a loss what to do. She could feel herself starting to panic, and she had to fight it-

Without warning, Erlina ran after Nerissa.

"Erlina, what are you doing?!" Lucinda called, taking off after her. Charming was barking orders at the assembled men, ordering them to climb the trees and tie themselves on with rope and vines and anything else they could find.

"Queen Nerissa, please wait a moment," Erlina was calling to the retreating mermaid. Catching up to them Lucinda heard Erlina say, "I shall go and look," before donning her feathered robe. As Erlina turned around to face Lucinda again, the cloak gleamed, appeared to be blown upwards in a blast of wind, and became a pair of shimmering wings. Erlina sprang lightly from the ground and flew away over the trees. Lucinda stared after her. Charming approached her, having finished ordering the other men about.

"Is something wrong, Miss Prince?" he asked.

"Where's Erlina gone, do you know?" she asked, trying not to sound desperate. Erlina was meant to be her last resort, and this seemed pretty last resort-ish. What the heck did she think she was doing, taking off without telling her?

"I'm afraid I don't know. It was Nerissa she spoke to," he replied, pointing down the beach, where the mermaid was waiting at the edge, holding counsel. As the men had gathered before, now there was a growing crowd of mermaids trying to keep themselves steady in the increasingly violent waves. They clung to the beach to try and stay still, but the sand fell away, so they scrambled onto the shore. The beach was filled end to end with mermaids trying to get out of each other's way, their shining tails flashing in the sunlight. As the two humans ran down the beach to join them, Erlina returned.

"What did you see?" Nerissa shouted above the roar of the waves.

"There was - " Erlina paused and shuddered, "there was a *wall* of serpents, I've never seen so many! They're thrashing about making waves and striking the seabed, it's most unnatural behaviour!" Erlina reported. "I would have gone closer, but I didn't want the man to see me."

"What man?" asked Nerissa sharply.

"There was a man flying above the water," Erlina explained, "I may be mistaken, but he seemed to be commanding the serpents. There is magic afoot."

"When is there ever not?" Charming sighed. "Well, Nerissa. This is your territory. What should we do? I've got all the villagers secured in the trees, but that's the best I can do. We can't swim away in time and only Erlina here can fly. And that won't help the villagers still in town."

"I don't know," Nerissa answered him. "We need to lessen the wave somehow, but we aren't big enough to counter it, not even with every mermaid here."

"Could you stop it with magic?" Lucinda suggested. "Mermaids know magic, don't they? Couldn't you, I don't know, sing the serpents to sleep or something?"

"Using magic against magic does seem to be our only option," Charming agreed.

"We'll never get close enough to enchant them or

this man, the seas are too rough!" Nerissa massaged her temples as she tried to think of something. Lucinda put her head in her hands. She couldn't think of anything, either. How had she ended up on a doomed island again? Were plane tickets really worth it?

"Mermaids have some control over water and weather, do they not?" Erlina asked.

"That's true, but it's not the weather causing the problem. We can't calm the sea," Nerissa replied.

"Can you not make your own wave?" Erlina suggested.

"You suggest fighting fire with fire? Or rather, water with water?" Nerissa replied.

"If you mermaids can build up a wave to send back at the serpents, I can help you by making a barrier to keep it up until we loose it at them," Erlina explained. "If we crash one wave into the other, they may cancel out."

"Is that even scientifically possi-" Lucinda began, before her logic fizzled out under the glares of a beach full of fish women and a fairy, "-never mind."

"We'll have to get our wave going before theirs! Start building it just in front of the island, facing out to sea!" Nerissa shouted addressing every mermaid on the beach. "If we don't get there first, it'll suck away all our water and we'll never stop it! Pull up all the water around the bay! All of it! We need every single one of you to help! Go!" The beach emptied as quickly as if a wave had carried the women away.

"What should we do?" Lucinda asked, running after Nerissa.

"I should ask your fairy friend," Nerissa replied, "though I would have thought a good hero would know what to do." The mermaid slipped into the water. Lucinda stared after her for a few seconds.

"But I'm not a good hero . . . " she mumbled, her feeble protest lost amongst the roar of the ocean.

"I think we need to get to the other side of the island," Charming said, grabbing her wrist and pulling. "Your friend might need help."

"But what can *I* do?" Lucinda wailed as she was led through the undergrowth. "I can't even get a teacup to turn a different colour, never mind control the weather!"

"What do princes do, Miss Prince?" Charming asked her as he continued to lead her through the trees. "Not to be rude, but do you always panic like this?"

"Yes, unfortunately," replied Lucinda, feeling her face turning crimson. "Johann told me I shouldn't, though. But it's hard, I'm not used to this! I'm used to learning how to ask for a cheese omelette in French and fixing it so that my wig doesn't fall off!"

"Answer the question, Miss," Charming demanded, bringing her back to reality. "You'll never be a good hero if you can't answer a simple question. What do princes do?"

"Is this really the time for hero trivia?" she groaned.

"It's the perfect time for hero trivia," he replied, still clutching her wrist. "Calm down and think. Townspeople panic, heroes think." This was another test, like with Gerda and finding the location of the secret door. What did princes do? The answer seemed painfully obvious, since it was ninety percent of the work Lucinda had done so far.

"They rescue the princess?" she answered, with only a slight tremor of doubt.

"That's right!" Charming replied, sounding pleased. "And part of rescuing the princess is making sure she doesn't get into a situation that she needs to be rescued from!"

"You think we need to protect Erlina?" Lucinda deduced. "But how?"

"By being her lookouts for a start! She'll be concentrating on the barrier for the wave, she won't see those serpents coming if we don't warn her!" Charming answered. "Though I'm more worried about the man she saw. It's probably Stollenheim, and he's going to be pretty sore that we're trying to stop him. We need to be ready for him."

"R-right," Lucinda replied, feeling as unready as ever, particularly for King Stollenheim. "It would be helpful," she hazarded, "if you would just tell me stuff for the rest of this . . . adventure. I'm new at this prince thing, remember? So if you've got any more questions, it would be best to ask me them now instead of waiting until we're in even more peril." Charming slowed down as he thought about this, allowing Lucinda to shake off his grip and stride alongside him.

"I do have one more question," he said, sounding slightly puzzled.

"Go on then," Lucinda said warily, "let's get it over with."

"What use, exactly, is a spell that turns a teacup a different colour?"

When they arrived on the other side of the island, the mermaids were already at work. From their vantage point on the cliff, which curved around the bay, they could clearly see the mermaids, holding hands in a row. The water in the bay itself was still; they were singing a spell to control it. The sea water was boiling up in front of them, forming a huge wall. Erlina was floating above, channelling the wind or some other force into a barrier. She could see

178

the water bouncing off it. The water built up slowly at first, but soon the captive wave was even taller than the cliff. The water level was dropping and dropping . . . Lucinda and Charming watched like hawks for any serpents or flying men coming their way, but for what felt like hours, there was nothing. Until;

"Oh blast it! *It's coming!*" Charming shouted to the fairy, as he spotted the enemy wave coming the other way. "Run!" he commanded, heading for the trees.

"We'll never make it!" Lucinda shouted, watching in horror at the approaching wave. She wanted to run, but her legs refused to work. The mermaids' wave was let loose. Charming swore, ran back towards her and knocked the frozen Lucinda to the ground as the waves collided. The result hit even the high cliff, sweeping the two of them away.

Lucinda came round on a beach. Erlina was shaking her awake and she could hear voices; the mermaids, and the men. She struggled into consciousness. She coughed violently and spat up sea water.

"Lucinda, you have to wake up!" Erlina whispered urgently. She muttered something, a spell, and Lucinda snapped awake. She looked around and tried to get her bearings before staggering upright. There was debris everywhere; she saw a boat embedded in what used to be the town hall, that she'd visited barely two hours ago. There were men and mermaids everywhere, coughing and groaning and trying to rouse each other.

"We were washed all the way back to the town?" Lucinda croaked, not sure how long she'd been out or if she was seeing things.

"Shh, quiet! That's not important right now-" Erlina whispered.

"So you're awake," came a chilling voice from behind the two girls. Lucinda looked round and almost fainted again from the shock. Floating in the air above the wreckage-strewn beach, was a pale man in evening dress and a cape. He had short black hair, thickly streaked with grey. There was no doubting who or what he was. This was King Stollenheim, the vampire she had first seen in Johann's castle. "I wasn't fast enough. Wretched fairy, I could have been and gone if weren't for you. But I suppose I can get some information out of you this way."

"Fairies have spells for everything," Erlina replied, narrowing her eyes at the vampire, "unlike vampires, who mostly use their spells to run away. You should try one now."

"I'd hoped my meddling step-daughter would be here by now, but instead I find her incompetent minions," he sniffed, ignoring Erlina's slight. "I was at least expecting the snow woman or her other general. I'm very disappointed. At least the real prince was still here."

"You flattened a whole town just to get to Sara and Charming?" Lucinda spluttered, still coughing up water. "Just two people? And Sara's your daughter!"

"Step-daughter," he corrected, with no more emotion than if he'd been correcting an equation, "I think you'll find I flattened a whole town to get rid of a rebel army. Sara and her peons are a threat to my throne. Besides, this is a *story*," he said, infusing the word with loathing, "I think you'll find this is perfectly acceptable behaviour." He gave her an unpleasant smile. "It's normally the step-mother's job to bump off unnecessary children, but I don't see why I should bother with getting married again when I can do the job more efficiently myself."

"That's against the rules!" shrieked Bubbles, dragging herself and an unconscious man ashore. She was covered in seaweed and scratches. "You aren't *supposed* to do it efficiently! That's the *point!* How *dare* you break the rules! Do you *want* us to end up like Earth?!"

"The point is to win, young lady." The vampire looked down his nose at her. "I have no interest in your rules. Why should I, when they will only result in my death?"

"We were just getting everything sorted out!" Bubbles actually began to sob. "Half the town is destroyed, and they'll blame it on us, we know they will! Humans always blame everything on us! If a man drowns in the sea, it must have been us. If a child drowns in a pond, it must be our fault that they haven't been warned to stay away!"- she pummelled the sand -"We worked so hard to change our image - *so hard!* We rescued people and we sang and we sat around looking pretty! The humans weren't scared of us any more-"

"No, they *weren't* were they?" The King sneered. "They weren't scared, so they took your fish and damaged your homes and ruined your crops."

"We were *working* on it!" she screamed. "Then you had to come along,"-she pointed an accusatory finger at him-"and ruin *everything!* We were so close-!"

"Close to an understanding?" he finished for her, sounding almost bored. He surveyed the beach, where many of the men were being helped or hauled ashore by the mermaids. "Oh, they respect you now perhaps, when catastrophe has brought you together. But in time, their respect will fade. Mermaids have been hunted for their meat, they've been captured and put on display. That's what looking pretty will get you my dear, and nothing more." He stretched in a leisurely way, before continuing, "Now if you'll excuse me, I have some business to take care of. I refuse to fight with mermaids, it's most unbecoming." He turned his back on the enraged Bubbles and addressed Lucinda, "Are you going to tell me where my step-daughter and her cronies are, prince girl, or should I just kill you now?"

"I don't know! And even if I did, I wouldn't tell you!" Lucinda yelled defiantly. Terror had rooted her to the spot and now the adrenaline was kicking in. Fear had made her angry, and she wasn't going to run.

"That's quite enough of that," came a man's voice from behind her, and she was pulled gently backwards as Charming stepped forward to face the King. "You've lost this one, Stollenheim. Sara has avoided your trap, and I'm still alive. And now you've gone and destroyed a town, how very stupid of you."

"Ah, the *real* prince," King Stollenheim greeted him. "I see you aren't dead, more's the pity. But you are incorrect, this town is part of my kingdom. I can demolish as many peasant dwellings as I please."

"Oh, I think not," Charming responded. Lucinda couldn't see Charming's face from where she was, but he sounded oddly pleased with himself.

"Do enlighten me," the vampire responded, "I just can't stand it when heroes get that smug look on their faces. I shall enjoy wiping it off. Go on, tell me your heroic reasoning, I'm all ears."

"Charming!" shrieked Nerissa, erupting out of the water and glaring at the both of them. "Get on with it! Don't just stand there and listen to him gloat!"

"It's considered rude to interrupt a villain's monologues and or gloating, Nerissa." Charming leant on his sword nonchalantly, but his eyes remained on the vampire. "And I'm sure you could have hit him with a spell or two yourself by now."

"I'll give him gloating!" she yelled, then turned to the vampire. "This is entirely unacceptable conduct, you floating parasite!"

"You know, I don't think the townsfolk will think it's acceptable either," Charming carried on in the same easy-going manner. "You know what happens when the townsfolk don't approve of a vampire's behaviour. I don't think they use pitchforks much by the seaside, but I'm sure they can find some somewhere. They've certainly got a lot of material for flaming torches now, don't they?"

"I am not here as a vampire," Stollenheim replied stiffly.

"You think so?" Charming continued. "Flying, controlling animals, that outfit you're sporting . . . you look like a vampire to me. Tough to break out of these habits, isn't it?"

"Nonsense," the vampire replied. Perhaps she was still dizzy from the wave, but Lucinda thought he actually sounded worried. " . . . I shall concede that it would be foolish of me to try to win a fight against a Charming when I am indisputably here as an overlord," he tutted. "Even I can't fight that kind of narrative momentum."

"You aren't running away because the angry townspeople will see that their King isn't as benevolent as he has been painted, then?" Charming continued to watch the vampire.

"You win this round, Charming," he muttered, before turning to address the mermaids. "Mermaid Queen

Nerissa, my apologies for any damage to your Queendom," the vampire announced suddenly. "One day you will thank me for my actions." He exploded into a cloud of bats that shrieked and wheeled away into the sky in a great spiral.

"Coward!" Nerissa and Bubbles both screamed after him. Charming shook his head in disgust. Lucinda finally found her voice again.

"That-" she started, struggling to get the words out. She sank to her knees. Erlina gave up trying to support her and joined her on the floor. "That's the guy we're supposed to be taking down!" she blurted out. "I couldn't even move! He can destroy villages, and I couldn't even move!"

"Calm down, Miss Prince," Charming said kindly, patting her on the shoulder, "it's normally trained vampire hunters who deal with his sort, and correct me if I'm wrong, but *you* are a prince in training. You could hardly be expected to take him on." What had Sara been thinking when she hired her? What use was she? She could think of only one thing . . .

As the last of the men were being hauled ashore and counted up, the village women appeared. They had fled to higher ground when they saw the wave being built. The force of the incoming wave had been greatly lessened by the mermaids' efforts, but the first row of houses had been completely washed away, taking down the majority of the second and third rows with them. The boats that had been idling in the harbour with no men to pilot them, had been carried inland and smashed to bits on the rocks. There was one left intact; the one sitting in the debris of the town hall.

"You!" screamed the head woman from before. "You merwomen! And you, outsiders! This is all your fault! Are you happy now? Are you happy now we're starving *and* homeless?"

"Madam, please calm down," Charming implored her, "Nerissa and the others had nothing to do with this. It is your unworthy king you should be blaming. He engineered all of this. I doubt he expected the village to survive his assault, given your quarrel with the mermaids. Luckily they were most cooperative."

"Cooperative?!" the woman shouted. "They took our men!"

"Martha, we took their food," interjected a man from the crowd. He was one of the men Bubbles had dragged to shore. "We took their food, Martha," he repeated sadly. "They had no choice."

"What, the fish? But we had to-" the woman replied, taken aback. "Th-there are plenty of fish!"

"Not any more," he replied, his voice tinged with regret.

"But they took you away!" she protested, clinging to her argument. "They took you all away!"

"Martha, what do you do when foxes are taking all your chickens?" he asked her.

"You get your gun and-" she started. "Oh." There was silence. "We didn't have a choice, we had to keep to the one boat rule, it was made . . . " she protested feebly, " . . . it was made the law." She put a hand quickly to her mouth and understanding dawned on her face.

"Looks like you've only got the one boat now, at any rate," Charming observed, looking around at the devastation.

"What are we going to do now?" asked one of the

younger women. "We can rebuild our homes easily enough . . . what with all this . . . spare timber . . . " She prodded some boat wreckage with her foot. "But what will we do for food?" The mermaids looked around, and then looked at each other. Then as one mermaid, they looked to Nerissa.

"I think we have a solution," she volunteered. The women looked worried.

"Go on," Martha responded nervously.

"We'll fish for you," Nerissa announced. There were gasps from women and mermaids alike. "In return-" she continued in a slightly louder voice to discourage the mumblings that had begun, "-you will farm crops for us. That way, we can keep an eye on the fish stocks, you can manage with only one boat and it's a fair exchange for everybody. Law or no law." The villagers looked at one another.

"That does sound like a good idea," the older man who had confronted Martha agreed. "Don't you think so?" He nudged her.

"It does," Martha agreed, giving the mermaid a firm nod. "It would be very kind of you." The townspeople murmured agreement.

Lucinda went and sat on the beach, Erlina clinging to her arm, as the negotiations and congratulations went on. There were building schedules and re-planting plans to be drawn up, lots to draw, building materials to gather. Everyone was glad to be alive, and most were happy to cooperate. Lucinda looked from one end of the debris-strewn beach to the other. Just one vampire had done this. Just one. It had taken all these mermaids and Erlina to combat him. And what use had she been? She watched the mermaids relaying messages and throwing wreckage out of the sea, the villagers scurrying about collecting it into piles and picking through the rubble of the houses. She felt completely useless. She stood up, determined to be of some help, even if it was only cleaning up - she felt a tug on her shirt.

"My lord, I do not feel well," came a quiet voice. It was Erlina. Now that she came to think of it, Erlina had barely said a word since she'd woken Lucinda after the wave. That was rather unusual. If Lucinda had thought she was ill this morning, she was certain now. She was almost white.

"Let's get back to the office then," Lucinda said, standing up. Erlina stood up shakily with her. The two of them made their way over to the ocean's edge where Charming and Nerissa were deep in conversation.

"I need to get back to the office and report this to Sara immediately," he was saying. "And let her know I haven't run off and got married, of course."

"More's the pity," she responded, smiling. "We'll keep you posted. Where's the best place to contact you?"

"Probably here," he answered, "Stollenheim looked suitably rattled. Nothing like the threat of flaming torches and pitchforks to get a vampire nervous. I don't think he'll be back any time soon. And there's always the barrier on the island if we want some privacy."

"Indeed," she replied, smiling. "We'll check out the other towns that were affected and see if we can't work something out with the villagers there. Though I suspect the one boat law won't be a problem for much longer, will it?"

"Excuse me," Lucinda interrupted, "we're leaving. Erlina doesn't look so good." Charming and Nerissa looked at Erlina.

"My goodness, you're right. Come here," Nerissa beckoned to Erlina. Erlina obeyed, walking to the edge of the waves. Nerissa reached out and took her chin, turning her face this way and that. "Hmm. I think you should see a doctor, as soon as you can."

"A doctor?" Lucinda started. "Do you think it's something bad?" The mermaid felt at Erlina's forehead.

"I'm not sure . . . you do have a mild fever." She took her hand away. "Magical creatures don't get sick very often. It may be something serious. The sooner you see a doctor, the better." Lucinda felt her stomach knot. Something serious? What if they were too late . . ?

"That's our cue to leave then, I'd say," said Charming. "I'll be back, though. Thanks for all your hard work." He took Nerissa's hand and kissed it. Then he made an extravagant bow, waved, and turned, ushering the two girls up the beach.

IN SICKNESS AND HEALTH

They found the door back to the offices easily. It had been protected from the tidal wave by its magic, and was left standing by itself, only its frame intact. Just as they got to it, it opened. It was filled by Gerda, who gasped and dragged the two girls inside. Charming stepped inside after them and carefully closed the door.

"'Ere, you look dreadful!" she exclaimed, eyeing the three of them. Their clothes had dried off considerably in the hot sun, but they were still covered in sand, bits of seaweed and debris. Lucinda had a large bruise at the top of her left arm and on one side of her chin.

"Long time no see, Gerda," Charming greeted the valkyrie.

"Charming!" Gerda squealed, sweeping the prince up in a bone crushing hug. "We thought you were dead, you 'ave no idea how happy I am to see you!" Charming tried to laugh, but he was having all the air squeezed out of his lungs.

"It'll take more than Stollenheim and his tricks to get rid of me, Gerda you know that," he wheezed, "but I fear your hug might finish me off. Is Freya here? What about Sara?"

"We have to go," Lucinda cut in. "We need to find a doctor for Erlina. Now." It was too bad Sara wasn't back. She wanted to give the woman a piece of her mind. It would have to wait.

"Lina's got worse?" Gerda's face fell as she studied Lucinda's expression and then transferred her gaze to Erlina, who was clinging to her arm. "You all right, Cinders?

189

Did something 'appen?"

"Oh nothing major, we just nearly died is all," Lucinda replied impatiently. "I'm glad Charming is back and everything, so you can all catch up, we'll just leave. See you later." She led Erlina down the corridor to the door leading to Bad Schwartz. She opened it and darted through before Gerda could stop her. She didn't want to talk to anyone right now. It would only make things harder . . .

It was dark in Bad Schwartz. Erlina, with her pale blonde hair and white attire was easy to spot in the moonlight, but the rocks and steps on the way down the mountain path were not. She would have liked to wait until her eyes adjusted, but there was no time. She pulled the fairy after her down the slope. She didn't say anything. She was too worried. The last few hours had brought some things to light, and try as she might, she couldn't blot them out. Her pathetic performance in Polvan was preying on her mind, but not half as badly as what Nerissa had said about magical creatures getting sick. If it was something serious and something happened to Erlina, it would be her fault for not noticing it earlier.

"Are you all right, Lucinda?" Erlina asked. There was a tremble in her voice. She hadn't flinched when townspeople were threatening to throw her in the cellar, or mermaids mentioned kidnapping her or having nearly been drowned, but she was concerned about Lucinda now, whose fault it may well be that she was ill. It seemed strange, and somehow unfair.

"Are *you*?" Lucinda asked back, avoiding the question. "You looked really unwell back there."

"I feel a bit better now," Erlina replied. "Where is this place? May we stop for a minute? I'm very tired." Lucinda stopped. She was torn between letting Erlina rest, and carrying on. If she didn't rest she might get worse, but Nerissa had said to find a doctor as soon as possible. She took one look at Erlina's face and relented, sitting down grudgingly on a convenient boulder.

"We're near a place called Bad Schwartz," she explained, "we need to find you a doctor, and I only know one."

"I didn't know we knew any doctors," Erlina replied, sitting next to Lucinda and leaning on her, quite heavily. Lucinda looked sideways at her. Something was odd.

"I suppose she was never a qualified doctor, but she is a witch," Lucinda replied. She frowned at the top of Erlina's head, trying to work out what was out of place. "A normal doctor might not be able to help a fairy anyway. But Rosie should be able to." She wanted to let Erlina rest more, but they really needed to press on.

"If we're looking for Rosie, why are we not in the Blue Forest?" Erlina questioned her.

"Rosie still isn't home, she's staying with Johann remember? That's why I don't have potions lessons this month," Lucinda replied. They needed to move. She stood up. "Come on, we're nearly there. Rosie will know what to do." She said it as much to reassure herself as to reassure Erlina. If Rosie didn't have a solution, she'd be completely lost.

As they came to the edge of the village and the dim lamp light fell upon them, Lucinda finally realised what was bugging her. "Your hair looks weird," she blurted out, feeling awkward. It wasn't as if Erlina's hair was a priority right now.

"I am sure it does," Erlina replied, unconcerned. "It is dark. You also look different in the dark. You look rather grim, as a matter of fact."

"Oh, no I didn't mean - " Lucinda stalled. "It just looks like there's something different."

"It is surely a trick of the moonlight," Erlina replied. She took Lucinda's hand, slightly leaning on her as they walked. " . . . If we see a water fountain in town, I should like to get a drink," she added, as an afterthought. Lucinda kept glancing sideways at Erlina. The fairy's discomfort was becoming ever more apparent; she kept biting her lip and her steps were heavy and uneven. Perhaps it *was* just a trick of the light, but right across Erlina's brow, her hair appeared to be streaked with white.

The two of them stopped by the fountain as Erlina scooped up a few handfuls of water. Lucinda pulled her face at this, and said that Johann would have clean water at the castle, but Erlina complained that she was too thirsty to wait and that she wanted to sit down again. Unhappy as she was to lose more time, Lucinda agreed. She'd expected the town to be dead as it was after sunset, but there were windows and doors flung open everywhere. Light poured onto the street from the tavern, and a few sheepish villagers had the decency to shuffle into the shadows when she looked at them. The light streaming through the open door revealed that Erlina's fringe really did have a white streak through it. It looked as though it had been dipped in white dye. Perhaps it had happened at the beach? She remembered reading somewhere that they made purple dye from some kind of sea creature, so perhaps there was one that bleached hair and she'd landed on one . . . Lucinda was brought out of her thoughts by a not-so-whispered conversation at the tavern door, along the lines of "No, YOU tell 'im!" There was some murmuring and a man was shoved out into the street. He gave Lucinda a nervous grin. Three other men peered around the door.

"Go on then!" one of them hissed. The man made his way slightly hesitantly to Lucinda, where he took off his cap;

"Evenin' milord," he said, bobbing down in what was meant to be a bow but had turned into a curtsey.

"Good evening," Lucinda replied politely. Erlina was staring at the fountain with a puzzled look on her face.

"Er, you, er . . . " the man stuttered, scratching his head. "You er, you shouldn't be out after sundown milord. It's, I mean, 'tis a terrible time, when much evil is afoot." Lucinda looked askance at the open pub, which from the sound of it contained half the village.

"*You're* all out after sundown," she pointed out. She really wasn't in the mood for this.

"Ah well, we're sorta, um." He gave her another awkward grin. "We're sorta afooting our own evil. Yeah. Indoors, like." He coughed nervously. "But a young lord like yourself don't want to be out. You want to be goin' indoors."

"But not indoors like the castle, I suspect?" Lucinda sighed. Clearly this was not one of the villagers she'd seen last time.

"Oh, er. No," he said. Then he said, "I mean, yes. Er, I mean,"-he took a deep breath-"'tis a *terrible* place, where evil stalks the rooms, with hair of black and eyes of red, and-"

"He's got blue eyes and red hair actually," Lucinda replied levelly, "and I only stayed there one night, but he didn't stalk."

"Oh, well, *fine* then," the man said, folding his arms. "I don't know why we even bother. We've got all these lovely brand new pitchforks and things, and we never get to use 'em. He just skulks around up there with his wolves, lollygagging I've no doubt! We go to all this effort right, but can he be bothered to even afoot a *tiny* bit of evil? Can he 'eck!" the man tutted. "Well, you please yourself mister. He's got good wolves, but you go up there and not be in any peril whatsoever and you give him a good thump from me." The man walked back to the tavern, muttering under his breath. The other three men had mysteriously disappeared. Lucinda sighed and tapped Erlina on the shoulder. She was still staring forlornly at the fountain. The two of them made their way towards the forest, with Erlina throwing the fountain dirty looks as she went.

The two of them made their way up the steep mountain path. Lucinda just wanted to get Erlina to Rosie and go home. Yesterday she would have been excited to visit Johann, but not now. They walked in silence. They were roughly halfway up when Erlina stumbled over and grabbed Lucinda's arm. There was a rustling in the bushes.

"They're just guide wolves," muttered Lucinda, who hitherto had never thought she would ever utter such a sentence.

"It's not the wolves," Erlina replied, "I can't walk properly. I think there was something wrong with that water. I'm still thirsty."

"I told you not to drink it," Lucinda scolded her, feeling rather unsteady herself, "I just hope it didn't make you worse." A wolf emerged from the bushes. "We know the way," she told it. It promptly disappeared back into the undergrowth, wagging its tail.

It seemed to take forever to climb the mountain. The road got steeper and steeper, and Erlina's grip seemed to be getting tighter and tighter.

"Lucinda, I need a drink," Erlina piped up. She was breathing a little too deeply.

"I don't have anything on me," Lucinda replied, catching some of her anxiety. "We aren't too far from the castle now, don't worry." Lucinda wished they could walk faster, but it was impossible. A few minutes later, Erlina spoke again, and this time she sounded as if she was in tears;

"Lucinda, I'm very, *very* thirsty." Erlina's grip was weakening.

"Just hang on, we're nearly there-" Lucinda replied as calmly as she could manage.

"Lucinda-" the fairy began weakly. Lucinda fell forwards as Erlina collapsed, the pressure on her arm having been suddenly released.

"Erlina!" Lucinda shouted, scrambling back up and losing what little composure she'd had left. "Erlina, talk to me!" The fairy was out cold, but she was breathing heavily. Lucinda tried again, "Erlina, wake up! What do I do? *What do I do?!*" As she attempted to pick Erlina up with very little success, a wolf emerged from the bushes once more. Lucinda yelled at it, "Get Johann, *please* get Johann!" She was almost in tears and shaking all over. "My friend fainted and I don't know what to do! I can't move her and she won't wake up!" The wolf disappeared.

Every second seemed like an hour. Lucinda tried to calm herself down, as Johann had advised her what seemed like so very long ago. She wondered if he would laugh. She decided she'd punch him if he did. She tried to stand up. The hill was too steep and she was too tired, so she had to crouch instead to keep from losing her balance.

She heard a strange noise and looked up. A flock of bats was flying overhead. No, flying towards them. They formed the outline of a person . . . She flung herself over Erlina and screamed;

"Leave us alone! I'm going to quit anyway, just leave us alone! I've had enough!"

"I can't very well leave you alone, can I?" came a familiar, if slightly irritated voice. "Even if you *hadn't* sent for me." Lucinda looked up into the blue eyes of Johann. She burst into tears.

"Johann, Erlina fainted and I don't know what to do!" she sobbed. "She's really ill and-"

"Calm down," Johann commanded, gently pushing her to one side so he could inspect Erlina. "What did I tell you about panicking?" Lucinda took a deep breath and smacked him across the back of the head. "Okay," he said in an even tone, continuing to examine Erlina, "what was that for?"

"I swore to myself I'd punch you if you laughed at me!" Lucinda replied hotly. "Don't you dare laugh at me! I don't know how to handle this yet, you've no right!"

"I'm not laughing and that wasn't a punch," Johann replied. "She's a fairy, isn't she? Where did you find her? She's not been living here, has she?"

"No, she's been living with me," Lucinda replied.

"You live on Earth though!" Johann replied, sitting back up suddenly. "That's even worse. This could be bad. "

"Why, what's wrong with Earth?" Lucinda asked. "Erlina kept complaining about it, but I thought she just didn't like the weather and stuff."

"Earth has very little magic," Johann explained. "Where did you meet? How long have you known her?"

"A few months now," Lucinda answered, "I met her in

the Blue Forest. It was right after I met Rosie the first time." Johann started.

"Oh, I see. I see . . . " Johann reached into his waistcoat and pulled out a little red bundle tied with ribbon. He untied it and took out a few small, green pills. Lucinda thought she'd seen Rosie making them. He patted Erlina's face with his free hand. "Erlina, you need to wake up." Erlina groaned and moved a little. Johann tried again. "Erlina. Wake up, just for a moment. You need to eat this." When he got no reaction he cursed and put his fingers on her forehead. "Wake up," he commanded. Erlina eyes flickered open, but she wasn't conscious. He lifted her up with one arm and opened her mouth with his free hand, then popped in two of the pills. "Chew," he commanded, again. When Erlina had finished he said, "Sleep." He removed his fingers from her forehead. Her head dropped back. Her breathing was more normal now, but Johann still looked concerned.

"I-Is she going to be okay?" Lucinda asked.

"For now, but we have to get her to the Blue Forest as soon as possible," he replied. He popped a few of the strange, green pills into his mouth.

"What *are* those?" Lucinda asked tentatively. "I've seen Rosie making them a few times." She felt considerably calmer now that Johann was here, despite the unnerving magic she'd just seen.

"Medicine," he replied, crunching on them, "for mana deprivation."

"Is that what's wrong with her?" Lucinda replied, feeling worried again as she had no idea what that was. "Is it bad? What about Rosie?"

"Forest first, Rosie later," he replied, picking up the

197

unconscious Erlina and tilting his head to indicate that she should follow him.

They arrived at Rosie's house roughly half an hour later. They had taken another door a little way from the village. It was in a ruined, little hut, hidden away. The Rent-A-Legend door took them out quite far away from Rosie's cottage, but this door was mercifully close. Johann told her he'd ordered it made to make visiting her easier.

"You stay here, I'll go back and get Rosie," he explained, taking Erlina right through into Rosie's bedroom. He laid Erlina gently on the bed. Then he left without another word. Left alone, Lucinda started to fret again, worrying about Erlina's condition and going over what had happened at the seaside town again and again . . . What was taking them so long? She paced between the bedroom, kitchen and front room, unable to sit still.

After what seemed like an eternity, the pair of them burst through the door. Rosie gave Lucinda only a cursory nod, walking right past her and into the bedroom where Erlina lay. Lucinda followed her. Rosie felt at Erlina's forehead, took her pulse and stroked the white hair back from her face.

"She seems to be in a stable condition, at any rate," Rosie said, looking up. "I think we caught it just in time. It could have been nasty."

"What's wrong with her?" Lucinda asked.

"She's suffering from mana deprivation," Rosie explained. "It probably would have been worse if she were a human, but as she's a fairy she *should* recover if she gets plenty of rest. I can't say for certain. But it should never have got this far in the first place. How did this happen?"

"Lucinda told me she's been living with her," Johann explained, joining them. "The problem is pretty clear."

"Is it?" said Lucinda, to whom it was clear as mud.

"You took a fairy to live on Earth?" Rosie groaned. "It's one of the driest places there is. There's hardly any magic there at all, except for up mountains and in deep forests. Fairies can't live there for long, especially if they use up their magic . . . " She paused and gave Lucinda a sharp look. "You were learning magic, weren't you? After what I said?" Lucinda looked at her knees.

"We weren't doing anything dangerous!" she protested. "Just things like invisibility and little spells, but I wasn't any good at them anyway!"

"The spells you were using aren't the problem," Rosie replied. "It's the environment. If you use magic where there's a lot of it, like Fairyland or this forest, you're fine. Because there's plenty around to use. But if you use it somewhere barren of magic, or dry as we say, you use up your own magic quickly and then you're in trouble."

"Why don't you just stop being able to use it?" Lucinda asked. "How come I'm not sick?"

"You couldn't use magic because you weren't skilled enough to draw on your own in the first place," Rosie answered. Lucinda looked politely baffled. "How do I explain this . . . " Rosie paused, " . . . say someone hurts their back carrying a heavy box wrong. You can't hurt yourself carrying the box if you're not strong enough to pick it up in the first place." Johann joined in;

"Magic is sort of like oxygen," he explained, "Everything alive creates magic. It's all around the place. Using magic is like lighting a fire. If you can't create a spark, you can't light the fire."

"Yes, oxygen!" Rosie agreed, snapping her fingers. "Very apt. It's in the air and it's in your blood. You have your own magic, and the environment has its own. There are different levels of magic in different places, just like there are different levels of oxygen on different planets."

"Right," Lucinda nodded slowly.

"If there's a lot of magic about in the environment, the spell uses that. Normally a fire goes out when it burns up all the oxygen in the room, but imagine if it could pull the oxygen out of your body. If there isn't enough magic around you to complete the spell you cast, it pulls on your own supplies, and you get *burned*. You have to know your limits or . . . this happens." Rosie flicked out her white hair.

"Your hair turns white?" Lucinda asked.

"It's merely an outward symptom of the destruction of your body," Rosie explained. "Magic-overuse sucks the colour out of you, but it also sucks the life out of you too. It's almost like a form of evolution . . . in a bad way. The more you get used to magic the more you can tolerate, but if you use more magic than you can handle, you damage your body. Damage it too much and you die. That's what usually happens in such circumstances."

"Die?!" Lucinda sat bolt upright, "Erlina isn't going to die, is she?"

"No," Rosie reassured her, "she's just exhausted her magic. In the case of humans or elves, the more damaged you get, the more your body needs magic to compensate for the damage. But fairies, unicorns and other magical creatures adapted to magic use a long, long time ago. Using magic doesn't damage them. They're practically made of it. But it means they have to live in a high magic environment to survive," she continued. "It's like fish and water. We drown in it, but they need it to live. There's a reason you don't see fairies and unicorns on Earth any more. The mana level is just too low."

"So if white hair is sign of . . . of magical damage,

then that means . . . " Lucinda trailed off. "Is . . . is that why you won't use magic? Why you live in this forest?"

"Yes," Rosie replied, "I live here to keep away the final stages of mana deprivation. I don't use magic any more because I *daren't*. I'd die. At least technically. You see, the change in your hair and eyes isn't the only thing mana deprivation causes . . . it alters your body to let you survive . . . " Rosie took a shuddering breath, " . . . by taking magic from others."

"I don't get it," Lucinda frowned. "What are you saying?"

"You wanted to know about vampires," replied Rosie. "This is where they come from." Seeing Lucinda still wasn't quite clear, Johann added;

"Rosie is a few spells away from becoming a vampire."

Lucinda listened in shock as the two of them explained the symptoms of mana deprivation, the final stage of which was turning into a vampire. The unfortunate magical creature or damaged human, once they had exhausted their own magic completely, should die, and usually did. But as the dehydrated desire water, so too did the mana deprived desire magic. The quickest and easiest way to get it was to drain it from other living things - in the case of animals, via the blood.

Rosie was living in the Blue Forest because of the extremely high magical background, where she could use the mana-rich plants to make medicine to combat the condition. It was Rosie herself who had discovered most of these things through research, and why she had asked Johann to be her research subject when they met.

"We're trying to eradicate vampires, you see," Rosie explained. She was wandering between the rooms as she talked, gathering ingredients. Lucinda looked from Rosie to Johann in confusion. "Not by killing them, silly," Rosie continued, correctly interpreting Lucinda's expression. "We want to cure them. If we can find a way to reverse the effects of mana deprivation before it's too late and find a way to stabilise mana levels in vampires, we could wipe out the condition in a few generations."

"In a few generations . . ?" Lucinda asked.

"You might have noticed I'm not sporting white hair and red eyes," Johann said. "When vampires have children, they pass the mana damage onto them – thus the children are always vampires, and the condition spreads. Vampire children are hard to raise and parents can usually only manage one, but still . . . "

"There are people who end up alone with a vampire child they don't want, or that they do, but the townspeople don't," Rosie said.

"Vampires get their abilities from whatever magic they know, so without a parent who can teach them magic, they won't survive in a hostile environment," Johann added. "The villagers in Bad Schwartz might complain that I don't bother them, but in places where fear takes over, vampires are killed."

"There are people who go mad and people who get so disgusted with themselves that they just won't . . . eat . . . and starve themselves to death. Not to mention some of us just plain don't want to be vampires in the first place," Rosie finished.

"Can't you just drink animal blood or something?" Lucinda asked nervously. "You don't *have* to drink human blood, do you?"

"I'm afraid we do," Johann replied. "There's not a vampire that hasn't tried animal blood, but it doesn't have a high enough magic yield. Humanoid creatures have high magical potential, and thus a high magic content, but animals do not."

"With the exception of dragons and unicorns that is, but dragon blood is highly corrosive and a unicorn would kill you first," Rosie explained. "Animal blood is to a vampire like artificial sweetener is to a humming bird - they can drink it, and it satisfies them after a fashion, but it doesn't have what they need. Incidentally, *never* give artificial sweetener to a hummingbird."

While Rosie busied herself concocting a potion to revive Erlina, Johann and Lucinda were left to their own devices in the front room. Their own devices included tea. And a plate of cookies. They were special herbal cookies, made with the same herbs and spices Rosie used to make the mana medicine.

"So," Johann began, dipping a cookie in his tea. "Back in the forest, you thought I was my father. What was that you shouted about quitting?" There was an awkward silence before Lucinda replied;

"We were attacked by him today." She shuddered. "At a seaside town. The whole thing was a trap. He's trying to kill Sara. Because she's a threat to his throne and it's *traditional*." Lucinda *loathed* that word now. "I never thought I'd hate stories, but I think I might now."

"What's so traditional about trying to kill your boss? That is your boss you're talking about, isn't it?" Johann stared down his tea. "Father must be even worse than I thought if he's trying to kill random women."

"There's nothing random about it," Lucinda scowled into her own tea cup. "She's his step-daughter. She's been trying to raise a rebel army to take back the throne from him. And he's been spying on us somehow-" Johann looked sharply up at her, almost spilling his tea all over himself.

"He's got a *step-daughter?*" he asked, still staring. "Father? I've got a step-sister?"

"Yes," Lucinda replied, "her name's Princess Saharaleia Something Something Stollenheim."

"I'm sure it isn't, but that's great!" Johann leaned round to shout into the other room. "Hey Rosie! Did you hear that? I've got a sister!"

"Oh yes," Rosie said, appearing in the doorway, "I forgot about that." Johann looked offended;

"You knew and you didn't tell me?" he complained. "Well thanks a lot. I won't tell you if you've got any long-lost, royal relatives."

"I'd say 'ha!' and that it's not likely, but I just remembered where I live," Rosie replied, smirking. "I'm sure I would have told you if I'd thought about it more, but I was distracted at the time." She disappeared from view again.

"I'm sure you weren't that distracted," Johann grumbled, pouting.

"You didn't know about her?" Lucinda asked him.

"No. I was . . . how shall I put this," he hesitated, " . . . *aggressively* uninterested in Sheva and my step-mother. Step-mothers are bad news, particularly if they're queens, and in any case, I didn't want to know about this woman and this country my father had abandoned us for." He sighed. "It was petty and unfair of me, I suppose, but I was hurt and I still haven't forgiven him. I told him that as far as Sheva was concerned, I didn't exist. When I didn't go to the wedding, he didn't speak to me for years. I honestly thought he'd disowned me." He scratched at the surface of the wood with a fingernail. "Then he reappeared, trying to

204

get me to marry into royalty. He was a changed man, and desperate. We thought he was distraught over his wife and the pressure of ruling was getting to him . . . " Johann sighed. "Perhaps if I had not been so stubborn back then . . . if I had just met with my step-mother . . . " Johann fidgeted with his teacup, clearly struggling with some internal dilemma.

"It's not your fault Johann," Rosie said, standing in the doorway. "You couldn't have stopped what happened. He wouldn't have listened to you. He never listens to you."

"Still . . . " Johann took a sip of tea. He was mollified for a moment, but then he sat up straight, brow furrowed. "You're right. I can't change what happened. Maybe I wouldn't have made any difference. But I could make one now. I can't let him go around trying to kill my sister. That really is the last straw. Stories don't allow that sort of thing for long. But I can't . . . ugh." He tapped his fingers on the desk while he thought. Lucinda remembered the incident on the beach and shuddered. It looked like King Stollenheim could do whatever he wanted, story momentum or not. "You say she's raising a rebel army?" he asked her suddenly.

"Yeah," Lucinda explained, "he exiled her from her own country when her mother died and she wants the throne back."

"I see," he paused and added, "If he attacked you today, how are you still alive?" he asked. "No offence, but my father is not the sort of villain who leaves heroes hanging above a tank of sharks with just enough time to escape. He'd stand and watch. And not for long, because he'd cut the rope himself."

"Prince Charming stood up to him. Flaming pitchforks were mentioned," Lucinda explained. "He said he couldn't fight a story that strong, or something like that anyway, and he left."

"He couldn't fight the story . . ?" Johann drummed his fingers on the desk again. "He can't fight stories after all . . . I see. Now I understand. If only I could join your quest!"-he slammed his cup down on the table, making her jump-"Damn it! But I can't fight stories either. Wait a minute-!" He stared straight in front of him. He stared back down as his cup again, but now it was in the manner of someone who has just won the lottery and is making quite sure that the numbers all match up before they jump around screaming.

"Don't you go breaking my cups!" Rosie scolded, appearing in the doorway again as she mixed something furiously in a bowl without looking up. "I got those from my mother, and you know perfectly well that I can't replace them. What's so dramatic?"

"My father hasn't been fighting stories head on," Johann twisted around on his stool, almost falling off in his eagerness to explain, "he's just changed his *role*, that's all!"

"His . . . role?" Rosie asked temporarily slowing down.

"Don't you see? He's a vampire, and there's nothing he can do about it, because he won't relinquish power and fit in. He can't wield power as vampire because it ends in flaming torches if you do that. So instead, he got a different kind of power," he continued, as Rosie stopped beating altogether, "by marrying a *queen*. He's a *king* now, Rosie!" He beamed triumphantly. "My father is *King* Stollenheim, yes?"

"Yes, that *is* the problem," she replied, still not quite up to speed, "I don't quite- oh. *Oh*." Understanding dawned on her face. "I see. We thought we were dealing with a broken story, but it was just *twisted-*"

"We've been trying to deal with a *vampire*, and I've been trying to act like one . . . to a point," he carried on excitedly, "but that was all wrong!"

"He's not a vampire any more . . . not as far as the story is concerned . . . " Rosie put the bowl she was holding down so that she wouldn't spill it during this epiphany.

"He's a king!" Johann stood up stabbed his finger in the air. "An evil *king!*" Rosie clapped once and pointed at Johann;

"And that makes *you-*" she started.

"*A prince!* I can join the quest!" Johann finished. The two of them kissed in an inappropriate fashion for if there is someone else in the room.

"I'm still here," Lucinda pointed out. "I don't have a clue what you're going on about. Does it matter if Johann is a prince?" Rosie nodded and looked a little embarrassed, having shown a crack in her teacher-like façade. She was flushed, but she was wearing a huge and slightly creepy smile.

"Of course!" she answered. "A vampire taking on an overlord is a bit . . . odd. But a prince, taking on his father, intent on bringing his tyrannical rule to an end and saving the kingdom, well. Even he can't fight story momentum as old and established as that!" She turned to Johann looking like a tiger that had just seen its lunch. "Let's nail his hat on!"

"I'm going to *drag* him home and handcuff him to the couch!" Johann declared, looking almost as scary. Lucinda felt she'd missed something.

"*Excuse me?*" she asked incredulously. "You're going to what him to the what now?" Johann looked confused before it dawned on him what the problem was;

"Oh. I mean I want to take him home to my mother's place," he answered in a much more sober manner. "Someone has to take care of him when we sort him out. He . . . All this started when I was only a child. His cousin Heinrich was killed by a mob and he blamed it on 'humans and their stupid rules'," he explained. "He started to hate them and he started to hate mother. As if she had anything to do with it. He left her and married an elf queen, but when the queen died . . . I suppose he felt threatened and he started this ridiculous power struggle. He clings to power like a raft. But it's power that will drown him . . . "

"Johann . . . " Rosie put her hand on his shoulder. "It's going to be okay. We can make real plans now. You can stop all this worrying."

"Rosie, I know you don't like him. Part of me wants to just leave him to it to get what he deserves. But he's my father. Maybe if I'd just stuck by him . . . I can't help but think it's partly my fault . . . " Johann put his hand on hers. "I think all he wanted was to escape the rules, just like I do. He's doing it all wrong. I just want him to understand that."

"I know . . . "

"I'm just going to check on Erlina," Lucinda excused herself. She felt uncomfortable, like this was a moment she shouldn't be intruding on.

Once alone with Erlina though, she regretted her decision as the dark thoughts came flooding back. They were mixed with ever more conflicting emotions. She wished she hadn't heard that. It didn't make her hate King Stollenheim any less, but it did make her feel sorry for Johann and moved that he should try and help someone even though all they caused him was grief. At least she wouldn't have to worry about these feelings much longer . . .

Rosie finally finished preparing Erlina's medicine. Johann seemed to be off in his own world, undoubtedly thinking about striding into the castle and challenging his father for the throne and other tactically unsound things that princes did when confronting their despot parents. Erlina woke up just as the medicine was ready, and Johann left the three girls alone.

"Erlina, are you all right?" Lucinda asked, tearing up in relief. She blinked them back. "I'm so sorry, this is all my fault . . . you shouldn't have been using magic and you shouldn't have been living with me. I should have found you somewhere to stay sooner, but-"

"I would have refrained from using magic if you'd asked Lucinda, but I wouldn't have left," Erlina argued. She didn't appear inclined to sit up. " . . . Why should I not, again? Where exactly are we, anyway?"

"You're in my house," Rosie explained, reappearing with a cup of steaming, blue liquid. "Drink this." She handed Erlina the medicine. "You fainted due to 'mana deprivation'. I don't suppose fairies know anything about it?" Rosie asked hopefully. Erlina's face was blank. "It's caused by serious lack of mana, as the name suggests. That's magic, to you."

"I don't understand," Erlina replied.

"You've been living on Earth, an environment devoid of magic. Fairies' bodies are adapted to areas with a high magic content. Your body couldn't take it. It's like how salt water fish can't live in fresh water," she continued. "You made it worse by using large amounts of magic, draining your body's remaining supply." Erlina looked to Lucinda for a translation.

"You're not going to be able to stay at my house any

more," Lucinda explained, feeling wretched. Erlina didn't really have anywhere else to go, and she knew she'd be lonely. Lonely and ill. And she didn't want Erlina to feel like that, but it was for her own good . . . and every minute it was getting harder and harder to say what she needed to say.

"I suppose not," Erlina replied turning her head away. "I do not know where to go. If I understand you correctly, this means I have to return to Fairyland. I do not want to. I suppose somewhere equally magical would do, but the only other place is here in this forest and I won't survive on my own in this condition." She sighed in a resigned manner. "I suppose I have no choice . . . "

"You can stay here," Rosie announced, startling them both. She put her hands on her hips. "What? You think I'm doing all this research and potion-making to get rich? I'm trying to help people in your situation. Not to mention mine," she added. "I've got a spare room here for patients anyway. You can help me with my experiments and my other work. You'd be a valuable research subject and a big help."

"I'm sorry Erlina," Lucinda apologised.

"That's all right," Erlina reached out and squeezed Lucinda's hand. "I suppose this is why people don't leave Fairyland for long. At least I can stay here. So I can still see you, Lucinda." She gave her a warm smile. Lucinda felt like a spike had been driven through her heart. She had to try and explain what she'd decided-

"Sorry, but I'm going to have to shoo you out," Rosie said, laying her hand on Lucinda's shoulder. "Erlina needs to rest. You can come and visit any time. You'll be round for your potions lessons anyway."

"I don't think I'll be needing them," Lucinda said

quietly. Rosie's brow creased a little. She hesitated and then patted Lucinda on the shoulder.

"We can talk about it later I'm sure." Lucinda stood up, bid the two of them farewell and went to find Johann.

A DIFFICULT DECISION

Johann went with Lucinda back to the Rent-A-Legend office.

"I'm not so sure this a good idea," Lucinda warned him before they stepped through the door. "Sara hates vampires. She's not going to trust you."

"I don't particularly blame her, I must admit," Johann said. "I don't like vampires either, and there's no reason for her to trust me. I'm hoping she trusts *you*." Lucinda didn't reply. Sara's trust of her was unsure, but she did seem to trust Gerda and Freya. Perhaps if they could just talk to them first . . .

There was no such luck.

Sara was back, and she sounded decidedly unhappy. Lucinda wanted to turn right back around and disappear through another door, but she made herself walk towards the main room. After all, Sara could shout all she wanted, it wasn't going to matter any more.

"This is all my fault," Sara was pacing up and down the office, clearly distraught. "Again. *Again*. My people's lives destroyed . . . I thought I was doing the right thing-"

"It's not your fault, Sara, don't be ridiculous-" Charming tried to console her.

"How many casualties were there?" Sara demanded, still pacing.

"Sara-" Gerda tried.

"*How many?*" Sara repeated.

"We don't know, but listen-" Charming started.

212

"Father should have thrown me to a dragon," Sara almost collapsed onto the desk, her back to the corridors. "And mother,"-she slammed her fist down-"I should have stopped him from marrying her in the first place!" Sara was digging her fingers hard into the side of her head, and she sounded as if she was on the verge of tears. "But that damn Grand Vizier was eyeing *both* of us up, and he saw him off. At first I was *grateful*, can you imagine? Mother liked him, maybe if I had bit my tongue instead of telling her he was just using her, she'd still be alive, now he's using my people like bait, and *nothing* I do will ever-"

"Sara, I was there, it was *not* your fault, casualties were minimal, now please, there's something I-" Charming tried again. Lucinda would have liked to wait until this was over, but it looked like the longer she left it the harder it would be.

"I'm back," she announced as loudly as she dared. Sara and the others snapped their heads round to look at her.

"Did you find a doctor for Erlina?" Gerda asked. "She all right?"

"A doctor?" Sara asked, "Please don't tell me Lina - "

"Erlina is staying with my girlfriend, the Silver Witch," Johann explained. "Her condition is stable, don't worry." Sara took in Johann's attire and narrowed her eyes;

"And just who are you?" she demanded, giving him an icy glare.

"My apologies," he said, bowing to them all, "I am Count Johann Von Stollenheim the Third." Sara's reaction was explosive; she lunged at him, removed a dagger from under her dress and slammed Johann into the wall in one fluid movement;

"You!" she hissed, holding the knife to his throat. "It

must have been you! How *dare* you show your face in *my* office! Your abomination of a father just destroyed a village and *you-*"

"Sara-" Lucinda began.

"And you!" Sara tried, unsuccessfully, to glower at Lucinda whilst still looking Johann in the eyes "Why would you bring this cretin back with you?" she asked, highly frustrated. "You are *so* fired."

"Johann and his girlfriend have been helping me out with potions lessons and things, and he just helped save Erlina's life too!" Lucinda explained desperately. "He's the vampire I told you about a few months ago. The one you told me to 'fix'." Sara lowered the dagger a fraction as she turned to glare at Lucinda properly.

"You *knew* he was Stollenheim's son and you carried on associating with him? And you didn't even have the decency to tell me? My step-father, *his father*, attacked Polvan today! Flattened the place! Because he thought I was going to be there! What I want to know is, *how* did he find out? *You-*"

"That's what I'd like to know!" Lucinda replied hotly, cutting Sara off. All the fear and anger of the day finally boiled up inside her and she practically screamed, "You never tell me what's going on, and then we get a threatening phone call and you aren't even here, then next thing I know your family members are trying to kill us with serpents and tidal waves! Why did you employ me, anyway? I'm clearly useless! I'm just *bait*, aren't I? *Aren't I?*" There was an uncomfortable silence as the two of them faced each other, both taking steadying breaths. Johann opened his mouth to say something, but he shut it again when Sara pressed the knife to his throat without even looking back at him. He was trying not to breathe.

"You're saying I knew an innocent village was going to be wiped out and I did nothing to prevent it?" Sara almost whispered. "That I'd leave my own people to *die*? That I care so little about my company and its employees that I just send them to slaughter?" She was now trembling with barely suppressed rage. "I sent you to rescue the villagers from the mermaids! They were running out of food, and any men I sent were just getting captured! You were my best and *only* option!" Lucinda faltered.

"Then why did the King think you were there?" she asked, "Why did you send *me* out to look for Charming instead of someone more capable?"

"I told you, there was *no-one* else! As for how that bloodsucker knew you were there-" Sara turned to snarl at Johann again. He tried very hard to become one with the wall. "-that's what I want to know!"

"He *knew* about me! He said on the phone, he said 'Is that the prince girl?' He *knew!*" Lucinda yelled.

"Of course he knew, you little fool!" Sara hissed. "You were passing on information to *this* son of a-"

"I wish it were that simple, Sara, but it isn't," Charming interjected, laying a hand on Sara's arm, "Stollenheim knew of our movements before Miss Prince here started working for us. If his son really was passing him information, it would have been old by the time he got it. He's been listening in on us, and I finally figured out how. It just clicked when she mentioned the phone-"

"*How?*" Sara demanded. Charming indicated the assortment of receivers hanging above the desk.

"The shells," he said, "I learned about it from the mermaids. You can add extra shells to a shell line and keep it open. 'Tapping' it's called. The mermaid clans were using this method to hold conferences and things during the fish crisis," he explained. "I'm sure it could easily be used to listen in on people. Anything you say in this room, he can hear. He must have been listening in on us for months now." All six of them looked up at the assortment of horns and giant conchs that made up the Rent-A-Legend phone system. Sara finally dropped her arm.

"Let's have this conversation somewhere else." She nodded towards the armoury. Johann was understandably hesitant to step into a room that contained so many pointy things as well as Sara, but he didn't have much choice. He situated himself at the far end of the room, putting plenty space between them.

"I know you've no reason to trust me," he said once the door was closed and everyone assembled, "I assure you I haven't been passing information to my father-"

"Just because it seems unlikely under the circumstances, doesn't mean it didn't happen," Sara snapped. "I've no doubt you have a good explanation."

"I've been trying to get my father to step down as ruler of Sheva for some time," Johann tried to reassure her. "Look, you know how you hate my father for what he did to your mother and your home?" Johann asked.

"And how did you know about that?" Sara asked suspiciously.

"Lucinda might have mentioned something about it," Johann said sheepishly, aware that this was just the sort of information sharing Sara was accusing them of. "It's just that *I* hate him for what he did to *my* mother and *my* home, and when I heard we wanted the same thing, albeit in different ways, I thought we might be able to cooperate." Sara subjected him to a critical look. "He's just using me as a pawn to keep his old territory under his thumb," Johann insisted. "I couldn't care less about power and keeping the peasantry in thrall. I just want to live a quiet life. I'm aware that it's not done for vampires to live with their girlfriends in cottages covered in flowers but frankly, I'm sick of everyone else trying to dictate how I live my life, my father included." Sara stared at him for a long moment. That wasn't the reason he'd given at Rosie's, but Lucinda supposed that he didn't want to bring up compassion at this point. Though it was a far less noble reason than the other one, it was probably just as true.

"I still don't trust you," Sara said quietly, looking away from him. The venom was gone from her tone. "Go home, Count Stollenheim. Blood is thicker than water."

"I'll leave," Johann conceded, "but if you need our help, we're here . . . " he trailed off. Sara made no reply. "Well, bye Lucinda," he said, patting her on the shoulder. "Come by and see Erlina in a day or two." The silent party watched him walk past and exit the armoury. Charming had the presence of mind to watch him through the door and along the corridor. There was a quiet clunk as the Blue Forest door shut behind him.

No-one wanted to be the first to speak. Sara still had a dagger in her hand. She half-sat, half-leaned on an empty spear rack and nearly sat on the dagger in the process. She looked at it like she'd never seen it before, then blinked and put it away.

"Fool," Sara muttered to herself. "Idiot," she carried on. "He's got no idea. No idea at all. He comes waltzing in here, ruining my plans . . . and he says he wants to *help*. Moron. Why don't people think?" There was a polite cough as Freya cleared her throat;

"I know you don't want to hear it, Sara-" she started.

"I don't," Sara sighed. "But *someone* is going to say it, so you may as well get on with it." Determined, Freya plunged on;

"I think you should let that boy join us," she urged. "He could be very useful. He's a dissatisfied prince and, of course, he is a vampire. He can do all kinds of magic we've no hope of doing, and think of the story momentum! A good prince versus an evil king!"

"He could march in there with nothin' but a rusty poker and win!" Gerda agreed. "But I dunno . . . "

"I believe that's the nature of the problem, isn't it, Sara?" Charming suggested.

"He'd win all right," Sara said, "I'd have defeated that old tyrant, but I still wouldn't have my kingdom back."

"Why n- oh," Gerda stopped.

"You think that boy would argue over who gets the throne?" Freya asked, "I don't think so. He would get more power cooperating with his father than with us."

"He doesn't *need* to argue over it," Sara's tone could have curdled milk, "he's the heir. I'm not sure if he's older than me, but in any case he's *male*. The throne will pass to him when the king is deposed. Unless I defeat my step-father without him, that is. Then I've got right of conquest."

"What they don't know won't hurt them, Sara." Freya shrugged, "Sheva doesn't know it has a prince. Just don't tell them."

"You can't do that, it's terribly dishonest," Charming objected. "What sort of ruler will you be if you begin your reign on a *lie?*"

"Sara has been workin' hard for years to get her country back, and this new prince comes waltzing in, just as we're ready to move?" Gerda scoffed. "How can you say-"

"Enough!" Sara slammed her hands on the rack and regretted it. She rubbed her sore palms. "Enough. We should be fighting Stollenheim, not each other. One thing is clear. I need to *think* about this. Now all of you get out of my sight, I'm tired and angry. Lucinda!" she called out as Lucinda made to head towards the door.

"*What*?" Lucinda replied, louder and sulkier than she had intended. Sara gave her the invisible glasses look, which was, in a way, reassuring. At least she was back to acting like normal. Sara *looking* daggers at people was an everyday occurrence; seeing her actually pull one on someone had been quite shocking.

"I've got something for you," she said. "Wait here a moment." Lucinda waited. A few minutes seemed to stretch into forever. She either wanted to get this off her chest or just go home and sulk, preferably both . . . Sara returned carrying a small, silver sceptre and a few coins.

"Your wages," she explained, handing them over to Lucinda. "I thought it was about time you got some. I don't have any currency that's usable in your world, so this will have to do. It took me forever to dig through that blasted hoard, looking for something of the right value," she complained. "Right. Be here tomorrow, same time. All of you." Sara went to the door and put her hand on the door knob . . . Lucinda bit her lip. It was now or never. Or be a coward. And she was determined not to be a coward, at least in some small way;

"I quit," she announced. The others, who had also started towards the door, froze. Sara appeared not to hear her. She left the room and headed over to the desk. Lucinda followed her, feeling like she was going to explode. Sara dragged a fresh piece of parchment towards her on the desk and wrote furiously. She seemed to be mumbling something. "I quit, Sara. I'm sorry," Lucinda repeated. She fancied she could *hear* the others peering around the door frame behind her.

"I heard you the first time," Sara replied, matter-of-factly. She wrote something else on the paper with a final flourish, then folded it up. "Here." She handed it to Lucinda. "Open it when you feel like it. Now go home." Lucinda waited, but Sara ignored her, grabbing whatever paper it was demanded her attention next and pulling out some quills and ink supplies from behind the desk, as she daren't work at it any more. Lucinda turned around, heading for the door. She hesitated as she put her hand on the door handle, just in case. No-one called out to stop her. She opened the door, slipped outside and down the alley.

Lucinda was determined to avoid her mother when she got home. She was bedraggled, bruised and she was on the verge of tears, not to mention the odd things she was carrying. For once, she shunned the strange looks people gave her, crossing the street if she saw anyone who was paying her close attention or hiding her face as people came close, pretending to tie her shoelace or look around to see where she was.

She opened and closed the door as quietly as possible and sneaked into the kitchen. Anxious as she was to avoid explaining her appearance to her mother, she was desperate to get something to eat. It was now evening, and she hadn't had anything since breakfast. She was also hoping she'd feel better after food and a cup of tea. She had no job, had lost all her friends after finally making some in this boring town, had almost been killed and was probably in trouble with her mother, but somehow it would all look better after a cup of tea. She wondered if Rosie could make some kind of magic tea. She blocked the thought out. She didn't want to think about anyone connected with Rent-A-Legend right now. She quietly opened the fridge, slowly opened the cupboard and slid out a plate, making sure not to knock it against anything else, and silently made herself a few jam sandwiches. Then she ruined all her good work by thoughtlessly switching on the kettle. It immediately began to hiss, and she heard footsteps cross the hallway.

"I *thought* I heard someone come in," It was her mother's voice. "Lulu, is that you? Where have you *been* all day? You should have called!" Lucinda groaned inwardly. She didn't like to worry her mother in any case, but now that she should genuinely be concerned it was even worse.

"I've been at work," she answered, trying not to let her voice tremble, "I'm really tired, I just want to get something to eat and go up to my room." She kept her back turned in the hope that her mother would leave before she had to turn around.

"I'll say!" her mother exclaimed. "You look like you were dragged through a, a *reef* backwards!"

"You don't know how right you are," Lucinda mumbled into her tea.

"Whatever were you doing?" her mother asked in the same high-pitched, disbelieving tone. "Let's have a look at you." Lucinda's mother spun her around. There was no avoiding it, she would just have to talk her way out;

"There were mermaids and a tidal wave," Lucinda explained hastily.

"That's why you look like you live in a sand-pit, is it? And is that-" Her mother's eyes widened and she touched the bruise on Lucinda's chin. Lucinda winced a little. "It's

221

not make-up, is it? And your legs! There's scrapes and bruises all over them!"

"During the tidal wave I got knocked about a bit-" Lucinda protested.

"'A bit'?" her mother repeated. "You look like you've fallen off a cliff! I'm going to go down to this workplace of yours and have a word with your boss, this is ridiculous!"

"No!" Lucinda protested. "You can't do that, it was part of the job and anyway-"

"*Part of the job?*" her mother scoffed. "I'll give you part of the job, what if you'd broken a leg-"

"Well, it doesn't matter, because I quit, all right!" Lucinda shouted, seizing her plate and mug. "I quit, so I'm going to be staying home and not going to see my other friends either, so you're probably pretty happy about that-" She stormed off upstairs, spilling some of her tea and cursing.

"Lucinda!" her mother shouted after her. Lucinda ignored her. She threw herself onto her bed, buried her face in her pillow, and sobbed. After about five minutes, she sat up, got herself some tissues and drank her tea. She left her plate on the dresser; she just wasn't hungry any more. She'd gone out through the other side of hunger, where she couldn't stand to eat anything. She stared at the ceiling, the events of the day running through her head. A few more minutes passed, and there was a knock at the door.

"Lucinda?" her mother said softly, opening the door a crack. "Do you want to talk about it?"

"You'll be mad at me," Lucinda replied, wiping her eyes a final time in the vain hope that she wouldn't look like she'd been crying.

"I might not," her mother hazarded.

"That's not a very helpful answer," Lucinda sniffed. Her mother opened the door and walked in to sit on the bed.

"I promise not to get mad," her mother tried, her tone gentle, "not even at your boss."

"I just feel so . . . so useless!" Lucinda bit her lip. "I can't do anything right. Erlina got sick and it's my fault. She's the one real friend I've made here, and now she's ill because of me." She tried to fight back a second wave of tears. "I couldn't help anyone at all today, I never can, all I do is panic! I didn't deserve the job, I can't do it, so I quit!"

"And did you *think* about quitting?" her mother asked. "You've come home with cuts and scrapes and bandages before – don't think I didn't notice - but you never seemed like you were hating it. You'd have said."

"No . . . " Lucinda sat up and hugged her knees, "I didn't hate it at all. My boss is kind of annoying . . . she doesn't tell me anything and she just seems to expect me to know when I do something stupid. It's so frustrating!"

"And is everyone like that?" her mother questioned.

"No!" Lucinda replied. "Everyone else is really nice! Freya and Gerda tell me stuff all the time, and Johann and Rosie have been teaching me all sorts of things, and they really helped me out today . . . and Erlina . . . Erlina is my best friend . . . "

"You didn't want to quit really, did you?" her mother said kindly, laying a hand on her shoulder. Lucinda couldn't answer. *Had* she wanted to quit . . ? Her mother gave her a hug. "If you want to quit, you quit," she said. "If you don't, you march back to that boss of yours and tell her you changed your mind. If she won't listen, you tell me." Lucinda nodded automatically. She had no idea what would happen if her mother and Sara faced off, but apocalyptic visions filled her head. "By the way. What's all that stuff on the kitchen table?" her mother asked. "They look like props."

"Oh!" Lucinda sat bolt upright. "Those are, um. My wages. It's sort of a voluntary thing, so we don't get paid in actual money." That about summed up being a prince, although what they normally got paid in was princess.

"I see." Her mother folded her arms. She pressed her lips together for a moment. "I promised not to get mad." She sighed. "I should check that stuff out if I were you, see if it's worth anything. If your boss is ripping you off, tell me," She took hold of her daughter's chin. "You know, I thought that going to the other side of the world would be too much for you, but then you went and got a job where you're out at all hours and you come home covered in cuts and bruises and you don't bat an eye. Except for today . . . Your sister was never like this." She looked off into the distance for a moment, before continuing, "So there you have it. I don't like it, but if that stuff really will buy you a plane ticket, you buy it. At least you won't have to come home looking like this any more." Her mother hugged her again and then stood up. "I'll take your cup. Just take your time to think about it."

When her mother left, Lucinda lay back down and stared at the ceiling, feeling almost completely different. She was still upset about Erlina being sick, and letting everyone down and not being able to do anything in the face of King Stollenheim . . . but cutting through all that, slowly burning it away was the realisation that she might have enough money for a ticket. She struggled with the conflicting emotions for a while, but eventually she could stand it no longer and she hauled herself off the bed and ran downstairs to grab her loot. She gathered it up, and headed back upstairs. She laid the stuff out on her bed. The coins looked like genuine gold but she didn't how to tell. What if it was fairy gold? Fairies were perhaps not as dishonest as they were made out to be. If fairy gold was magical, it was no wonder it disappeared overnight if taken into a low-magic atmosphere. She prodded one. It remained distinctly unmagical, and most importantly, did *not* turn into a blood-thirsty monster. If humans and fairies could become vampires, maybe magical objects got turned too. Vampiric currency sounded *terribly* magical, quite literally, and was possibly one of the worst things she could imagine.

She booted up her laptop, grabbed one of the coins and put it on the counter. Enthusiastic as she was, working at Rent-A-Legend had taught her some caution. Before she made her decision, she was going to check whether or not she really had enough money for a ticket. All she could do was estimate, but an estimate would be good enough.

"Okay," she said to herself, "If I have enough money for the tickets, I quit. If not, I don't. Maybe." She looked around on the internet and found similar items to the coins. She counted them. She did the maths in her head. She double checked using a calculator. She scribbled down the sums, walked as calmly as she could downstairs and looked around for her parents. Her father was watching TV in the living room.

"Dad?" she asked. "Can you check these for me?"

"Check what?" her father said, staring at the TV for a moment, before turning to take the paper she was offering him. "What's this? Bit simple for maths homework, isn't it?"

"It's not," Lucinda replied, "I think-" she stopped, barely able to contain her excitement, "I *think* I might have enough to buy my plane tickets. But I wanted to check first before I tell everyone."

"*You* want to check something?" he replied, his eyes widening, a disbelieving look on his face. "You never check anything, you just run off and start yelling, like when you thought we'd won the lottery and I'd only matched three numbers. Our neighbours were very disappointed." Lucinda rolled her eyes. Parents brought up the most awkward things, sometimes.

"I don't want to upset my friends by telling them I can get a ticket if I can't," she said. Her father took the paper and checked it.

"Your maths seems fine," he said. "This is what your tickets are going to cost, is it?"

"Yeah. I looked them up ages ago," Lucinda replied. "I can afford a ticket. *I can afford a ticket!*" she shouted, hugging her dad and then jumping up and down on the spot. "I'm gonna go tell Pens and the others!"

"Before you run off," her father stopped her, "I found this on the kitchen table. Is it yours? It's just a blank piece of paper, but it looks like a prop so I didn't want to throw it away in case it was from your work." He reached over to the coffee table and picked up a yellowish piece of paper, which he handed to Lucinda. It was a letter. Privately thinking that her father's eyesight must be going, she took the paper and raced off upstairs again, far too excited to bother with stray letters right now.

She jumped straight back onto her laptop, opened her messenger and was dismayed to see that all but one of her friends was offline. Pens was online though, and she was looking forward to telling him the most.

'Hey! Guess what?' she typed.

'No. :P' came the sarcastic reply.

'Come on, guess,' she typed, not willing to give up so quickly.

'Why? You're obviously dying to tell me, you'll crack sooner or later! XD' he responded. Pens was right of course, but she couldn't let him spoil her fun as easily as that.

'Fine, you big meanie. Maybe I'll just leave and not tell you. Then you'll be dying to know what it was, and I'll tell everyone else and demand that you're left out of the loop. That'll show you.'

'Ha ha! That would be annoying. Okay I'll guess,' he replied. Lucinda waited. 'Did something good happen?' he asked.

'Yes. Something really good,' she typed back.

'REALLY good?' he typed. 'Did you get a raise at work? Ha ha, did they pay you yet?'

'Yes they did!' Lucinda typed back. 'AND I have enough for a TICKET! How awesome is that?'

'No way! That is TOTALLY awesome!' he replied. 'So how is it going at work, anyway?'

'Actually I quit today,' she typed, after a pause. There was another pause before Pens typed back;

'That's a shame. Why?'

'Because I'm no good at it. I couldn't do anything today, and it was a really bad situation,' she typed. 'Why is it a shame?'

'That's dumb. You quit because you suck? That's the point of getting experience, silly. Besides, they would have fired you ages ago if they thought you were that bad,' he chided. 'It's a shame because it made you happy.' Lucinda stared at the last sentence.

'Happy?' she typed back.

'Yeah,' he replied, 'you've been much happier the

227

past few months. You used to just talk about how school sucked or how your mum was getting on your case, but lately you've been talking about Erlina and your boss and stuff.' There was a pause and then, 'And I can tell you're happy anyway, because when you aren't, you're never offline! You've been online less and less lately.' Another pause. 'I'm starting to get a bit lonely!'

'You think so?' she asked after staring at the screen for a full minute.

'Oh come on. How long have I known you? Since forever, was it?' he typed. 'I think you should go back and say you changed your mind. Besides, then you can have money to come visit us another time! And build up your costume collection! XD'

Pens had to log off, so Lucinda lay on her bed again. There were all kinds of thoughts swirling around in her head. Maybe Pens was right. Before she'd started working at Rent-A-Legend, her life had seemed to be about how much she disliked her new town, how she didn't fit in and a constant longing to see her old friends again. But lately it had been fun; Erlina was always there to keep her company, and she'd met some new and interesting people who actually *encouraged* her to dress up and act like a moron.

Would Sara let her come back? Sara wasn't the forgiving type. But she hadn't seemed angry. Not angrier than usual, anyway. Lucinda had wanted to keep the job, even back when she thought she wasn't going to get paid. Now she had been paid. This whole thing had started because she needed money, but it had ended up somewhere else entirely. She could walk away and go to America and see her friends and go to that convention . . . but then what? Then she would go back to her old life, only having decent conversations online and lonely for her old friends.

'But they don't need me there,' she thought to herself, turning onto her side, 'they have a real prince again. Prince Charming is worth a hundred, no a *thousand* of me. I can't even handle a sword properly yet, and I always, panic.' She glanced up at her loot. The piece of paper she had brought upstairs with it caught her eye. Her dad had given it to her, but she'd seen it before. She stared at it for a moment, before it clicked. It was the piece of paper Sara had handed to her before she left. She'd left it on the table when she'd taken the sceptre and the coins upstairs. She leapt up, seized it and read;

'Dear Cinders,

I think you'll find that there's such a thing as 'giving notice'. You can't quit for a certain period of time after you announce your resignation, but I don't intend to accept it anyway. If you want to be a fool and sulk just because you almost died, then fine. You understood the job when you signed up, and almost dying is in the job description. For a hero, it IS the job description. Never forget that it's the 'almost' bit that's important. If you can't be the hero, I'm sure I can at least use you as the idiot who inadvertently saves the day or comes up with a brilliant idea.

If you can read this, I expect to see you at work on Monday. If not, I never should have hired you in the first place. It also makes you a filthy liar. You told me that you believe in stories. If you don't, you can't read this and I never liked you.

If you can read this and you don't turn up, remember I know where you live.

  Sara.'

  Lucinda stared at the parchment. She turned it over to see a map to the office. The same one that had been on the advert for the job in the first place. She finally understood something.

  "I guess I still believe in stories," she said to herself, " . . . I guess Dad doesn't."

TO ARMS!

Despite having a late night due to excitement and anxiety, Lucinda woke up early and paced around the kitchen after breakfast until about eight-thirty. She didn't know what hours the office actually operated, but nine am seemed like a reasonable hour. Her father wasn't awake and her mother had gone out. When she couldn't stand to wait any more, she grabbed her things and headed to the office.

"You want me to go back home?!" Lucinda gawped at Sara, who merely gave her the invisible glasses look. Sara had set up a makeshift desk in the armoury.

"I believe the letter said Monday," Sara explained. "I'm not ready for you today. Unless you can get yourself ready?"

"Sure!" Lucinda replied unthinkingly, eager to prove herself. " . . . What do I need to get ready for?" she asked, sounding a lot less confident.

"I need you to go home, dye your hair or wear a wig. *Don't* wear your prince uniform," Sara commanded, "but you do have to look like someone from around here. A commoner. I need you to look as *not* like you and as *not* like a prince as possible." Lucinda couldn't believe her luck.

"Blue face paint isn't a good idea though, I suppose?" she asked. Sara put her head to one side.

"No," she replied, making an effort to keep a straight face. "No, it isn't."

Lucinda ran home, running into her father in the kitchen.

"Getting ready for this convention thing, are you?"

he asked, turning the page of his newspaper. Her father always seemed to be reading the newspaper. She suspected it was a dad thing. She'd never got the attraction of newspapers. It seemed like all they did was blow everything out of proportion. The way they talked, all celebrities were either angels or the worst scum you could scrape from the barrel of mankind, all animals were smarter than us and the world was going to end next Tuesday. Games and books might give the impression that every orphan in the world is a mysterious heir with magical powers and that it's perfectly okay to take other people's stuff, but at least they didn't expect you to take them *seriously*.

"It's a bit early yet," Lucinda replied. "It's for my boss, I'm in a hurry, sorry!"

"Well done, by the way," he said, "I didn't think you would do it, you know." Momentarily stunned by such double-edged praise, Lucinda froze. That was a dad thing, too. Praise wrapped in an insult.

"Well *thanks*," she said sarcastically, forgetting she was in a hurry. "It's no wonder you couldn't see that letter." Her father's brow furrowed. She continued, "Don't you know that whenever a child is determined to do something difficult that their parents don't approve of, they're guaranteed to succeed?" Lucinda gave him an invisible glasses look Sara would have been proud of.

"Are they now?" her father replied, returning to his newspaper.

"Yep," Lucinda said confidently, "I'm pretty sure it's a law of the universe."

"Is it a law of the universe that children striving to do things their parents don't like won't get in trouble with their boss for not getting a move on?" he replied smoothly.

Lucinda jumped and ran off up the stairs hearing her father chuckling affectionately as she went.

She dug through her costumes, throwing them on the bed. Most of them were too fancy, or too obviously fake. Finally she found something suitable. It had been a peasant costume for a school play at one time, but she'd added bits and pieces to it herself. It didn't look great, but it should pass for normal in the Otherworlds. She grabbed her desk chair and rummaged around on top of the wardrobe for a wig. She was quite worried that she wouldn't have a suitable one. They were mostly for cosplay and other convention stuff, so they were pink and curly or white and sparkly. But right at the back, with a light covering of dust, was a long, plain, blonde wig. She had to stretch pretty far and she almost fell off the chair, but she managed to snag the end of it. Once safely back on the floor, she shook it out and tried it on. It fitted a lot better than she remembered.

She got dressed, affixed the wig firmly in place with a few hair clips, grabbed her make up bag for good measure and rushed back out.

Back at the office, Sara was clearly trying to decide whether or not to be impressed. She compromised and went for pleased.

"That was unexpectedly resourceful of you," she commented. "Bit of a speciality of yours, is it?"

"You have no idea," Lucinda replied, noting that it wasn't only dads who could give you a poisoned compliment.

"Here's your assignment," Sara handed Lucinda a piece of paper and, unusually, a photo.

"I didn't know you had cameras," Lucinda said, studying it.

"I've got access to this place called 'Earth'," Sara reminded her, "they've got cameras there."

"So . . . what's the assignment exactly?" Lucinda asked. The photo showed a young man talking to a white-haired woman. They looked as if they were at a royal ball or other courtly event; everyone was wearing massive, puffy dresses and fancy shirts. The scene was obscured though – the photo had been taken through a window.

"I want you to find this man and hire him. It *has* to be him," Sara explained. Lucinda wasn't usually given such clear instructions and this didn't even sound like a story.

"Is there some kind of catch?" Lucinda asked warily.

"I'm afraid so, yes," Sara confirmed. "The name Stollenheim is going to be a problem, and that includes mine. The other document is a contract. I need him hired, and I need him hired *immediately*. He's a vampire hunter. That little incident yesterday made me think. We need to make a move against my step-father *now*, when we should be reeling from that last attack," she explained, "not to mention, if he was listening in last night he thinks I attacked his son and that you've quit." A light went on in Lucinda's head.

"So that's why you asked me to dress up!" she exclaimed. "Even if he doesn't think I've quit, he won't be expecting me to look different. But are you sure you shouldn't send Gerda or Freya? They could put on disguises too, couldn't they?"

"You couldn't disguise either of those two, even with plastic surgery," said Sara, "Freya has her little temperature problem, and Gerda . . . well, it doesn't matter what you do to her, she's still Gerda. You're my best bet. Now get going."

Lucinda had extremely detailed instructions. The

entrance door and the hidden door back to the offices had been clearly marked out, there was a map of the town she was going to and a description of the man she was looking for. All in all, she was rather suspicious. Sara hadn't told her the whole story, even now. Lucinda wondered why this man would refuse to work for her.

She found herself a little way from a town. The door opened out under a huge, hollow tree that was carved and strewn with decorations. The town itself looked like Bad Schwartz. That wasn't the only similarity;

"Stranger, if ye be new in town," an old man approached her, sounding like he had a sore throat, "I warn ye, ye'd do well to stay away from yonder manor." He indicated a fantastically creepy mansion that was clearly visible even from the other side of the village. It looked like a haunted house; a stark contrast to the rest of the village, which was full of flowers and brightly painted houses.

"Has it got a vampire in it, by any chance?" Lucinda asked, before he could ramble on about how doomed they all were. He snorted;

"HA! I *wish*," he replied, using a normal voice. "It's just full of ghosts now. Lot of good they are. Couldn't doom a hovel, never mind a town, not the whole lot of 'em. They keep *wavin'* at people through the windows. We had a vampire, but she moved to a cottage in the country, said she couldn't be bothered with the stresses of town life, the swanky cow." He sniffed. "It's all right though, I suppose. For just having ghosts, I mean. But what you *really* want in a town-" Lucinda cut him off;

"Yes, sorry, that must be annoying," she said, "but I'm looking for this man." She pulled out the photo to show him. "And the . . . Van Kresnik offices?"

"Vincent?" the man chuckled. "In a spot of trouble, are you? He's a decent bloke Vincent, but he can be pretty useless." Lucinda waited politely for more information. "Oh, you're serious, eh?" he said eventually. "His office is over on the other side of town, I reckon you can see into the mansion from his upstairs window. Head for the mansion and you'll find it."

"The mansion you told me to stay away from, you mean?" Lucinda replied, smiling.

"That's the bunny," he said. "If a sad and terrible fate befalls ye, you were told. If you're looking for Vince, I suspect it already has. Good day to you, Miss." He gave her a little nod and went on his way.

The mansion dominated the village, so it was easy to find. It stood in front of a suitably spooky forest. The forest looked as if had been planted as an accessory to the mansion; it had a maintained look around the edges, all flat, bare ground and trimmed trees. The office wasn't so easy, and Lucinda had to check the map and ask another person for directions before she found the stairway up the side of a completely unrelated shop.

There was a sign above the stairway with the name 'Kresnik and Co.' Lucinda nodded to herself and climbed the stairs. She knocked on the door at the top. No-one answered.

"Hello? I'm here on business?" she called. She opened the door cautiously and peered around. She found herself in a little office. The place gleamed. The wood was polished, the windows were clean. There was a desk in the middle of the room and three chairs lined up against one wall, presumably so customers could sit and wait. They were so shiny, anyone who sat on one might well slide off. There was another door on the opposite wall. Should she try knocking on that one instead? It was behind the desk, which was a signal to her that it was off limits. Better leave it alone. This Vincent was going to be hard enough to recruit as it was.

"Hello? Is anyone in?" she called as loudly as she could without being rude.

"Sorry, sorry!" the door opened and a skinny, young man slipped out, smiling. He had short, mousey brown hair. He was wearing a brown tunic and trousers made of a rough, dark material. "I was in the other room, I don't normally get many customers . . . ha ha, I shouldn't tell you that, I suppose. It might give you a bad impression."

"Are you Vincent?" she asked. As for bad impressions, the old man had already seen to that.

"Yes, that's right," he confirmed enthusiastically and sat behind his desk, "Vincent Van Kresnik at your service! Now what seems to be the trouble? Tell me your case."

"Case? Um," Lucinda hesitated, "there's this vampire we need to fight-"

"Oh, you want to hire me as a hunter?" Vincent jumped. He sounded surprised.

"Are you not?" Lucinda replied, in much the same tone. He scratched his head.

"Oh yes, I am. But I'm mostly a lawyer these days," he explained. "I inherited the vampire-hunting trade from my father, but it's gone downhill since he retired. Most vampires nowadays want to live in peace and the ones who are really evil are far too good at it. So you're either going after someone who doesn't deserve it and won't stand a chance or someone who *does* deserve it who's going to eat you for breakfast." That certainly seemed to be the case with Stollenheim. But there was something far less relevant she was dying to ask about;

"So . . . I have to ask, why did you choose to be a lawyer . . ?" Lucinda asked him, baffled. To her surprise, he went red.

"Well, I uh, I wanted another way to fight evil and stand up for folks who can't do it for themselves, but . . . " he hesitated, "let's just say being a lawyer turned out to be a lot like being a vampire hunter." He sighed. "But I do my best, either way. Tell me about this vampire."

"I've got a contract here," Lucinda said, fishing it out of her pockets and handing it over. He spent a minute reading it and re-reading it. He grimaced.

"This contract is for a Stollenheim?" his cheery tone had vanished completely. "I don't take contracts out on the Stollenheims, Miss." He pushed the contract back across the desk. "Any of them. I haven't heard of this one, but I don't care." So this was the obstacle. No wonder Sara hadn't wanted to hire him herself. The Stollenheim name was her own as well as her target's. But even without him dealing with Sara herself, their target's name was on the contract, clearly. Was she going to get in trouble for letting him read it? She didn't see how there was any way to *stop* a lawyer reading a contract. She hadn't bothered to read it herself, but she didn't need to, she already knew what it was about.

"Why *not?*" Lucinda asked. "I *have* to hire you and I have to hire you *today.*"

"I don't take contracts on the Stollenheims!" Vincent insisted. "Now if you don't have any other business, you should leave."

"Please!" Lucinda persisted. "Why won't you take the contract? I don't understand!"

"Contessa would never forgive me!" he explained. "I'd never forgive *myself!*"

"Contessa?" she asked, with a sense of foreboding. This didn't sound good.

"Sh-she was, um . . . " He looked down at his knees, presumably trying to hide that fact that his cheeks had gone pink. "Um. She was the village vampire for a long time. She used to live in the mansion over there." He pointed to the mansion, the only thing visible from his window.

"And?" Lucinda encouraged.

"She used to have battles with my father all the time," he explained. "At night, they'd have shape shifting battles, the traditional way. *He*'d turn into a wolf and *she*'d turn into a wolf-"

"Wait, wait," Lucinda stopped him. "That's traditional is it? What about all the stakes and the garlic and stuff?"

"It's traditional here," he said, and shrugged. "We inherited it from some place called 'Sentrel Yoorup'. She did a bit of garlic and stake stuff too, though, so as not to disappoint anybody. She was very good like that. What with the press and mass literacy, people have started to expect different things."

"So she fought with your father, but it was . . . sort of . . . a business thing?" Lucinda surmised.

"Yes, exactly, " he said. "He was injured badly, fighting a foreign vampire in another town, and he had to retire sooner than he wanted," Vincent continued. "I-I wasn't really ready, but I took over from my father . . . " He went crimson again. "I, um, I really screwed up my first battle, but she just laughed and, er," he stuttered, "s-she said it was cute."

"So . . ?" Lucinda prompted.

"Well, she was really nice and she taught me a lot

239

about fighting vampires, even stuff my dad didn't know," he explained, "but the better I got, the more I didn't want to fight . . . "

"I don't see what this has to do with the Stollenheims though," said Lucinda.

"Oh, didn't I say?" he said, looking up from his knees. "Her name was Contessa Von Stollenheim. She's related to all the Stollenheim vampires out there. She's the head of the family."

"You refuse to take out a contract on a Stollenheim because you'd be making an enemy of this Contessa lady?" Lucinda summed up.

"I'm afraid so," he said. "I won't make an enemy of Contessa for anyone. I'm sorry."

"Not even if the vampire is terrible?" Lucinda asked.

"And what shall I say to Contessa?" he replied. "I killed your grandchild because they were terrible?"

"Well, yeah!" Lucinda stood back up. "He tried to kill me and my friend, and he flattened a whole village in the process! And he was *trying* to kill his own step-daughter! And that's just what he did to *me*." Vincent pursed his lips together. He stood up and stuck his chin out in a determined manner.

"I really am sorry, but this is what we call a conflict of interest. I must ask you to leave."

After arguing with him for several minutes, Lucinda hadn't made any progress, so she left and sat down on the fountain in the town square to think. She understood Vincent's dilemma all too well. Much as she loathed Stollenheim, Johann didn't want him dead, and Johann was her friend. Her heart just wasn't in this quest. What if she had hired Vincent and then Johann had found out she'd basically assassinated his father? He'd never speak to her again. She was staring into the middle distance when a shadow fell across her path.

"Vincent not up to the job, then?" It was the old man from before. Lucinda sighed. Great. An audience for her misery. "'Fraid he's the only lawyer in town," the man continued. "I can't stand to see a young lady look so depressed. If it helps, I could try lawyering for you if you'd like," he offered. "I don't know anything about lawyering mind, but I can't be much worse than Vince, and at least you'll have someone to argue your case, right?" Lucinda stood bolt upright. That was it. Someone to argue her case.

"You're absolutely right," she announced. Seeing the hopeful look on the man's face she added, "Um . . . not about you though. But you did give me a great idea! Thank you!"

If Vincent wouldn't help with Stollenheim because of Contessa, then the person she needed to talk to was Contessa herself. She sounded like a decent sort. To find Contessa, the easiest thing to do would be to ask Johann. Then she could also talk to Johann about it and have a clear conscience instead of feeling like she was sneaking around behind his back. That would mean having to dodge Sara, but she already had an excuse for that. She had to visit Erlina, after all. If she happened to bump into Rosie and Johann while she was there, possibly by taking a little detour to Bad Schwartz, then that was hardly her fault, was it? If she played her cards right, she might even be able to wrap this quest up all on her own, without anyone having to kill anyone. If she could just find Contessa Von Stollenheim . . .

241

Lucinda rushed through the offices and was almost at the the right door when Sara opened the door of the armoury.

"And just where are you going?" she asked sternly. "Did you hire that kresnik I asked for?"

"I'm working on it!" Lucinda replied. "You know how quests are. 'I'll do this for you, but only if you get me this thing or talk to that person' etcetera."

"And you're going where?" Sara repeated pointedly. That wasn't encouraging.

"To the Blue Forest," Lucinda replied, "to see Erlina. It's on my way to do the quest thing." It really was, but would Sara buy that?

"Good," Sara replied. "I was hoping you would."

"You were?" That caught Lucinda off balance. She'd expected to be denied because of Rosie's relation to Johann. And because she hadn't actually explained herself at all.

"Yes." Sara retreated into the armoury and returned with another letter. "I've changed my mind. I want to ask Stollenheim's son and the witch to join us. We'll need all the help we can get."

"Oh, all right then," Lucinda replied, flooded with relief. Sara peered at her suspiciously, but remained silent. She handed over the letter and disappeared back into the armoury.

Lucinda stood in Blue Forest wondering how on Earth she had just gotten away with that. Now she practically had permission from Sara to ask Johann about this Contessa woman and find a way around killing his father. She spent most of the time walking to the cottage wondering if Sara would see it that way. She knocked on the cottage door, which was promptly answered by Erlina, who squealed and almost bowled her over with a hug.

"Lucinda!" she cried. "I thought . . . I . . . I knew you wouldn't leave! They said you'd quit, but you came back!" She sniffed. Lucinda looked down to see that her eyes were welling up with tears.

"I did, actually," Lucinda admitted, slightly ashamed, "but only for about three hours." She hugged the little fairy back.

"Is that Miss Prince I hear?" came Rosie's voice from the other room. "I take it you didn't quit then? Johann said you were going to."

"I did, but I *un*-quit, okay?" Lucinda shrugged.

"Good for you then," Rosie congratulated her. "Is this a business visit or are you just here to see Erlina? She's been helping me about the cottage, she's very good."

"I know," Lucinda said, feeling a sense of pride for her friend. "Um, I'm here for both? Sara gave me a letter."

"'The enemy of my enemy is my friend'?" Rosie guessed as Lucinda handed it over. She opened it and read it. "Pretty much," she said, tossing it onto the sideboard.

"Will you help?" Lucinda asked. "You can let go now," she told Erlina, who was hanging onto her as if for dear life. "I'm not going anywhere, not for a bit anyway."

"I don't think I'm ever letting go of you again," Erlina replied, all too seriously. Then she laughed and broke away. "I'm just so glad you're back. I'll make tea," she told Rosie, skipping off into the other room.

"She's a sweetheart, isn't she?" Rosie said, when she was sure Erlina wasn't listening.

"I feel awful that she got sick because I wasn't paying attention," Lucinda replied.

"If I'd taught you about magic like you wanted, she

wouldn't have gotten sick," Rosie replied. "You shouldn't keep blaming yourself. Besides, she'll be fine so long as she rests up, takes some medicine and stays away from dry areas for a while. I'd rather she wasn't up, but she wouldn't stay put. She said she had to do something or go crazy."

"I know that feeling," Lucinda smiled.

"She was waiting for you," Rosie told her. "She was adamant that you would come back, even after she overheard Johann telling me you were going to quit. She couldn't sit still, even so."

"So what are you going to do about Sara's letter and King Stollenheim?" Lucinda asked, changing the subject.

"We'll help," Rosie replied. "We were trying to find a way to dethrone him in any case. I'll contact Johann in a bit. He's really pleased that he's a prince, you know. It's not that he minds being a vampire as such, he's just annoyed at the restrictions it puts on him."

"The drinking blood thing?" Lucinda asked.

"No, that's . . . I don't believe that's ever been much of a problem," Rosie laughed. "It's the solitude, the dingy castles and . . . you know. All that. He finds it depressing." Erlina came back in carrying three cups of tea. She set them on the side board and beamed.

"I remembered where everything was!" she said proudly.

"You're a fast learner and no mistake," Rosie praised her. "While you two catch up, I'll call Johann. He'll want to know about this."

"Wait! I need to talk to him," Lucinda told her, "to both of you I think." Rosie looked intrigued.

"This isn't about your boss, huh?" she asked.

"We-ell. It sorta is?" Lucinda hesitated. "I need

information. I'll explain when I talk to him."

"Understood." Rosie gave her a nod. "Just come through here then." Lucinda was led through into a storage room, full of boxes, spare flasks, weird looking bottles and brooms. There was a large mirror hung at the far end. It looked like an antique, but it was polished up and completely flawless. It could have been made yesterday.

"Mirror, mirror on the wall, I now need to make a call," Rosie said to it. Lucinda snorted into her tea.

"Seriously?" she asked, with a grin on her face.

"Oh, shut up," said Rosie. "It's the only way you can use them. They have to be activated in the proper way and then they only respond to rhyme. Blasted things."

"And whom are you calling?" the mirror boomed in a deep, masculine voice.

"Count Johann Von Stollenheim," Rosie answered it. There was a pause.

"That name is not recognised," the mirror replied.

"Oh *come on,*" Rosie complained at it.

"That name is not recognised," the mirror repeated. Rosie groaned.

"J-Johnny Von Snugglebuns," she stated.

"Calling . . ." the mirror responded. Lucinda fought back a laugh.

"Oh, *shut up!*" Rosie complained, turning crimson. "You think I ever expected to have to call my boyfriend in front of people? I live alone in the middle of a damn forest!"

"What?" Lucinda replied innocently. "I didn't say a word."

"Yeah, you better not, either . . . " Rosie grumbled. The mirror filled with smoke. Then it cleared. It reflected a bedroom, but there was no-one there.

"Johann!" Rosie shouted. "Answer the mirror, damn it!"

"Yeah, Johnny!" Lucinda giggled, grinning like a maniac. "Get in here!" She earned herself a filthy look from Rosie, but she was far too amused to care. There was the creak of a door, and then Johann appeared in the mirror.

"Sorry, I was cooking!" he apologised. He looked askance at Lucinda.

"Miss Prince wants to talk to you," Rosie explained stiffly.

"Sara wants you to help out after all," Lucinda explained, "and there's something else. First, you will help out right?"

"Of course," he replied firmly. "This makes things much simpler. So what's this 'something else' you need my help with?"

"Do you know where I can find Contessa Von Stollenheim?" Lucinda asked. "I need to talk to her."

"Grandma Connie?" Johann's eyes widened. "Gosh, you have been digging things up. What do you need to talk to her about?" Lucinda blinked.

"'Grandma Connie'?" she repeated in disbelief. "She's your grandma?"

"Not my actual grandmother," he clarified, "she's my great, great, great . . . great . . . grandmother. I might be missing a great. If we went around calling her that, we'd never get anywhere."

"I see. Do you know where she is?" Lucinda asked.

"She's currently living in a cottage on the plains adjacent to the Blue Forest. Not terribly far for me, but you'd have a heck of a walk."

"I think . . . I think I have a solution to that problem," Lucinda replied. "Now that that's sorted out . . . I don't think Sara will want me telling you this, but she asked me to hire a vampire hunter today."

"Let me guess. To kill my father?" Johann said. "It's sensible, but I don't like it. Wait . . . she asked *you* to hire the vampire hunter?"

"He doesn't take contracts against Stollenheims and I'm guessing that one Stollenheim taking a contract out on another is a double no-no," Lucinda explained. "She's adamant that I hire him and that's why I wanted to talk to Contessa. I had this idea, though. I don't suppose she'd be able to talk your dad out of fighting would she?"

"I don't think so. But . . . " Johann rubbed his chin in contemplation. "It might be worth a shot. And don't worry about the vampire hunter. I'll stop him myself if I have to. Father must be stopped before he gets any worse and I can't do it without my sister's help. I'll have to play along for now."

"If you're sure," Lucinda replied. That was a great relief. Of course now she was on the wrong side of Sara, but surely as long as they won, it would be fine. At least that was what she was going to keep telling herself.

"Is that everything?" Johann asked, glancing sideways to something off mirror.

"I think so," Lucinda confirmed.

"Only I think my dinner is on fire . . . "

Erlina was disappointed that Lucinda had to leave so soon, and wanted to go look with her. But both Lucinda and Rosie insisted that she stay at the cottage and rest. Erlina grudgingly agreed. Rosie was reluctant to leave Erlina alone, so she pointed Lucinda in the right direction and sent her on her way.

'Maybe I should have asked Johann to come with me,' Lucinda thought to herself as she stared out at the vast expanse of the plains. 'But he has stuff to prepare for and the unicorns said they'd help me . . . so how do I call them?'

"I'd sure like some help right about now," she announced to the world at large. Nothing. "Maiden in distress over here." Still nothing. "Come get your bona fide maiden? You know I wouldn't have to do this if people would just give me *proper instructions!*" She heard something rustle.

"Maiden, what ails thee?" came a musical voice. She looked around and saw nothing. "Down here," the voice said. Lucinda looked down to see a small man with goat legs and a flute. Wrong magical creature. "Maiden," he repeated, "what troubles thee so? It may be I can help ye in some small way." Lucinda eyed the little fawn.

"I don't think so," she answered cautiously. Accepting help from fairy-like creatures was usually more trouble than it was worth. He would want her first born child or something, and that probably seemed like a great idea until you actually had the baby, goodness knows how many years later.

"Yes, get lost you," a second voice said.

"Indeed," another joined in. "We saw her first. We joined her quest *ages* ago!" Lucinda turned to see two unicorns standing at the edge of the forest.

"Go on then," the first unicorn told the annoyed fawn, tossing his head in the direction of the forest. "We have this." The fawn made a rude gesture and scampered off into the forest.

"Maiden!" the second unicorn exclaimed. She was

the filly who had taken Lucinda to Rosie's house her first time in the forest. "Maiden, you look like a maiden today!"

"Yes, we were very surprised when we saw," the male agreed.

"'Tis most appropriate," the filly said approvingly. "With what may we assist you, maiden?"

"I need help finding a cottage. It's out on the plains and it's too far on foot for me." The unicorns exchanged glances.

"Is this an important cottage?" asked the filly politely.

"Yes, are you sure you aren't looking for a castle or terrible, gloomy keep?" the colt asked.

"No, it's definitely a cottage," Lucinda replied, to their apparent disappointment.

"Does the cottage contain an important artefact, perhaps?" the filly tried.

"No, but it might contain an important person," Lucinda reassured her, "possibly the most important person for the quest."

"That's more like it!" the colt said, stamping his hooves and snorting enthusiastically. "Shall we depart?" There was a brief argument over who got to carry Lucinda, but the colt gave way, saying that carrying humans was a soft, girly thing to do anyway and insisted that he had only been trying to be a gentleman.

Lucinda rode the filly along one side of the plain, while the colt ran parallel to them far enough away to be seen, but so that he could see as far away as possible. After about thirty minutes, he came galloping straight towards them.

"Maiden!" he whinnied. "I have located the cottage! 'Tis over yonder!"

The two of them followed the colt at an easy trot back the direction he had come. They were near the 'cottage' within ten minutes, although 'cottage' was a terrible word to describe the huge building in front of them. It certainly had thatched roofs and white walls. There was even a pretty garden and a white picket fence. There was a pink flamingo in it, and a large collection of gnomes. However, it was at least three storeys tall and twice as wide as a regular house. There was a moat around it.

Houses not being very unicorn friendly, the filly and colt waited at the edge of the garden. Lucinda walked timidly up to the door and knocked, using a ridiculously oversized, overdecorated brass knocker. The door creaked open with a noise like nails down a chalkboard.

"Come in, my child," came a sultry voice. This voice had *the* accent. There was no mistaking it. This was a vampire you were talking to, and she wanted you to know it. Lucinda took a deep breath and walked inside. The door swung shut, unaided.

"Hello?" Lucinda called nervously. "A-are you Lady Contessa Von Stollenheim?"

"Vhy yes, child." the voice answered. "I am honoured zat you have heard of me. To vhat do I owe ze pleasure of your visit?"

"I came to tell you about what one of your relatives is up to," Lucinda stated, sounding much braver than she felt.

"Ah, I am alvays happy to hear of my grandchiltren," Contessa replied. "Very vell. Come into ze drawink room, and ve vill discuss them." Lucinda didn't move. " . . . Ze drawink room is to your left. There's a little plaque on it, you can't miss it," the voice prompted. Lucinda looked to her left, following the wall until she found the door with 'Drawing Room' on it.

When she opened the door, she was overwhelmed by the richness of the room. Everything was red and heavily embroidered. There was a roaring fire, in an expensive-looking fireplace, with a lavish, intricately carved mantelpiece. There were countless framed pictures covering the walls, both landscape paintings and portraits of people Lucinda presumed were family members.

"Come in, come in!" came a voice from the other side of the room. There were plush-looking chairs upholstered in leather. The candles on the mantelpiece were black, and they burned with blue flames. Lucinda suspected there was a scientific trick to it rather than magic, but then again, a vampire could probably get candles to burn whatever colour they wanted. "Come closer, my dear. Sit by zer fire. I do not bite," the voice paused, "I am obliged to add zat I mean zis metaphorically." Lucinda obediently made her way to the fire and sat on a sort of couch. It was very long. A chaise longue in fact, she thought to herself. The kind that posh women were always fainting on in romances and dramas. Contessa was lounging on the one opposite it.

"Grandma Connie" was an incredibly young-looking woman with a figure like an hourglass. She was wearing a clingy, dark red dress and a red, translucent scarf over her shoulders. She was wearing some seriously elaborate jewellery and she was lounging like a pro. She had a glass of what Lucinda could only hope was red wine in one hand, her other was draped daintily over the side of her chair. She looked only a little older than Rosie, and the resemblance was remarkable. Her hair was long, and white as snow. Unlike Rosie, her eyes were red, and they shone in the firelight.

"So," she said when it was apparent that Lucinda was not going to make the first move, "tell me about this grandchild of mine. I presume zey have done something foolish?"

Lucinda recounted what had happened to herself, and how King Stollenheim had treated Sara and Johann, his own children.

"Zis is indeed troubling to me. He is going zer way of Heinrich . . . " she took a sip from her wine glass, and then elegantly reached forward to place it down on the table. She delicately rearranged her dress and scarf as she sat up properly. "He has given in to hatred, and vonce zer hate sets in, zer rot sets in." She gazed into the fire. " . . . I appreciate the information, child," she said, "but I vill not help you."

"Why not?" Lucinda pleaded. "People almost died, in fact, I think some people did, I don't know . . . You could save us all a battle if you'd just make him stop. I don't want to see my friends hurt."

"I understand zese things, child," Lady Contessa replied, tucking her long hair over her shoulder. "Neverzeless, I cannot interfere vith zis. The heirs must battle. How often do you hear of an evil tyrant's grandmother turning up and telling him to knock zis nonsense off right now? Never, zat is how often. These things, they must run zer course."

"You won't help us at all?" Lucinda asked sadly. "I came all the way here for nothing?"

"Vell, I don't know about *nothink*," the woman answered smiling, "you have brought me news of my grandchiltren. But I vill not help you fight him. You must

252

do zis yourselves. You should go now." It wasn't a suggestion. Lucinda found herself standing up.

"There is another thing I came here to ask," Lucinda was hesitant.

"Ask avay." Contessa picked up her wine glass again.

"I tried to hire Vincent Van Kresnik today, but he refused because he didn't want to make an enemy of you," she said, fidgeting with a strand of her hair. "I was hoping if you won't stop the battle . . . " her voice got quieter as she spoke, " . . . at least you can tell Vincent to fight with us?" The effect was electric. Contessa slammed down her glass again and stood straight up, throwing her long hair out of her face.

"Oh for goodness sake! Vhat is *zis*?" she thundered. Lucinda took a step back and almost fell back onto the chair. "Vincent, *vhat* are you doing? Refusing to fight, you silly boy, I don't believe zis!" Contessa regained her composure and plopped back down on the chaise longue. She coughed. "Vincent is anozer matter. I am going to scold zat boy something awful."

"You . . . you really don't mind if we hire a vampire hunter to kill your relative?" Lucinda asked.

"As I understand it zer plan vas *not* to kill him," Contessa replied, "but if he has really gone to zer bad, you may not have a choice. My children did not choose to be vampires, child, but they chose how to behave. In zis vorld you reap vhat you sow. If ve expect people not to hate us just for being vampires, zen ve must not hate vampire hunters just for doing zer jobs."

"And even though we might kill him you still won't try talking to him first?" Lucinda asked. "Even though people might die fighting him?"

"I am four hundred and seventy two years old, child.

People die all zer time. Zis is var, and even one as young as you knows how zey go." Lucinda sagged back in the chair. So there really was no hope for it. Contessa caused a quill, ink and parchment to come floating in, with which she scribbled a letter, signing it with a flourish. As she handed it over she said, "You vorry for nothink. Fighting evil overlords is easy. You have Prince Charming, you have two angry heirs, you have more good guys. It vill be piece of cake, child." She patted Lucinda on the head. "Do not vorry. You have good friends."

"What makes you say that?" Lucinda asked.

"That's simple enough!" the vampire laughed. "You vould not come all the vay out here for *bad* friends, now vould you?"

Lucinda smiled and bid Contessa goodbye. She was disappointed, but now she had a way to hire Vincent, and a new found confidence. This was a *story*. They were the *good guys*. They were *bound* to win. It stood to reason.

STORM THE CASTLE

Nearly a week later, and nothing was even sitting to reason. Sara had gathered almost everyone together. Vincent, Erlina and Rosie were missing. Vincent had read Contessa's letter with a pained look on his face, apologised profusely and signed the contract immediately. Erlina had insisted on accompanying Lucinda to the battle - Rosie had only agreed on the condition that she do nothing but rest until then. Sara and Charming had come up with a plan. It sounded like a video game plan. The sort of thing that really shouldn't work. In a way, it gave her confidence. These things worked in stories. The rational side of Lucinda however, was insisting that they were all going to die.

"We're just going to bust in the front door?" she summarised, her voice betraying her disbelief.

"Correction," Sara replied, "*you're* going to bust in the front door."

"I am?" Lucinda was taken aback.

"Not you personally," Sara said. "We will split up into teams. Cinders, Lina, Freya, Gerda and Johann will attack the front gate. Myself, Charming, Rosalind and Vincent will break in the back way, though the kitchens. We'll get to the throne room and take my step-father down there."

"I didn't know the Silver Witch was actually joinin' us on the battlefield," Gerda remarked. "She can fight, can she?"

"Rosie is an accomplished alchemist," Johann reassured her. "She might not use magic any more, but she has an array of offensive potions at her disposal."

"As long as they don't go offendin' any of us," Gerda

said. "You're comin' too then, Count Stollenheim?   You sure you want to?"

"My father must be stopped," Johann replied. "As his son, I have a responsibility to help stop him."

"Huh," Gerda rocked backwards and forwards on her heels.

"If you've got something to say to me madam, I suggest you get it out of the way," Johann prompted. "I'm sure I don't need to tell a shield-maiden that the middle of battle is not a good time to air out any concerns."

"Well, it occurs to me . . . " Gerda began, as she thought about what she wanted to say, "it occurs to me that *we* need an army to take on ol' Chalkface, and yet here you are, needing our help to take him on when presumably you've got the same powers and things."

"Gerda brings up a good point," Charming joined in, smoothing out the castle map on the table "Why *do* you need our help? If you've decided to resort to force, surely you'd be better off without us?"

"It's not that simple," Johann replied. "Aside from the fact that he's older, cleverer and more practised in magic than I am, plus that army that you might have noticed he's got, dragging him home by his ear just wouldn't work," he said, sighing. "As horrible as it sounds, I think that making sure he doesn't have anything to return to is the only way. If I merely tip him off his seat of power, he'll just climb back on again, no?"   Gerda nodded thoughtfully, but she didn't respond, so he asked, "Is there something else?"

"Well, I dunno," Gerda replied non-committally. She was absent-mindedly rubbing her neck.

"Go on, ask it," Johann said. "*Someone* should ask it already. You know. About me and the b-word." Gerda realised what she was doing and guiltily put her hand down to her side.

"So . . . " she said, "there's generally a lot of the b-word about on the battlefield and it's not goin' to be pretty if you go all berserker and start bitin' people. You aren't goin' to start bitin' people are you?" she continued. "I reckon we need to instigate some sort of 'no bitin' people' policy."

"Finally," Johann said under his breath. Then he said in a louder voice, "Rosie gets very testy about that sort of thing," he reassured them. "If I bite anyone else, I'll be in the doghouse for a month. It would ruin her research. I assure you, it's not worth it."

"You're tellin' me you're a vampire who takes orders from 'is girlfriend?" Gerda's face lit up. "Well done, that woman." Johann coughed.

"Yes, well," he said, avoiding the subject, "I just want it to be perfectly clear that I'm on your side and not a loose cannon that's going to get set off by a little blood. Lucinda here can attest to that." Lucinda would indeed have attested to it, but she had other things on her mind;

"Where's Vincent, anyway?" she asked suddenly. "Shouldn't he be here? I would have thought we needed our vampire hunter when we're planning to go vampire hunting?"

"I sent him his orders earlier in the week," Sara replied in a clipped tone.

"Wouldn't it have been better for him to be here in person though?" Lucinda asked, frowning. Erlina and Rosie's absences she could understand.

"No, he's a busy man," Sara replied. "The instructions and directions are very clear, he should have no trouble. He's a professional. He's done this before, he doesn't need to be told how to do his job." Lucinda's frown deepened. Wasn't Vincent something of a beginner? And from what she'd understood, he didn't get much business. But Sara was the one who had requested him, and she'd known he'd be difficult to get. Maybe he *had* just given her a bad first impression.

"Can we get on, please?" Sara complained. "If anyone else has a stupid question, ask it now." No-one did. "Back to the strategy then. I want you to cause as much trouble as possible. Cause as much *noise* as possible. Block any kind of communication you can. If you see any messengers, take them out. The guards need to have their hands full with you, so they won't have time to come and tackle us. If you can break through or convince anyone to give up, do it, and join us in the throne room. If we aren't there, look for us."

"So, we're the distraction but we have to break in anyway?" Lucinda pointed out. "What's the point in that?"

"If no-one actually tries to get in, then it will be blatant that you're a distraction. Besides that, it is possible I'll need reinforcements. We'll be catching him in a scissor attack-"

The talk went on for about half the day; they discussed strategies for how to cause the most noise, how to recognise messengers, what to do if it became apparent that Sara's party had been discovered and the best routes to the throne room from either side.

The next day, Lucinda and the others found themselves not in a gloomy forest like she had expected, but in the middle of a desert. The group was gathered in a small oasis, in sight of a huge palace, surrounded by a town. Sara's army was a motley bunch. There was a giant, a blonde girl who appeared to be a princess, a man and woman dressed like pirates, a few soldiers and some heroes she'd never seen before. It looked like Sara had called on every story contact she had.

Standing with Freya were two women who, like her, were bundled up despite the heat. She wondered, and not for the first time, what Freya looked like under all that fur. Perhaps today she would find out. They were jabbering away in a foreign language, together with some large, ogre-like creatures with red-coloured skin and black horns, dressed in tiger print loincloths. From what Lucinda could tell, they were complaining about the heat. There was something about the way they were fanning themselves furiously with their hands that gave it away. There was still no sign of Erlina and Lucinda was restless. Sara and the others were busy, so she wandered over to Freya, desperate for a friendly face, even if it was hidden under a scarf. As she got closer, she realised something.

"Is that Japanese you're speaking?" she asked Freya.

What little of Freya was showing looked surprised. She asked, "You know Japanese?"

"No, I just hear it on games and things a lot." Lucinda replied. "I kept meaning to ask you . . . you're a snow woman, right? How did a snow woman end up in Iceland?"

"My grandmother moved to Iceland because she hated Japan's hot summers. Iceland is *never* hot."

Freya introduced Lucinda to her aunt and cousin, and to the ogres, who were old friends of theirs. Finally Erlina turned up. She ran up and hugged Lucinda. She was wearing a thick, white cloak as protection from the sun.

"Rosie still didn't want me to come, but I insisted," she said.

"I didn't want you to come either," Lucinda replied. "Are you sure you're well enough?"

"I've just not to use any magic if I can help it. Rosie gave me some potions to use," Erlina explained, opening the cloak a little to reveal rows of pockets filled with bright little vials. "Besides, who will protect you if I'm not here?" Despite her worries, it was a great comfort to have Erlina here, and she had an alternative to magic, thank goodness. But everyone was still standing around and Lucinda was restless again, so she went to find Sara.   .

Sara was standing on a rock scanning the horizon. She looked like she was waiting for something. She was dressed in some kind of battle outfit. It was shorter than her usual dress, and dark green. She had a pair of thin daggers strapped to her legs. She was wearing bracers, metal knee pads, and thick, knee high boots. She was sporting some vampire hunting equipment too; she had a crossbow strapped across her back, a cross and a bottle of what Lucinda presumed to be holy water around her neck. She was wearing a crown-like band around her head.

"You look like an inappropriately dressed video game character," Lucinda observed.

"Good," Sara replied.

"Because it fits with the story, right?" Lucinda guessed. "But I expected us to be battling a vampire in a dark, dank castle. *That*,"-she pointed at the brightly painted, gold coated palace in the distance-"does not say 'vampire's castle' to me."

"We're not going on a vampire hunt," Sara replied, "we're bringing down an evil overlord. Doesn't matter what kind of castle he's in."

"Then why did you hire Vincent?" she asked, trying

not to sound irritated. That wasn't what Sara had said last week. "What's that cross and holy water for?"

"I'm hedging my bets," Sara explained. "If he decides he's a vampire after all, and believe me, if he starts losing, he will, I'm not going to be caught out. And this isn't holy water."

"What is it then?" Lucinda asked.

"Acid," Sara replied.

"*Acid?*" Lucinda replied in disbelief.

"Holy water doesn't work," Sara said. "Acid does. Did you want something?"

"It's just . . . " Lucinda hesitated. There was something different about Sara today. She had weapons. Sara with weapons was a terrifying prospect, as she had already demonstrated. Lucinda on the other hand, was *not* a terrifying prospect, weapons or no, and with the battle looming, she was increasingly nervous.

"You aren't going to say you're quitting again, are you?" Sara asked. "It's a bit late for that. And in any case, I need- ah. We were waiting for you!" This last comment was aimed at a group of townspeople who had walked up. "Did anyone follow you?" she asked them. There were about ten people in what Lucinda thought of as 'desert clothes'; white robes and head coverings, shading their faces from the scorching sun.

"No, Your Highness," one of the men answered. "We left on the other side of town and doubled back."

"That must have been hard on you," she acknowledged. "Are you ready? Is everyone set?"

"Yes, Your Highness!" the man pulled a salute and the others murmured agreement.

"When the time is right, you'll spread the word that the King and his army have been defeated," Sara instructed, "then you'll bring as many people as possible to the palace."

"I don't get it," Lucinda said. "That's not very helpful, is it?"

"It is if we haven't beaten him yet," Sara explained. "The soldiers won't fight civilians and their morale will be destroyed. I'd like to win this battle with as little bloodshed as possible. These are my own people I'm fighting, I don't want them slaughtered." She raised her voice, "Attention everyone!" she bellowed. "We're all assembled! You all know your roles, so let's get in there and kick old Bat Face in the teeth!" There was an answering cheer.

The party split up. Sara's group, including the townspeople, went back the way they had come. The main party was told to wait until they were out of sight, and then make their way towards the town. As they got closer, Lucinda began to swing between excitement and horror. She was going to be in a battle. It was exciting because she knew they were the good guys, and good guys tend to do things like win and have really witty dialogue. It was horrifying because in the real world, things didn't work that way. In the real world, people died, and it didn't matter what side they were on. They'd been told not to kill anyone if possible, so she didn't have to worry about that particular dilemma, but she suspected that the enemy hadn't been given the same orders. She had Johann and Erlina and the others to help her, but they'd be busy fighting. As if she'd been speaking aloud, Johann addressed her concerns;

"If it gets too dangerous, just pull back," he advised, touching her shoulder. "No-one expects you to get killed." There was a noise that was something between a snort and a squeak.

"If you ask me, that elf woman had no business letting little girls onto the battlefield in the first place!" a high-pitched voice complained. "It's a disgrace, this. She should be breaking in there in the middle of the day with just the vampire hunter, while he's asleep."

"Father doesn't sleep much during the day, you know that," Johann complained back. "She'd be walking into a palace full of armed guards too. Vampires don't employ armed guards - father is cheating."

"I wouldn't say cheating, exactly," the voice continued, "he doesn't come back to life like the proper sort, if he gets killed he's a goner. You can't blame the man for having a back-up." Johann looked very much like he would blame his father for having a back-up, but Lucinda interrupted;

"You're that bat," she said flatly, "from the first time I went to the castle. What are you doing here?"

"Hark at the child!" the bat clambered over Johann's shoulders so that he was on the same side as Lucinda. "Unlike you, I'm actually useful. I'm practically a *requirement.*"

"What requirement?" Lucinda asked testily. "Are you going to nag the enemy into submission?"

"No," the bat said and puffed itself up, "I am the talking animal familiar, who gives important advice and scouts out the area and whatnot. Very important. Can't quest without one."

"You're sure about that are you?" Lucinda asked.

"He has a point, Lucinda," Erlina put in. "You have to have a talking animal for quests."

"A bat though? In the daylight?"

"Oh shut up," the bat sneered. "Respect your elders,

young lady. I was learning all this before you were born!" Lucinda considered this. She asked;

"How long do bats live again?"

"He's not a bat, as such," Johann explained. "He's my Great Uncle Lamprey. He turned himself into a bat one day and he couldn't turn back. Didn't have enough magic to do it. Can't obtain enough as a bat either, they're too small."

"I can turn back any time I want!" Lamprey snapped. "I just don't want to. Now if you'll excuse me, I'm going to go ahead to the castle so I can get out of this blasted desert sunlight." He fluttered off, a little unsteadily.

"Don't mind him," Johann sighed. "He just gets annoyed easily, and he was brought up as a traditional vampire. He doesn't appreciate all this modern thinking."

Without the shade provided by the oasis and especially now that they were moving, it was absolutely sweltering. The town was in sight now, but the heat haze made it difficult to judge distance. Lucinda hoped they would get there soon . . . much as she wasn't looking forward to actually fighting, the suspense was killing her. Erlina squeezed her hand, and she turned to speak, but-

"Got your battle cry all ready, Cinders?" Gerda asked cheerily, giving Lucinda a mighty slap on the back and making her cough.

"B-battle cry?" she asked, trying to get her breath back. A hearty slap from Gerda was like having a punching bag smacked into you.

"Yep," the valkyrie beamed. "Got to have a battle cry, even if it's just 'Rraaaaaaargh!!'"

"I think I'll just go with that," Lucinda wheezed.

"I dunno if you've got the lungs for that," Gerda replied doubtfully. "I reckon you need something bloodcurdlin' to shout."

"I'll shout something blood-curdling then," Lucinda replied, not really in the mood for difficult questions regarding her lung capacity. The heat was oppressive, and every step closer to town she was feeling more and more nervous.

"Thinkin' it up on the spur of the moment, eh?" Gerda replied in a conversational tone. "That's the way! It'll probably have some good swears in it." Lucinda merely nodded. The *start* of the battle wasn't what was worrying her . . . She jumped again when someone laid a hand on her shoulder.

"It's going to be all right, you know," It was Johann again. The other three were looking at her in concern as well.

"You look like you're off to the gallows, Cinders," Gerda observed. "Cheer up all right?"

"I've never been in a battle before!" she protested. "I really don't see how I'm going to be any use. I don't know why Sara wants me here." Freya gave her a pat on the shoulder. She wished people would stop trying to comfort her in the form of physical contact, it was starting to bug her. "Can't you give me any useful advice?"

"Like what?" Gerda asked.

"How not to die would be favourite," Lucinda replied. Gerda and Freya exchanged a look.

"Do you think we should tell her?" Gerda whispered.

"I don't think that's a good idea," Freya whispered back doubtfully.

"Tell me what?" Lucinda asked.

"Well, you weren't hired for your fightin' abilities, exactly - " Gerda hazarded.

"Look, this is story country," Freya pointed out,

265

before Gerda could continue. "We're the good guys. The good guys win. It's only justice, right?" Lucinda felt a little comforted, but she still thought that something was off. Before they could discuss it further, they arrived within charging distance of the castle. The soldiers were now also in plain view, lined up in front of the palace. They had curved swords, and spears. There were some higher up, armed with bows.

"Ready with that battle cry?" Gerda leaned over towards Lucinda. Lucinda quailed.

"I thought we were doing a surprise attack?" she hissed.

"No, we're the distraction." Gerda clicked her tongue. "It's our job to go 'Hey, look! We're over here, coo-ee!' while the *others* do a surprise attack. Weren't you payin' attention?"

"Yes," Lucinda replied impatiently, as the air thickened with tension around them, "but I thought it was a surprise on both sides! I wasn't expecting them to be *ready* for us!" Both sides stood and waited, glaring at each other.

"You can't march an army up to the front of a castle without bein' seen Lucinda," Gerda told her. "It's all right, we'll look after you. Besides, these are just minions. Minions are *easy.*" Raising her voice she addressed all the rebels, "Everyone ready?" she shouted. There was a murmur of agreement. *"Let's give 'em Nifelheim!"* she screamed raising her sword. Various rebels around her yelled things with really good swears in.

"Something bloodcurdling!" Lucinda screamed at the top of her lungs. As the rebels rushed forward, Johann grabbed her wrist. Freya and Erlina hung back too.

"Let them go first," he said. "Once we've gotten their

attention, we have to sneak in and back up my sister. They're more experienced than we are, we'll just get in the way." The rebels rushed forward and clashed with the guards. The giant merely picked up the enemy soldiers, plucked away their swords and dropped them in the moat. "Let's get to the gate!" Johann continued, "I can get us past the guards easily." They spied a gap through the warring soldiers and ran for it. They dodged round one pair of fighters and then another, weaving and ducking, keeping the gate in their sights. Some of the guards noticed what they were doing, and converged on them, drawing their swords;

"Don't you even think about it!" Freya shouted at them, squaring up to fight. The guards paused, attempting to weigh up the situation. An unarmed woman in fur shouldn't pose a threat, and as story people, the guards were well aware that it's always the harmless-looking one that turns out to be the most deadly. Freya's gaze swept the circle of guards. Lucinda and the others got behind her.

"Stand aside," one of the guards commanded, raising his scimitar. "It would pain me to harm such a pretty lady." His companions looked at one another, and shuffled away from him. They already knew they were in trouble - spouting cliché dialogue was only going to make it worse.

Freya threw off her coat and hat, and violently kicked off her boots, catching one of the men on the head. Lucinda and the others were hit by a blast of freezing air. There were fresh waves of cold from either side as her aunt and cousin de-robed too, and the guards were surprised to find themselves facing a pair of dainty Japanese women wearing white yukata. Freya was not dressed in Japanese attire. She was barefoot, and wearing what resembled a bikini made from leather and chain mail; frost was forming on the metal. The only thing Lucinda knew about snow women was that they caused freezing weather. This must be why.

"That's not very good armour ma'am," one of the soldiers pointed out, shakily. Women in amazingly unsuitable battle clothing were even worse news than unarmed women.

"The less armour, the worse for you," Freya replied confidently, taking up a fighting stance and flexing her fingers. "Touch me, and you'll be *lucky* if you get frostbite. You better be good at dodging!" Freya lunged. She caught the line-spouting guard on the wrist as he raised his sword, and he screamed and dropped it immediately, clutching his wrist as if he'd been burned. It rapidly turned red and swollen, and he fell to the ground, clutching it and hissing. Freya leapt and twirled, agile as any dancer, disabling the guards quickly; a grab here, a jerk there, and all the guards around them were on the floor, whimpering in pain. The fracas didn't go unnoticed, and more guards were pushing through to try and apprehend them.

Johann grabbed Lucinda's wrist and pulled. There was the clang of metal all around them, and other than the circle of destruction around Freya, it was hard to tell which side was in more trouble.

"Our priority is to get in the castle and back Sara up, not stick around out here," Johann reminded her. They set off towards the gate again. Johann and Erlina used magic and potions to clear their way. Much like Freya, they were using precision, not force; the spells and potions were designed to disorientate, not damage. One man barring their way got hit in the face with a potion, abruptly dropped his arm and stared around as if he'd never seen the place before, until a rebel clonked him on the head, knocking him out. A woman who came at them screaming suddenly found one of her feet stuck to the floor, and came crashing to the ground, her weapon bouncing away to be lost in the crowd. As they continued to dodge and disable the enemy, they were followed by Freya, who didn't have to dodge in the slightest. The desert people were keen to avoid her, not only for the harm she could do, but the dire cold she exuded. Perhaps it was the story momentum that was to blame, but the rebels did seem to have the upper hand; the enemy forces were largely made up of elves and humans - they were no match for the magical creatures that made up the rebel army. The four of them quickly made their way to the entrance, where a few determined soldiers were barring the way. They didn't seem inclined to move, so Lucinda twisted round to address Freya.

"Isn't Gerda coming with us?" she asked.

"Gerda is leading our soldiers here," Freya replied, whilst staring fixedly at the guards. "Besides, you can't bring an army to a final showdown, it's in bad taste." The guards looked at each other.

"Final showdown, you say?" the senior one asked.

"That's right," Johann said. "We have come to topple the old, oppressive regime!" The guards shared a puzzled look this time.

"Well, I don't know about oppressive," the guard said, touching his head in a respectful fashion, "but a final showdown is a final showdown. If you could just overpower us, it would be much appreciated." The remaining guards took up defensive stances.

"Right-" Freya looked ready to pounce.

"Hang on," Johann stopped her. "Gentlemen, I am Johann Von Stollenheim the Third, son of King Alucard Von Stollenheim, the overlord around these parts. That means

I'm the prince, coming to challenge his tyrant father. I think you know what this means. Please step aside." The guards looked unhappy.

"We can't just stand aside," the senior guard argued. "We weren't hired to just *stand aside*. That's not what guards are for!"

"No, they are for the enemy to warm up on, before they get to the boss-" Freya threatened.

"Look, stop," Lucinda spoke up. "Johann here is the prince, right?" Everyone nodded, slightly knocked off balance by her interruption. People weren't supposed to be reasonable in this sort of situation, they were supposed to scream and run at each other. "If he's the prince, he's technically your boss, right?"

"He's with an invading army," one of the younger guards pointed out. "It's just not good sense to take orders from someone with an invading army, is it?"

"No," Lucinda agreed, "but what if we're here to assist the king? What if we've been working with the rebels in order to discover their plans?" The guards continued to look doubtful. "For example," Lucinda continued, hoping this would work, "there's a party sneaking around in the castle right now, trying to assassinate the king. What if we're breaking into the castle in all the confusion to stop them?"

One of the guards raised his hand. "Ah, but what if he is an evil prince, come to take the throne unjustly because he's tired of waiting for his father to die?" he said triumphantly.

"Evil princes don't break into palaces," Lucinda argued, "they use poison and trickery. When have you ever seen an evil prince gathering an army of rebels to take over a kingdom? Huh? I bet you can't think of one time." The guards scratched their heads.

"He is right you know," one said.

"Indeed, evil princes *always* use poison," another agreed, "'cause they don't need to raise an army, they just need their parents to die faster. Stands to reason."

"Very well, then." The senior guard waved them past. "Go on then, Your Highness. Please save His Majesty from the rebels!"

"I will," Johann told him sincerely. The three of them started down the hallway-

"*Grab them now!*" the first guard screamed. Making the mistake of turning to face the yelling guard, they found themselves grabbed from behind. Bad news travels fast, and these new guards were covered from head to toe in several layers of material to protect themselves from Freya's icy touch. They were each wearing several of the robes Lucinda had seen the townspeople wearing. Two guards were attempting to handle Freya, but one each sufficed for Lucinda and the others. Lucinda's arm had been twisted painfully behind her back. She tried to pull free, but she was no match for the wall of muscle behind her. Freya was; she aimed a backward kick at the groin of one, causing him to him to flinch and crumple, though he refused to let go. The other redoubled his grip as he avoided a second kick from Freya, to which her response was a backwards head butt. She was on the verge of breaking free, and would have done so if it weren't for the guard holding Lucinda. A sword was held to her throat.

"Either you stop struggling right now, or this boy does," he threatened, "if you know what I mean." Lucinda pressed herself as far away from the blade as possible. Freya swore and stood motionless. Johann didn't seem to have been able to put up a fight without his magic, but he stopped struggling too. Erlina looked like she was preparing a spell, but Johann managed to kick her on the ankle and she stopped. Lucinda felt the guard holding her nod, his chin grazing the top of her head. "That's better. I'm sure you could get away from us if you struggled hard enough woman, but not this one." He jerked Lucinda's arm, making her wince. "If you value the life of your comrade, you'll come quietly."

"I dunno, is this okay?" said the younger guard from the entrance. "This feels like bad guy stuff. Taking hostages and threatening people." The guard holding Lucinda shrugged with his sword arm.

"Do not worry. It's acceptable to do grey area things like this if you're disabling bad guys," the older guard reassured him. "Nice 'stupid guard' routine, comrades! I almost believed you were that idiotic myself!" The young guard's chest swelled with pride.

"I've been working on it!" He beamed. "I think I could do with looking about 20% more stupid, though."

"I thought it was spot on, boy," his companion slapped him on the back. "Well done. What shall we do with these rebels? You don't really think he's the prince?"

"See for yourself," Johann replied. Then he grinned as widely as he could, showing his fangs. The guards looked at each other, and the older one peered at Johann's teeth. He gave them a poke.

"They don't seem to be fake, so he certainly is a vampire . . . " the guard trailed off.

"Doesn't mean he's the prince, though," the guard holding Lucinda pointed out.

"I dunno," the guard holding Johann responded doubtfully, "vampires *are* pretty rare." There was a bang as something hit the palace walls, followed by some screaming from outside.

"There's no help for it," the older guard said. "You'd best take them to the king. It would be terrible if we threw his son in the dungeons by accident." There was a murmur of agreement as something else struck the wall, knocking a chunk out of the door. "Get going, we have our hands full here."

The three of them were escorted rather more gently than Lucinda had expected down several large hallways and small intermediary rooms. They came to an ornate, gold-leaf covered door carved with a phoenix emblem; it had to be the door to the throne room. One of the guards holding Freya relinquished his grip and slipped through the door. After a minute, he poked his head through again.

"Bring them in," he confirmed. That wasn't good. If the guard had found Stollenheim unencumbered in there, it meant that Sara either hadn't got that far, or worse-

"See, you have failed," the King's voice rang clearly through the hall. Lucinda shuddered. The last time she'd heard that voice, death threats had followed. This time was to be no different. "If you surrender now, I shall consider merely throwing you in the dungeon. Refuse and you and your rebels will die. Right here, right now. Don't think I'm going to gloat at you, I'm not that foolish." Now that they were in the same room as the king, the guard took his sword away from Lucinda's neck. Sara was not so lucky; King Stollenheim had her held aloft by the throat. Her face was contorted with hatred. Charming was stood in a fighting stance a few metres away, distracted by something above them. Vincent and Rosie were nowhere to be seen, but there was a large, white wolf growling and baring its teeth at the King. It had an ethereal quality, as if it weren't really there. Sara was attempting to prise her step-father's hands apart. She may as well have been trying to bend an iron bar.

"Father, put my sister down," Johann commanded, as boldly as he dared while still being held firmly by his arms.

"Ah, Johann," King Stollenheim greeted him, without taking his eyes off Sara, "I have to admit, I'm rather surprised. I didn't think you had the guts to oppose me so openly." He sighed, and made a disapproving noise. "I'm so disappointed that you had to come under the command of someone else. Your ancestors would be ashamed."

"I shall ask Grandma Connie when I see her father," Johann replied. "We'll see who she's more ashamed of."

"Is this boy truly your son, my liege?" asked the one free guard.

"I'm sorry to say he is," Stollenheim confirmed. "I would ask you to release him, but I'm worried he will do something foolhardy." Johann shot a look at Charming, as if berating him for his lack of action. Charming jerked his head upwards. They looked up. There was a gallery around both sides of the throne room, and each side was lined with soldiers, each one armed with a crossbow. One wrong move, and they would be skewered. Johann glanced up again, but appeared unphased by the archers. "Father, I ask you again. Put my sister down. You're not playing fair."

"She tried to assassinate me," the king replied. "I'm well within my rights to restrain her. Thankfully she's not very good with a crossbow. My archers however, will not miss." He snapped his fingers. "Guards, step away. And you archers, try not to hit my son." Lucinda and the others were released, and the guards stepped hurriedly away but there was no shower of arrows. "Problem?" Stollenheim raised his voice, still keeping a firm grip on the struggling

Sara, who was now making a spirited attempt to claw his eyes out. One of the archers coughed nervously;

"Er, we can't fire, Your Majesty," she shouted down to the king. "As, the man whom you have confirmed is your son, and thus His Highness, has said, that would not be playing fair."

"My step-daughter doesn't play fair either," he replied, remaining calm.

"With all due respect Sire, it doesn't matter if the other side plays fair or not," the archer persisted. "We're the good guys, we mustn't stoop to their level!"

"That's right!" another guard on the side of the gallery agreed with her. "We can't just shoot them Your Majesty, we must give them a chance to see the error of their ways!" There was a noticeable drop in temperature which had nothing to do with Freya. After a few moments of ringing silence, Lucinda burst out;

"*You're* the good guys?!" she screamed. "You have *got* to be kidding! *He's* the bad guy!"

"Who are you going to believe, my subjects?" King Stollenheim asked. "Your king or these invaders who come under the command of the princess who abandoned you?" He flashed Sara a nasty grin. Sara exploded;

"You murdered my mother and banished me, and then you have the gall to say I abandoned my people?!" she raged. "How dare you! *How dare you!*" Sara dug her nails into Stollenheim's hands as hard as she could. "You caused your subjects poverty by imposing stupid laws intended to root us out and you destroyed a helpless village!" she screamed. "You dare call yourself king, you aren't fit to lick my father's boots you *monster-*"

There was a soft popping noise, and a smash. Then another, and another. Thick, purple smoke filled the room.

275

It was rising from several smashed vials that had come raining down from the gallery.

"Disable the archers!" came a yell from above. It was Rosie's voice. There were more crashes and screams as she launched vials at the guards on her side of the gallery. Johann hurled spells at the guards on the other side, who were unable to see who they were aiming at. Erlina whirled round and barraged the guards on the floor with potions and Freya launched herself at the king.

"Enough of this!" The King made a sweeping motion that dissolved the smoke in his wake and sent Freya flying backwards into the wall, which she hit with a nasty crack. "Someone apprehend the witch!" he ordered. "Along with the rest of these pathetic rebels-" He made another sweeping motion as Charming and Erlina leapt at him; they fared no better than Freya. Johann had avoided the blow with a spell of his own however, and he advanced on his father looking determined.

"Father, please stop this. I don't want to battle, I just want you to stop this stupid quest for power and come home-" Johann pleaded but he was interrupted;

"Johann Von Stollenheim, I have heard enough!" Vincent screamed, striding through the doors and pointing a crossbow straight at the King. "I was instructed by Lady Contessa not to kill you unless absolutely necessary, but if you continue I have more than enough testimony to prove you perpetrated acts that qualify you for termination! I have here a contract for said termination and I will not hesitate to carry it out if you do not desist!" He flashed a piece of parchment at them with his free hand and then put it away just as quickly. "If you have anything to say in your defence, you have the right to say it now."

"So that wolf really was a kresnik," King Stollenheim

responded in a mild manner. Unlike everyone else in the party who were slowly looking between one man to the next, thinking they had misheard, he had a terrible grin spreading across his face.

"That's right," Vincent replied, "I am the last in a long line of kresniks. I trained under my father and also under one Lady Contessa Von Stollenheim. Out of respect to Lady Contessa, I did not hunt the Stollenheims, however, I have deemed you a disgrace to the name, and will terminate you as per this contract, which I have taken out with one Lucinda Martin." Lucinda goggled at him. Was that really what she'd signed?

"Young man," King Stollenheim replied coolly, "would you please restate the name of your client and intended target?"

"My client is a lady named Lucinda Martin and the target is one Johann Von Stollenheim," Vincent stated. "Which is you," he added helpfully, indicating the king with his crossbow. There was a chilly silence. Everyone turned slowly to look at Lucinda.

"You took a contract out on me?" Johann asked incredulously, raising an eyebrow.

"No!" Lucinda protested, horror-struck. "*I* didn't write it, Sara gave it to me!"

"You didn't think to *read* it before you got me to sign it?" Vincent asked.

"I'm a fifteen year old girl!" Lucinda made an expansive shrug. "What do *you* think? You're a *lawyer*, what was *your* excuse for not checking it was the right person?!"

"Lady Contessa demanded I accept it right away so I did!" he defended himself. "She told me she didn't care whose name was on it!" Stollenheim started laughing maniacally.

"It looks like we have come to a conclusion!" He dropped Sara, who merely collapsed in a heap. "You've *lost*, princess. No-one will accept you as queen now, even if you win." He grinned unpleasantly. "And would you like to know *why?*" Sara looked up through tear-stained eyes.

"I thought you said you weren't going to gloat?" she said in a hoarse voice.

"Gloating? Ha!" the king scoffed. "This is *teaching*. You lost because you didn't believe. Stories don't work for those who don't believe, princess. You never believed in your story to begin with, but I believed in *mine*." His face contorted. "You were born a beloved princess and handed everything on a silver platter! I was not. I was born a vampire, born to be loathed. And look where we both are."

"How dare you judge me!" Sara hissed. "I was supposed to be a stupid girl who got kidnapped at every opportunity and fawn all over princes I just met. My parents *died* because of my story, how do you think that feels? They died because it made a good story! I *despise* stories-" She broke down into sobs. Johann looked up at the guards, who had lowered their crossbows. Rosie was watching from the gallery. Vincent had also lowered his crossbow, at a loss for what to do. Johann stepped forward and raised his sword;

"Father, I challenge you for the throne," he announced.

"Are you serious, Johann?" King Stollenheim sighed. "You won't win. You're fighting for a disgraced, despicable princess. She even tried to kill you, using her underling as a scapegoat. And you still fight for her? Please."

"This isn't about her," Johann continued, his face serious. "You can needle my sister all you like, but you're

278

much worse. Princess Sara only just met me, and I'm the son of the cause of her troubles.   It's only natural she would suspect foul play and take precautions. It would have been stupid not to. But what excuse did *you* have to hurt all these people? To escape being a vampire? To get power over the humans you despise? You could've chosen a different path, but you chose evil." The King's easy-going manner vanished.

"Guards, arrest this boy," he commanded, "but do try not to hurt him, stupid as he is, I really will catch hell from my relatives if he gets injured."

"Begging your forgiveness Sire, but we can't do that!" the guard from before saluted. "This is a bona fide fight between father and son to see whether the modern or the old ways will prevail! Serious accusations have been made. Guards interfering in such a matter would be just plain rude, Your Majesty!"

"I don't care if it's rude, commander, I order you to remove my son from my sight!" the King demanded.

"Please forgive my insubordination Your Majesty, but I just can't do that," he replied. The guards all mumbled agreement. The King gave up and focussed his attention back on Johann.

"And just what are you going to do?" he asked. "Unless I am mistaken, you are no good with a sword. Vampires do not need swords."

"I'm challenging you as a prince, father," Johann explained, as the two began to circle each other "Princes use swords. If I want the story to work, I must stick to the rules." There were shouts along the lines of 'hear hear!' from the watching guards.

"It seems I've been too soft on you," the King bared his fangs. "I gave you a castle and a town to rule, and what did you do? Run off with that witch, pander to the peasants, join rebellions against me-"

Lucinda made her way over to Sara, who was still quietly sobbing. Much as she hated to admit it, the King was right. Johann *was* no good with a sword, and she knew *exactly* what sort of things happened when people weren't good with swords. She had to do something. What was *her* story? She certainly didn't qualify as a hero right now; at best she was an amusing if incompetent sidekick. She needed to be a distraction . . . She pretended to be comforting Sara, whilst she reached slowly for the bottle around her neck. She managed to undo the chain with some difficulty. She weighed the bottle, stood up, tilted her arm back and threw it overarm as hard as she could. The King had seen her obvious attempt though, and he whipped around and lunged at her. She cringed back as he transformed into a cloud of bats-

Everything seemed to happen at once. Johann tried to hold his father back, but was a fraction of a second too late to get a grip, Freya, conscious again, sprang across the room like a cheetah and Vincent hurled a bottle of what appeared to be actual holy water. Lucinda flung herself at the ground and there was a flash of light-

When there was no impact, no pain, no piercing teeth, Lucinda gingerly removed her arms from over her head and looked up. The bats were frozen in mid-air, covered in a faint, eerie glow.

"Rosie, stop!" Johann yelled. Rosie was standing with her arms outstretched, panting. Her eyes were closed, and she appeared to be shaking. There was a feeling like a release of pressure, and everything fell to the floor, including Rosie; she toppled right over the gallery banister, and Johann ran forward to catch her. He stumbled, but he managed it. He laid her on the floor and stood up in case his father was still mobile.

The acid had missed, but the bats had been splattered with Vincent's holy water. They dissolved into mist and then reformed as the King. He was wide-eyed, gasping for air and slightly smoking. He tried to get up, but he didn't appear to have the strength.

"Sara, you want me to freeze him to floor?" Freya asked, hauling herself up and over to the old vampire.

"Leave him alone, please," Johann commanded. "If he could move, he would be doing so. Trust me."

"No offence, boy," Freya said, folding her arms, "but I don't take orders from you."

"I think you'll find that I'm king now, and this is my kingdom," Johann pointed out, "so just at the moment, yes, yes you do take orders from me."

"Sara?"   Freya touched the elf gently on the shoulder, where her armour was thickest. "It's over now." Sara pushed her hair out of her eyes and rose like an avenging angel. In one movement, she stood up and removed a pair of long daggers from under her clothing, much as she had done that day in the office. She held them to Johann's throat, forcing him backwards-

"*Renounce the throne!*" she demanded, her voice harsh. "*Do it now.*"

"No," he refused calmly, "and if you would think for a few seconds, I should think you'll see why."

"Do it," she demanded again, "or I won't revoke the contract I wrote for the kresnik."

"Actually that contract is between me and him," Lucinda pointed out.

"It's already been rendered invalid because it's for the wrong person," Vincent took out the contract and tore it in half, letting the pieces fall to the floor.

"Then I'll do it myself," Sara panted. "I'll-" Charming seized both her wrists, forcing her back away from Johann.

"My apologies Sara, but we have other things to attend to," he indicated the now ex-king who was making further attempts to get up and the collapsed Rosie, who was in much the same condition. "I'm sure Johann will be happy for you to threaten him later." Sara relented, and once more sank to the floor in an impenetrable gloom. Freya sighed.

"I will stop Stollenheim from getting up," she told Johann. "He tries anything though, he becomes ice cube. You must attend to your witch." She looked down at the ex-king, a puzzled expression on her face. "It's strange though. I thought holy water didn't work on vampires?"

"It's not holy water," Vincent answered her. "No-one uses that any more. It's paralysing potion."

"It's too bad we didn't think of that," Freya replied, stationing herself by the king. Johann knelt down by Rosie's side.

"Rosie? I wish you hadn't used magic . . . " Johann touched her face. "Rosie? Are you all right? Please, open your eyes!" he begged. The realisation of what had happened hit Lucinda, and she raced to Rosie's side. Johann's words back at the cottage rang in her head - 'Rosie is only a few spells away from becoming a vampire'.

"Is everyone safe?" Rosie mumbled. "Did I stop him in time?"

"You stopped him." Johann leaned closer. "Everyone is fine. Rosie? Open your eyes."

"I don't want to, Johann," Rosie replied, her breath coming in short bursts. "I'm scared."

"Come on now, it's not that bad," Johann encouraged

her. "You'll be all right, no matter what. We'll think of something. Come on, please. Open your eyes." Rosie took a deep shuddering breath and opened her eyes. Johann and Lucinda inspected them.

"What colour are they . . ?" Rosie whispered, hardly daring to ask.

"They're . . . pink," Lucinda replied. "Does that mean she's okay?" Rosie sat up and stuck her finger in her mouth.

"They're realleh pinf?" she demanded, still feeling her teeth.

"Yep," Lucinda nodded.

"Like cherry blossoms," Johann agreed, "or roses."

"Stop trying to make it sound pretty," she complained. "They're really just pink?" She felt her teeth again. "I don't have fangs, at any rate. I think I'm safe."

"Excuse me, but if she's fine, we have big, bad guy over here still," Freya shouted. "Johann, get over here and king! You can stare into your girlfriend's eyes later!"

"Okay, okay," Johann replied, going a little red. He put a hand on Sara's shoulder, but she shook him off angrily.

"Don't touch me!" she snarled. "Don't you dare touch me! You stole my revenge and my kingdom, are you happy now?" Johann looked stung.

"Do you know how much effort it took to fight for you after you took a contract out on me? My own sister?"

"I am *not* your sister!" Sara snapped. "Stop calling me that!"

"You might not like it, but you are," Johann replied. "You ought to start acting like it. I don't want your kingdom, particularly. But someone has to step up and run it. Everyone saw you try to take me out and much as I hate

283

to admit it, my father is right. Your people won't accept a queen like that. You're going to have to wait until they forgive you before you can rule this place." Sara clenched her fists.

"And my revenge?" she said, flinging out an arm to point at the ex-king. "That man killed my mother! Where is my justice?"

"I never killed your mother," Stollenheim croaked, "she died of natural causes. I have witnesses."

"Oh she was ill, yes, but that was just the perfect excuse, wasn't it-" Sara began to weep again.

"Why would I be so stupid . . . " the ex-king wheezed, " . . . as to kill my new wife so soon, especially . . . when her heir still lived?"

"That's why you banished me after she died!"

"I banished you because you threatened my position, my power, my lifeline-" Stollenheim broke off in a fit of coughing.

"You liar!" Sara was shaking with sobs and rage. "You killed my mother, you hurt our people, you deny me even closure-"

"That's enough!" Johann commanded. "Sara, please, for the sake of your kingdom, believe him. And also believe me, when I say I will investigate his crimes, and he will be punished accordingly."

"*My* kingdom . . ?" Sara tried to wipe her eyes. "Don't mock me."

"I'm not," Johann assured her. "Vampires aren't meant to rule countries. Just small, isolated, paranoid villages. And all this sand just won't agree with me at all. I'll be glad to give it back. When the time is right," he added meaningfully. Sara stared at him for a long moment.

" . . . When the time is right, you say . . . If you'll

284

excuse me . . . " she said, and limped away.

"You will punish me, Johann? For trying to stay alive?" Stollenheim asked. He had his voice back, but now it was broken and dejected.

"If I do not," Johann answered him firmly, "then story karma will, and it will *not* forgive you."

"Story karma . . . I can never escape it . . . " Stollenheim's voice shook. "Everything I did to escape my destiny . . . for nothing . . . it bends to the will of humans so easily . . . *why?* *Pathetic* humans, they don't know how lucky they are. Humans may become anything, but a vampire can never be anything but a vampire."

"That's not true, father," Johann argued. "We're all trying to get along in our own way."

"Your own way, indeed," his father replied bitterly. "Humans expect us to be their attack dogs or bloodthirsty tyrants. You're stuck with one choice or the other. Imagine! Vampires acting-" he spat the word, "-*nice*. There is no middle road, no in-between. We either play human or we're hunted down like dogs," he growled. "We're *dogs*, either way! You chose *nice*. You *chose* to wear a *collar*. You're no better than me."

"I chose to be happy, father," Johann replied. "I don't require any human approval other than Rosie's." Johann supported his father as he managed to stand. "You took the role of a villain - your species was irrelevant," Johann berated him. "A vampire can't help acting like a vampire. But that doesn't mean they can't act like a decent person. Grandma Connie acts like a vampire all the time, but no-one seems to mind."

"Grandma Connie is one of the biggest hypocrites on the face of the planet," he replied sulkily. "It was *her* idea to name me Alucard. She might as well have spelled it the right way round and have done with it-"

"Oh that's right, blame everyone else for your problems," Lamprey the bat flew down from the rafters and took up his usual position on Johann's shoulder. "Grandmother will be very angry with you."

"Grandmother is always very angry with me, uncle," the ex-king whined.

"Yes, well, that's because you're an ungrateful brat, isn't it?" the bat chided. "And talk about a screw up! Grandmother says if you can't stay in one village for a few years without getting hunted down by an angry mob, then you aren't doing it right."

"I get angry mobs at the door all the time, uncle," Johann pointed out.

"That's because you aren't doing it right," the bat replied.

After some arguments and threats of the use of Vincent and Lady Contessa, it was agreed that the old King would move into Bad Schwartz with Johann's mother, under house arrest, at least for the time being. The girls lurked in the next room whilst the negotiations were going on. Contessa herself showed up towards the end; she'd decided it would be prudent to make sure her family wasn't ripping itself apart, or at least to make sure that if it *was,* it was doing it in a suitably traditional way.

"This all happened because of fear and misunderstanding," Lucinda was looking out over the balcony, feeling forlorn. "It's just like you said . . . 'Once the hate sets in, the rot sets in'."

"Vell then remember to teach zat to your children," said Lady Contessa. "I try to keep an eye on mine, but zere is a limit on vhat I can do. Magic does not solve everything.

286

I know zis first hand."

"You didn't start out as a vampire did you?" Rosie asked her. "So tell me, what stupid spell did *you* attempt?"

"I vas a sorceress, but my power got ze best of me," Lady Contessa replied, fanning herself. "I vas looking for eternal life, and I got it. Not vhat I vas hoping for, but I played ze part I vas handed."

"I still don't know why I'm here," Lucinda complained. "All I managed to do was hire Vincent, and that turned out to be the wrong thing to do."

"Did it?" Contessa asked. "I should think you vere hired for zer same reason. Vincent has a strong sense of justice. Zat is vhy he refuses to kill zose who do not deserve it. I expect he vas hired for his effect on story karma. Vhy else vould she hire somevon who has compassion for zose he is sent to deal vith? Vhy, out of all zer vampire hunters out zere, did she pick the von who von't take contracts on Stollenheims? You and Johann as vell. You believed you vere doing the right thing, so zer right thing vas done."

"Oh come on." Rosie looked extremely doubtful. "You don't really think we won because we believed in ourselves hard enough?"

"We'd have been killed by the guards if they didn't refuse to fire," Lucinda put in.

"And zey didn't fire because zey believed the von vith justice on zer side vould vin," Contessa replied.

"Leaving us fighting their king seven on one," Rosie pointed out.

"And? Vas justice not done?" Contessa asked. "Vhat people believe is important."

"Stollenheim said Sara didn't believe in her story," Lucinda said. "She said herself she hates them. I wouldn't want to believe in something if I thought it had killed my parents, either . . . "

"I told you, zat is vhy she hired you all," Contessa answered. "She did not believe she could vin, so she hired you to believe it for her. Vhen we lose hope in ourselves, zat is vhen zer hope of others is most important."

"So is story karma a real thing or not?" Lucinda asked her.

"Who can say?" Contessa resumed fanning herself. "All ve can do is believe zat if ve fight for vhat is right, ve vill vin. Othervise, how vould *anyvon* have zer vill to fight at all?"

The land of Sheva received the news of their new king quietly and with some puzzlement. The city folk, having been far away from the law altering suffered by the outlying regions, had quite liked their old one. Their old princess was back yes, but they'd never even heard of this new king. There was a great deal of work to be done restoring the country.

Lucinda had thought that Sara would have stayed in the palace, but she announced that she would continue as she had, running the offices of Rent-A-Legend. Someone had to get heroes where they needed to be, she'd said.

"Well, that's it then, Cinders," Sara concluded, swinging her legs over the ever-awkward reception desk. "You did what I needed you to do, and now you can carry on."

"With what?" Lucinda started. She'd expected some kind of backlash from siding with Johann, but Sara seemed to be pretending it hadn't happened.

"With whatever." Sara waved a hand. "You don't need to work for me any more."

"Why not?" Lucinda protested. "I did a good job in the end, didn't I?" Sara gave her a puzzled look. Things were definitely different if Sara was allowing herself to look puzzled.

"You mean you don't want to quit after all?" Sara asked. "I was under the impression that you got what you came for, and that once my step-father was defeated I wouldn't see you for dust. Am I wrong?"

"Yes!" Lucinda stamped her foot. "If you try to fire me, I'll . . . I'll set Vincent on you." Sara genuinely smiled. It was most strange.

"So I was right all along. You really do believe strongly. Enough to make up for me, even," she continued. "You make an excellent idiot. Even if the day is saved by accident, it's still saved." Lucinda was annoyed. She'd *meant* to save the day, after all.

"And here I thought I was the protagonist," she replied.

"I dare say everyone is their own protagonist," Sara replied. "You gave me your notice, Lucinda." Lucinda looked down at the floor and sighed. Was it really over? Sara was scribbling something on a piece of parchment. She handed it to Lucinda. "On your way out, you can do me one last favour. Stick this in that newsagent's window, will you?"

Lucinda read the advert she'd been handed;

> 'Young person wanted for part time job
> General Assistant
> Must be available on weekends.'

"You know what?" Lucinda looked Sara right in the eye. "I think I know just the person."

Back at home, Lucinda gathered up the coins to take them to the pawn shop. She was excited. She wondered how much she'd get, and her head was filled with fantasies of what she would buy with the leftover money. Her mother went with her of course, and ruined the mood slightly by telling her not to get her hopes up too high. But her mother's down-to-earth warning was nothing compared to the sales assistant.

"I can't take these," he said, pushing the coins back towards them. Lucinda was distraught.

"Why not?" she asked. "It's not like they're fairy gold or something."

"They might as well be," the assistant told her. "There's no hallmark, I don't recognise them at all, I can't find anything like them on the database . . . where did you get them from?"

"My boss," Lucinda explained.

"And where did your boss get them?" Lucinda bit her lip.

"I don't know," she replied fretfully.

"There's a lot of theft about you see," the assistant explained. "We can't just take anything. We have to be able to trace things, in case there's crime involved. I'm sorry. No-one will take these without some indication of what they are or where they've come from exactly."

Heartbroken, Lucinda trudged back towards her house with her mother. She was going to have to tell all her friends that she couldn't make it. They were going to be so disappointed, especially after she'd told them she could definitely come. Her mother did her best to cheer her daughter up;

"Lulu, I'll tell you what," she started, putting an arm around Lucinda's shoulder. "We can't afford to pay for it all, but we'll see what we can do, all right?"

"It's too late," Lucinda replied, on the verge of tears. "I don't have nearly enough money saved up. I'm just going to have to miss out. I hope they're not mad at me."

"Of course they won't be mad at you," Lucinda's mother comforted her. "You wouldn't be angry if they couldn't afford it, would you?"

"I suppose not," Lucinda replied.

"There you are then," her mother reassured her. After a pause, she asked, "What are you going to do with these coins? I ought to go and give your boss a thick ear-" Lucinda looked down at the bag she was using to transport the coins in.

"No, it's not Sara's fault." Lucinda sighed. "I'll just give them back to her, I suppose."

Sara didn't bother looking up as Lucinda walked in, but she did when she placed the bag of coins on the desk.

"What's this?" she asked pointedly. "I went to quite a lot of trouble for that, you know. There were dragons involved. Dragons, plural."

"You can have them back," Lucinda explained. "I can't sell them, so they're no good to me. I know it's not your fault. Sorry."

"Gold isn't worth anything in your world, then?" Sara frowned. "I could find you something else, but it would take a while and you'll have to give me an idea of what I'm supposed to be looking for."

"It's not that," Lucinda explained dejectedly. "They won't take it if they don't know where it's come from, and I can't tell them I got it from an elf." She plonked herself down on the floor, leaning her forehead against the desk. "I just wanted to go and see my friends," she mumbled. "I'm not allowed, apparently. The world just seems to not want me to." Sara peered over the edge and tapped Lucinda on the head;

"I didn't hire a pessimist. Get up off the floor," she commanded, "you're supposed to be a hero. What's stopping you seeing these friends? Because I know it isn't vampires or dragons else you'd be doing it already."

"Money," Lucinda replied huffily, getting to her feet and crossing her arms. "I don't know if you've noticed, but it doesn't grow on trees. Neither do plane tickets."

"Plane tickets . . ?" Sara replied irritably. "Where do these friends of yours live exactly? The moon?"

"No," Lucinda replied testily. "Pens lives further up North, Anna lives in Georgia which is in America and Copper lives in New Zealand. Pens isn't too difficult to visit I guess, but Anna and Copper might as *well* live on the moon. But it's America in particular I was aiming for." Sara gave her a genuinely concerned look. It was almost scary.

"I really don't understand what the problem is," she said, thumbing at the corridors that led to the various realms and worlds. "Why don't you just take a door?" Lucinda looked at Sara, and then at the corridors and back again.

"You mean to tell me," she said, "that we have doors here that I can take to the U.S *for free* and you never said anything all this time?"

"You never asked," Sara said. "Besides, Freya lives on

a glacier in Iceland. How did you think she was getting here every morning? Did you think she took a taxi?" Lucinda just stared, utterly speechless. "Seems you're sorted." Sara looked back down at the desk and shifted into a more comfortable position. "Just don't tell anyone about us and don't be flitting all over the place. I'm not a travel agency." Lucinda scrambled up and ran off to find the door map.

Several weeks later, there was a commotion outside the Rent-A-Legend door as Lucinda tried to get a large box through it and hold it open at the same time. It wasn't working.

"Is Sara there?" Lucinda asked, holding up her end of the box whilst Erlina held the door open.

"Yes she is!" Erlina replied. "She looks very annoyed."

"There goes the element of surprise, then," Lucinda laughed, finally managing to get the end of the box through the doorway. "Gah, why does this door have to be up a darn fire escape?!"

"What in blazes are you bringing into my office?" Sara complained. "And can't you do it more quietly? Some of us are trying to work." As she said 'quietly' two of the shells began to buzz and chime.

"How did you do at your contest, Cinders?" Freya asked cheerfully, scooting around the desk so that she could see what they'd brought in. "Was America fun?"

"We crashed and burned!" Lucinda told them. "They said the whole thing was too over the top. Ha! America was great though, we had tons of fun!"

"Aww, that's too bad," Freya sympathised, "but yes, fun is more important."

"Now what exactly have you been wrecking my door frame with?" Sara asked.

"I think you'll like it," Lucinda said, grinning, as she finally closed the door. "Phew."

With the help of Erlina, the two of them finally unpacked the thing and put it together. Then they stood either side of it like it was a prize on a game show.

"Ta-da!" they said.

"It's a chair," Freya observed.

"A *tall* chair," Lucinda corrected, "and look-" She jumped onto it and spun it around a few times. "-it swivels!" The two girls hoisted the black swivel chair into the centre of the desk. It was perfect.

"Now you can sit in the middle of the desk," Lucinda explained helpfully. "You'll be able to glare at people for interrupting you in comfort!" Sara swung her legs back over and sat in the chair.

"Yes, I believe this will do nicely," she said approvingly, reaching up to one of the shells and then reaching down to something under the desk. "I can reach everything and the desk is at a good height." The two girls waited expectantly. "Waiting for something?" Sara gave them one of her looks. "I do believe I gave you an assignment to do yesterday. Get on with it. You too, Freya." Freya obediently walked off into the corridors and disappeared.

"Glad it's useful," Lucinda said, scooting around the desk and heading towards the collection of doors herself. "We'll just be going then." Erlina followed her into the corridor. Lucinda walked along, picked a door at random and opened it. Then she closed it again. Erlina gave her a questioning look, but Lucinda merely put a finger to her lips.

After a moment of silence, there came the unmistakable squeaking of someone spinning a swivel chair around very fast.

THE END

Eggs, Butter, Sugar and Disaster

By Alicia L. Wright

Seralina didn't mean to become a goddess. Especially not the unimpressive sounding 'Goddess of Puddings'. But that's what happens when you go around ignoring perfectly clear warning labels.

In between working as a part-time valkyrie in the goddess Freya's new Ginza bar, Seralina and her cat-dragon-bird thing familiar Phin travel around the Afterlives, encountering gods, spirits and talking trees - sometimes not even as a result of being really bad at flying.

The gods are rather disturbingly like humans; some are kind and helpful, some are petty and jealous and some are more than happy to use a hapless do-gooder for their own ends...

ISBN 978-0-9567852-1-3

Available from all good booksellers

Emma's Stormy Summer

By Miranda Newboult

Dad thinks I'm a nuisance

It may be sunny but Emma's perfect world seems to be unravelling in front of her. First her friend Becca started being horrible to EVERYONE and now Daddy is ignoring her and acting weird.

Emma can't help but worry that it is all her fault and as the storm clouds gather over her Dad she feels more and more guilty and responsible. If only she could get everything back to normal.

This summer she realises that growing up can be a rollercoaster and maybe, just maybe, she should relax and enjoy the ride.

ISBN 978-0-9567852-0-6

Available from all good booksellers

Lightning Source UK Ltd.
Milton Keynes UK
UKOW03f1225300614

234282UK00001B/9/P